# Books By
# Misha McKenzie

**Burke Witches**
*Aria's Law*
*Anna's Knight*

**The Magic of the Heart Series**
*Magic Found*
*Magic Hidden*
*Magic Lost*
*Magic Revealed*

**Single Titles**
*RavenStorm Witches*

# ANNA'S KNIGHT
## BURKE WITCHES

## MISHA MCKENZIE

ICASM PRESS

SAVANNAH

Published by Icasm Publishing LLC
5710 Ogeechee Rd. Suite 200 #278, Savannah, GA 31405
www.icasmpress.com


Library of Congress Cataloging-in-Publication Data

McKenzie, Misha
Anna's Knight / Misha McKenzie
    p. cm.

ISBN-13:978-1-942318-20-0 (Trade Print)
ISBN-13:978-1-942318-21-7 (Mass Market Print)
ISBN-13:978-1-942318-22-4 (eBook)
I. Title


Printed and bound in the United States of America

10 9 8 7 6 5 4 3 2 1

# Burke's Prophecy

*"Witches born—two light, two dark*
*Each possessing an element's mark*
*Air and Water by the brightness of day*
*Earth and Fire by the moon's subtle ray*
*These signs will one day come to bear*
*And evil kept caged will wake and prepare*
*As every year passes the bindings grow weak*
*While the force within strengthens and seeks*
*Four babies born as foretold by this seer*
*They'll have until their twenty-fifth year*
*To mature, to learn, to find their right path*
*For it's up to them to end its wrath*
*Their destined arrival is the key*
*Personal sacrifice will set them free*
*On the anniversary of their birth*
*Four into one defeats the devil unearthed."*

# 1

Anna landed on her ass for what seemed like the hundredth time. She rubbed the tender spot on her hip, recognizing the fact that she'd have one more bruise to add to her growing collection. She'd endured countless beatings from this man in the last two months, and she'd probably take many more.

Hiding the marks he left on her body had become something of a challenge of late. She'd had to resort to long sleeves, and in the humid Florida heat, that could get uncomfortable fast. When a left cross had accidentally connected with her chin, she'd had to avoid her family until it faded enough for makeup to cover it. If they ever saw what lay underneath her clothes and concealer, they'd all go ballistic.

But she couldn't leave. Her life depended on it.

"Come on. Get that little ass up and come at me again," shouted a deep, hard voice she'd learned to hate.

Anna eyed him wearily and got to her feet. Her breath was sawing in and out of her lungs, and her heart was hammering hard against the inside of her chest. He just stood there and taunted her in a way he knew drove her to insanity as he crooked his finger at her.

With her petite frame and five-foot-four-inch height, this brute towered over her and outweighed her by an extreme amount. He was all long, ropy muscle with quick reflexes and attitude. He was built for fighting, and he did it dirty.

And that's exactly why she was paying him to teach her.

~~~

Anna couldn't believe how much difference a year made.

She ducked under Joe's long reach and sent a quick jab into his ribs. When his body reacted to the punch and bent in on itself, she grasped the back of his head with both hands. Using his own momentum, she pulled it the rest of the way down at the same time she brought her knee up and into his face.

If the blow had actually landed, he would have been laid out flat, bleeding profusely from his mouth and nose. Instead, he rose up to his full height of over six feet and grinned.

"Nice. That's good. But you'll need to move *a lot* quicker than that," Joe Conrad jeered at her. "There can be no hesitation. Your attacker is bound to be much larger than you. He'll think he can easily overpower you. Use that. Use his own weight and bulk against him. And when you *do* get the upper hand, wail on him with everything you've got. Make damned sure he won't get back up."

Anna took another drink from her water bottle and nodded her acknowledgement. After almost a year of one-on-one instruction with him, seldom did she have to hide bruises anymore. She was proud of the fact that she'd given *him* a few in recent months. Joe was an ex-MMA fighter who now coached future athletes at his gym in Daytona Beach called Knight's Place.

She'd come for a free self-defense class he'd offered and stayed to learn everything he could teach her.

If she were going to live to see her twenty-fifth birthday and beyond, she'd need to master her physical training. In addition to the arsenal of family magic she'd inherited through the Burke line of witches.

Her attention back on her session, they finished out her
~~~

daily regimen. Just as she was gathering up her stuff to leave, he approached.

"How's Aria doing?"

Anna read real concern in his question and thought about her identical twin. She could still recall the fear that had swamped her when her sister had almost been kidnapped a few weeks ago. The sick bastard who'd tried to take Aria was obsessed with her and had beaten her severely in his attempt to subdue and escape with her. She'd fought back, and that had given the rest of the family enough time to arrive and rescue her.

"She's good," Anna told him truthfully. "She's all healed now. Seth is keeping a pretty close eye on her, though. Noor still wants her, and we have no way of knowing when he'll show up again."

"There's been no sign of him? No evidence he's...possessed anyone else?" Joe had only recently discovered that the world of witches and magic and evil existed. It wasn't an easy thing to swallow, but he was trying. She had to give him that.

"No." She pushed some stray silvery-blonde hairs off her face. "Between him killing his favorite puppet and our attack on him after he assaulted Aria, he probably used up his entire store of energy. If his usual pattern holds true, he'll have to crawl back under his rock for a while and recoup. We just don't know for how long." Anna absently wiped at a drop of sweat sliding down the center of her chest as she considered. "Hopefully we did enough damage to keep him down for a few more weeks. We could definitely use the time."

"At least the killings have stopped." Joe's gaze followed the movement of her hand, and heat pooled in the amber depths of his eyes.

Anna saw his sudden need, and it gave her a shivery moment. She wanted him to act on the promise she saw in his eyes, but he held back. He always held back.

They'd been doing this dance for over a month now, and she

was about at her wits' end. When Aria had come back to town, she'd met Joe once and knew right away he had feelings for Anna. When Aria had told her, she hadn't believed it at first. But as the days went by and her awareness of him increased, Anna became more and more edgy around him.

How could she not, when the epitome of tall-dark-and-drop-dead-gorgeous wanted her? She'd always thought his tall, muscled frame and milk-chocolate skin were things of beauty, but out of respect for him as her trainer, she hadn't let her thoughts go any further.

Until her sister had blasted that door right off its hinges.

And now, all she could think about was his black goatee brushing over her sensitive skin, his light golden-brown eyes watching her. She fantasized about running her small, fair hands over his dark-skinned form. The contrast between light and dark drew her like nothing else ever had. *He* drew her like no one else ever had.

She dreamed of his rough, calloused fingers tracking over her naked body, and it haunted her to the point of waking up, all hot and twitchy.

When she'd finally found the nerve to tell him she knew of his feelings for her, he began avoiding her, as if just her knowing had pushed him away. Then to add to the confusion, out of the blue, he'd shown up at her house one night. A night she and her siblings had gathered together over maps and police data to try and find Noor before he struck again.

Whatever Joe had been planning to say to her that evening had been lost, pushed aside by other, more urgent matters. That was the night he'd learned who she really was and what she could do.

Now they were back to circling one another from a distance, and Anna was beyond frustrated.

Giving herself a mental shake, she brought her focus back to the conversation.

"The only good thing Noor has ever done is destroy JD. But that doesn't negate the fact that it was with his help that JD was able to rape and murder nine women. Luckily, when Noor learned JD had betrayed him by trying to kill Aria behind his back, his crazy took over and he wiped him out."

The longer Joe's attention lingered on her, the more restless Anna became. Her heart did a dizzying stutter in her chest, and her blood heated until her whole body felt flush. In order to keep her hands from trembling—or worse, planting themselves on his chest—she clutched her towel tight.

It was always like this, and she was getting damned tired of it. They both wanted, but neither acted on it.

"I'd better go or I'll be late for work." Anna grabbed her bag and practically ran for the door.

When she pulled into her driveway fifteen minutes later, she killed the ignition and slumped against the steering wheel. Why couldn't she just jump him and be done with it? She envied her sister in that regard; when Aria had finally decided she wanted Seth Lawson, she took him. She didn't let anything stop her.

But Anna knew the reason behind her own hesitation. Her empathic ability. Her shields were strong, and not much got through that she didn't intend. But what if, one day, she inadvertently relaxed those walls and breached his privacy? What if in doing so, she read something in Joe that ripped them apart?

She'd told Aria she was going to stop being afraid and go after what she wanted, but saying it and doing it were two entirely different things. And so here she was, weeks later, and still she and Joe hadn't come any closer to figuring it out.

On an aggravated sigh, Anna pushed out of her car and stomped into the house. Aria was on the couch sketching in her drawing pad but looked up when Anna burst through the door.

"Uh-oh." Aria set the book aside. "What happened?"

Anna dropped everything to the floor, walked over to the

couch, and flopped down next to her sister. "Same thing as usual."

Aria's pale blue eyes met their exact match in hers. "Anna—"

"I know, I know." She let her head drop back. "Ugh, why can't he just make the first move and take the decision out of my hands? It would be so much easier that way. This avoidance thing we're doing now is making me insane."

"And frustrated," Aria teased with a knowing grin. "Still having erotic dreams?"

"Yes. And that only adds to the stress." Anna blew out a breath. "But not all of us can have a real, live stud-muffin in our beds every night."

Aria snorted out a laugh. "Stud-muffin? Seth will love that. And you could have a sexy, mouth-watering pastry of your own if you'd just get over yourself. He's waiting for a sign from you."

Anna sat up and drilled Aria with narrowed eyes. "How do you know that?"

"Seth has started working out with him. They talk."

Anna would discern later how being talked about made her feel. Right now, she had to know exactly what he'd said. "What did Seth tell you?"

"Joe's not an idiot. He can tell there's something holding you back. He wants to be with you, but on your terms, and only when you're ready. He told Seth he'd wait. For as long as it takes."

"Great." Anna stood. Her fidgety body couldn't sit still. "More pressure."

Aria rose with her and took Anna's hands in hers. "Anna. The only one putting pressure on you is *you*. I know you're still worried about sensing something in him or violating his trust, but I really think he's exactly what you need." Aria gave her a sly smile. "And so does Dad."

"*Dad?*" Anna's brows shot upward. That was the last thing Anna expected her sister to say. "What does he have to do with this?"

"Didn't you ever wonder how you came across that pamphlet for Joe's class in the first place?" When Aria didn't say anything more, Anna figured she was waiting for her to come to it on her own.

Thinking back, Anna remembered how she had found it tucked under the wiper on her car one afternoon. She'd come out of school and there it had been.

She hadn't given any thought as to how it had gotten there. Until now.

It clicked, and her mouth dropped open. "He *didn't*."

Her sister nodded, grinning like a fool. "He most definitely *did*."

"Dad set the whole thing up?"

Aria nodded again. "He told me a few weeks ago."

She just might have to have a word with him. "That sneaky little..." Another unsettling thought occurred to her. "Does Mom know? Was she in on it too? Did they team up and try to find me a date?"

"Nope. This was all Dad." Aria pointed a finger at her. "And don't you tell him I told you. He'd kill me if he knew I spilled his beans." Aria sighed, and her features turned earnest. "I only told you because I thought knowing Joe had Dad's stamp of approval would go a long way to easing your mind."

Anna let that knowledge settle and found that it did indeed help. But there were still things she needed to work out for herself.

She reached out and hugged Aria. "It does, and I promise I'll think about it. But right now, I have to get ready for work."

"There's one more thing." Aria's tone changed, and her expression sobered. "I had the vision again."

Anna knew exactly the one her sister was talking about. In it, Aria sees her involved in a horrific crash. The force of the impact sends her over the side of the road. As the car comes to a rest, Aria sees her lying bloody and broken in the torn and smoking wreckage of her car.

"Was there anything new?" Anna asked. "Like where or how it happens? If I survive it?"

"No. Just those same few images over and over."

Anna nodded before taking a moment to force the fear away. She refused to let it consume her. She'd cheated death before, and she'd do it again.

"We've already altered the course of the last vision you had of me dying. We'll just have to make sure this one doesn't come true either."

# 2

When she walked into her classroom an hour later, the children were just arriving. She loved her work. She'd begun as a kindergarten teacher, but her career had slowly evolved into working with only a very special group of young students.

The five who were now in her class, ranging in age from five to nine, had needs that couldn't be met in a regular classroom. Whether it was autism or some other type of mental or physical disability, she helped them to be the best they could be. Her empathic ability allowed her to understand them in a way no other teacher could.

As time had passed and the school had taken notice of her success with these special cases, they'd approached her about shifting her schedule to focus on helping those who needed her most. She'd been glad to do it and, after several meetings to work out the details, she was given the privilege of teaching this wonderful group.

It was almost time for class now, and her children were being led or wheeled in to find their seats.

Until she had kids of her own, these five very special little people would receive all the love she had to give.

She was getting them settled in when the principal, Mrs. Steeple, stepped into her doorway. Beside her stood a small boy. All Anna could see of him was his seal-brown hair and his thin body. His head was bowed so far forward that his chin had to be touching his chest. He was completely drawn in on himself, and when Mrs. Steeple rested her hand on his slight back to usher him into the classroom, he flinched at the contact.

Anna's protective instincts immediately went into overdrive. When they made it into the room, Anna squatted down to put herself on the same level as the frightened child.

"Hi, there. My name is Miss Anna. What's yours?"

When he didn't answer, Mrs. Steeple spoke for him. "This is Jacob Murphy. He's six and he'll be joining your class."

Jacob just remained next to the principal, scared and alone.

"A word," Mrs. Steeple added to Anna.

Anna nodded and bent to Jacob again. "Would you like me to show you to your seat?"

Nothing.

She held out her hand to him and waited, but he stayed completely unresponsive. Anna let her hand drop. "That's okay. I know it's always a little scary meeting new people and being in new places." She stood and moved off towards an empty desk. "How about we put you right here in the front?" Anna laid her hand on the desk. "That way if you need anything, all you have to do is look up at me. Okay?"

Still no reply, but he shuffled slowly towards her.

After getting him settled at his desk, Anna went into the hall where the principal was waiting. She left the door partly ajar in case anyone required assistance.

"Jacob doesn't fit the usual profile of students we normally assign to your class, but I wasn't sure where else to put him." Her expression was full of concern and sympathy, but she smiled through it. "You're so good with the fragile ones, and I'd definitely classify him as that."

"What's going on?" Anna's intuition was screaming.

"I wasn't told much," Mrs. Steeple admitted, "but he's just recently been entered into the foster care program. His foster mother met with me and informed me that, though he's otherwise healthy and normal, he's not uttered a single word since he was brought to her two weeks ago."

"Is he able to?" If Anna were going to help him, she'd need as much information as she could get.

"From all accounts, yes. Whatever happened to him has traumatized him severely."

Anna turned to look through the small window in the door. Jacob hadn't moved. He sat with his head down and his hands clasped in his lap. For all intents and purposes, he was closed off to everything and everyone.

"I'm glad you brought him to me."

"Mrs. Pier, his foster mother, will drop him off and pick him up every day. She asked that we release him only into her care, and only when she personally comes for him."

Were they just being extra careful with this child, or could Jacob be in danger? Anna could only guess that whatever had happened must have been awful. And it could potentially still be a threat.

Well, not on her watch.

"In the meantime, I hope you can work some of your magic on him." Mrs. Steeple smiled sadly before swinging around to return to her office.

Anna knew her boss's words were only a figure of speech, but Anna hoped that her gifts would indeed help little Jacob.

She walked back into her class and got the day started. She kept a close eye on her new student throughout the afternoon, but he neither moved nor spoke. Not even when parents started arriving to take the other children home.

As the last one left, Anna went to him. She pulled up a chair and sat down next to his desk.

"Hi, buddy. Mrs. Steeple said that Mrs. Pier will be picking you up. How about I wait with you until she gets here?"

Anna felt such sorrow for the reclusive child, she vowed to help in any way she could. Taking a breath, she lowered her walls just enough to take in whatever might be near the surface of his mind.

And gasped as his terror and uncertainty swamped her. At the same moment, his head snapped up and his coffee-brown eyes speared straight into her soul. But before she could figure out what it meant, an older woman appeared in the doorway.

"Jacob, sweetie, are you ready?"

When Anna glanced up and then back at Jacob, he was again sitting with his head bowed like the moment had never happened.

As he rose, Anna pasted a smile on her face. "I'll see you tomorrow, Jacob."

~~~

Anna was preoccupied all that evening and into the next morning. Her workout with Joe passed in a blur while her mind was consumed with thoughts of a small frightened boy.

She came in to work early, she was so anxious to see Jacob again. She watched the door closely and just before the bell was about to ring, Mrs. Pier entered with Jacob at her side.

Anna breathed a sigh of relief. She didn't know why he had affected her so much at the first meeting, or why she felt if she didn't have him near her at all times, he'd disappear.

It was irrational, but if being a witch had taught her anything, it was that things happened for a reason. She'd just have to wait and see what Fate had in store for the two of them.

But right now, today, he needed care and tender handling.

Anna crossed to meet him and his caretaker. "Good morning, Jacob. I'm so happy to see you again."

She smiled and nodded at the other woman, and then, without touching him, guided Jacob to his desk.

The same routine continued through the rest of that week and into the following. Jacob made no advances forward—he
~~~

remained silent and withdrawn. And no matter what she'd said or done, he'd not looked at her again.

She hadn't been able to spend as much one-on-one time with him as she would have liked. The rest of her class needed her, and she refused to neglect any of their needs. Breaking through the fear that was wrapped so tightly around Jacob was going to take more. More than she could give him in the limited amount of time she had him in class.

Anna would have to get creative and find a way to reach past his fear to the innocent kid hiding underneath. And if it took personalized attention to do that, then that's what she'd give him.

Until she could figure that out, she included him in their usual routine. Anna used art therapy a lot to help these smart and loving kids express what they couldn't with their words. Jacob resisted though.

Every day she'd place a sheet of paper and a few crayons in front of him. But every day he'd only sit, head down, not moving.

Until today, when movement from his direction caught her eye. She watched, both hopeful and curious, as his little hand came up slowly to grasp a blue crayon. His chin stayed firmly tucked to his chest, but his gaze had risen to focus on the paper in front of him.

Anna subtly shifted away from him and pretended not to notice, continuing to talk encouragingly to her other students as they drew. The last thing she wanted was to distract him when he was finally making progress.

As drawing time came to a close on yet another day, she wrapped up the class as usual and said her goodbyes to the rest of her students.

After seeing the last child off, all that remained was Jacob. She approached his table nonchalantly and pulled up a seat, just as she'd done for a week.

As she sat down, her gaze was instantly drawn to the picture sitting on his desk. As she looked at it, her heart plummeted into her stomach. A lone man stood tall on the paper, but where his face and head should have been, was an image she was all too familiar with.

The beast. The horrific form Noor had taken to attack them on the beach, nearly killing her brother, Ethan.

Granted, it was drawn by a six-year-old, but there was no mistaking the massive head of a bear, the long bat-like ears that stood up and out to the sides, or the thick ram-style horns that grew up from the top of the skull and curved back over it.

Anna desperately wanted to make sense of the image and question Jacob about where he'd seen it, but Mrs. Pier came in at that moment to take him home. Anna hurried to gather herself enough to say a pleasant goodbye.

Once he was gone, Anna rushed back to the sheet of paper lying on his desk. She reached out to pick it up but stopped before making contact. Her hand actually trembled as it hovered over the shocking depiction.

Steeling her nerve, Anna grasped it and held it up for closer study.

Why had he drawn this? Had he seen this creature? If he had, it was no doubt the reason behind his silence and terror. Anna turned and looked out the door where Jacob had exited. Who was this child? And what connection did he have with the monster that wanted to kill them all?

Anna carefully folded the picture and took it with her when she left. Her family needed to see this, so she put out the call on her way home.

Aria and Seth were already there when she walked in. Evan and Ethan, the other set of identical twins that made up their quad set, arrived shortly after.

As her dark-haired, dark-eyed brothers found seats, she paced what little space was left in front of them.

Evan, her brother the cop, spoke first. "Anna, tell us what has you so worried."

"A new student came to my class last week," she began. "His name is Jacob Murphy." After sharing what limited information she knew about him, she continued with the events of the day.

"Today is the first time he's made any attempt at communicating." She crossed to where she'd left her bag and pulled the drawing out. She held it, still folded, in her hands.

"I've tried to read him, but his fear is so overwhelming that it has him completely locked down." Anna dropped her gaze and looked at the paper. "And now I think I know why."

She straightened it out and slowly turned it so her siblings could see it.

Startled gasps and curses filled the air.

"Is that…?" Aria pointed but left the question hanging.

"I'm pretty sure," Anna confirmed, distraught.

"He's tormenting children now?" Evan's teeth were clenched, and his voice sounded more like a snarl than words. His coal-black eyes glittered with fury and loathing.

"I don't know," Anna admitted. "But from what I *can* pick up from Jacob, it doesn't seem to be an ongoing thing. Rather than the echoes that usually accompany a recurring offense, this felt more like the isolated after-effects of an extreme emotional trauma. If this is it," she shook the paper, "it would make sense. We all know how sick and twisted Noor is."

"Wait a minute," Seth intervened. Aria's boyfriend and Evan's partner on the police force stood and scrubbed his hands through his hair. His face was ashen as he turned to the others. "If he's seeing the beast, then he has to be connected somehow." Stalking the same path Anna had followed just moments before, he swiveled and pointed at them. "Other than you four, I seem to be the only person that can see him. Since I can't think of how he could be tied to the prophecy, does that mean he's related to Noor like I am?" His eyes darted between the two identical men before turning to the women and landing on Anna. "What exactly do you know about this kid?"

The Burkes had always thought that, because the four of them were the ones destined to fight Noor, they would be the only ones affected by him while he remained imprisoned. But when they'd discovered that Seth could see the manifestations Noor projected, on a hunch of their mother's they'd probed into his past.

When Noor's wife, Isabel, had left him and disappeared in the late 1500's, she'd taken with her their two young sons. Seth's lineage had been traced back to one of them, and because of that blood link, he was able to see what the rest of the world couldn't.

Was that why Jacob was aware of Noor's presence? Or was it something else?

Anna thought back and tried to recall anything she might have missed. "The only details I know about Jacob's past are the ones I already told you. Last week, Mrs. Steeple said he'd been with his foster mother for two weeks. So whatever caused him to shut down must've happened not long before that."

"Why only the head though?" Aria glanced down at the drawing still clutched in Anna's hand. "Is this a ghastly new game for him—morphing just enough to scare the crap out of innocent children?"

"If that man's head was replaced with Noor's, that might point to possession," Ethan speculated. "What if Noor jumped him and wore him like a new suit?"

Anna worried her bottom lip. "We've never seen him take this abbreviated form any of the times we've met up with him." She turned to Seth. "When Noor was in JD, did you ever see anything like this?"

Seth shook his head. "No. The only indication I had that Noor was in there were JD's eyes. They were vacant and glassy."

"That's all we've noticed too. So why, and how, did Jacob

see him this way?" Aria's gaze searched each of their faces before locking onto Anna's. "This is a new wrinkle, and we need answers. Do you think he'll open up to you?"

"I'm trying." Anna knew she'd have to try harder. "I didn't get a chance to talk to him about the man in the picture. Maybe when Mrs. Pier drops him off tomorrow, I'll see what she knows."

"We'll look into it from our end too," Evan said, indicating himself and Seth. "If this is Noor's new MO, we need to shut him down. *Now*."

"What could his endgame possibly be? What could he stand to gain from this? Jacob's just a kid." Ethan looked bewildered.

"Whatever it is," Seth voiced, "it can't be good. We need to find out and protect this little guy."

There'd never been any doubt that Anna could count on her family to back her about Jacob. Above all else, he needed to be shielded from evil and protected from further harm.

<p style="text-align:center">~~~</p>

The following morning, Anna went through the motions of her workout while worries about Jacob filled her mind.

She'd just grabbed up her bag and was heading out when Joe cornered her.

"Can I see you in my office, please?" His tone was brisk.

She nodded and set her stuff back down, wondering what his problem was. When he turned on his heel and stalked off, she mentally shrugged and followed. He stopped and waited at the doorway at the end of the gym for her to enter first. She walked through, and as soon as the door shut behind them, he shocked her by grabbing her arm and spinning her around to face him.

"What the hell is going on?" His features were set and fierce as he demanded an answer. "You've been distant and unfocused lately. Is there something you're not telling me? Has

Noor returned?" His amber eyes were heated. "Damn it, if he's back and he's threatening you again, you can't shut me out. You may not want me involved in this part of your life, but that's just too fucking bad. I'm in it, and I'm not leaving you unprotected if that sick son of a bitch has surfaced again."

Anna was taken aback at the vehemence in his tone.

Her temper wasn't usually quick to flare the way her siblings' did, but Joe had it simmering in the danger zone. Between her worry about Jacob, speculation of what Noor's new plans were, and now Joe's accusations, it was very close to boiling over.

So she'd been preoccupied over Jacob. That didn't give him the right to jump all over her and get testy. Not everything in her life revolved around him or this mixed-up mess they found themselves in. It pissed her off that he would assume it did and that he'd get so jacked out of shape at the perceived slight to his precious ego.

"We haven't seen him." Her voice was clipped as she jerked free of his hold. "And even if we had, I don't remember asking *you*," she stabbed him in the chest with her finger, "to act as my guardian. I've had more than my fill of those my entire life, and I'm done."

"Well, I'm not. Not by a long shot," he said through clenched teeth. "And don't push me. You might not like the consequences."

She took a step closer, bumping the toes of her shoes into his. Anna looked up into his glowering face and dared him to do something about it.

The muscles in his jaw flexed, proof that he was at least trying to control himself.

Screw control.

"I wasn't shutting you out, you ass. I happen to have a hell of a lot on my mind right now and, *news flash*, it has nothing to do with you." She narrowed her eyes up at him and put the tip of her finger against his chest again. "And just so you know—if there ever comes a day I *do* decide to end your involvement in this, you can damned well bet I'll let you know."

He grabbed her forearm and jerked her into him. Their chests met with a thump and matched the one her heart gave. Anna gasped and made the mistake of looking at his mouth. Those full luscious lips parted—probably to blast her again—and she took advantage. Riding on anger and weeks of pent-up frustration, Anna grabbed the back of his head with her free hand and wrenched him down, locking her lips to his.

When she released him and stormed out, she didn't bother to look back.

# 3

When Joe's mind finally stopped reeling from that scorching kiss, he was stunned. And quickly came to the conclusion that he needed to piss off Anna Burke more often. It was the only time she'd ever dropped her defenses and just reacted.

And, wow, had she *ever*. Joe smirked and called to memory the feel of her mouth eating at his. The flavor of her lips was exotic and hot, and the sudden swelling in his shorts implied his brain wasn't the only part of him happy with this new development. His whole system was on board.

Though the hard-on was nothing new. He'd been living with that since the first time Anna had walked into his establishment. His body and mind had been tied up in knots over her for so long, he didn't remember what life had been like before her.

And now that he'd had a taste of her, there was no way he was going back to the way they'd been—wary and walking on egg shells, careful not to overstep. Nope, after what had just happened, he fully intended to capitalize on the recent advancement in their relationship.

As Joe left his office, he was aware of the cheesy grin still on his face, but he didn't care. Let the guys think what they would.

He headed straight for the locker room and changed into his street clothes. He knew in his gut that she'd neglected to tell him something, and chances were good that it involved Noor. In her current mood, he could pretty well guess that she wouldn't tell him now either. So that left Seth.

As he drove to the police station, Joe mentally rearranged his schedule, trying to free up more time during his days. If Noor was active again, she wasn't bopping all around town without a safeguard. She liked to think she was a bad-ass now, but there was still plenty she didn't know.

And if she didn't like it? Tough shit. That might just work to his benefit, if a repeat of earlier could be expected  Joe felt a rush of heat at the thought. That little witch had a mouth on her, and he planned on putting it to good use.

He found Seth and Evan at their desks. Anna's brother wasn't openly hostile towards him anymore, but he was still aloof and reserved. Evan really seemed to resent the fact that Joe had gotten so close to his sister without his knowledge.

As they'd trained together and gotten to know each other, Anna had told him that her family had always been overly protective of her. And that they'd treated her like a fragile piece of china—breakable with the slightest touch.

Her brothers' reactions when they'd learned she'd been taking classes from him just confirmed to Joe what she'd told him.

He hadn't ever seen that side of her himself, and couldn't understand their reasoning. She'd never displayed any tendency to be frail or soft. She worked her ass off in his gym and unabashedly returned whatever he dished out, never whining or crying over pain or bruises.

Even after he'd learned she was a witch with empathic abilities, she still showed no signs of weakness. She was strong and resilient and sexy as hell.

And that was something he definitely shouldn't be thinking about while facing her mammoth-sized brother. Joe was a stout six foot, but both of her brothers had him by a good four inches.

The first time he'd ever seen them, they, along with Seth, had been standing guard over Anna.

It had given him a moment's pause, but he'd never backed down from anyone. And they'd been blocking his path to Anna.

He'd known she had siblings and that the four of them were quadruplets—two sets of identical twins—but the first time seeing them all together had been startling. Anna and her sister were small and fair, both only a few inches over five feet. Their long hair was a blonde so pale it shimmered like silver in the sunlight as it fell to the middle of their backs. Their features were delicate and refined, and their eyes…the color reminded him of glacier ice he'd seen, but instead of being frigid and intimidating, they radiated only warmth and kindness.

The guys, on the other hand, were at least a foot taller. And in every way, the total opposites of their sisters. Every feature of the men was a stark contrast to those of the women. Dark to their light, and hard to their soft.

Approaching Evan's desk, Joe looked down into his face. As was the norm, it looked like it could have been cut from stone. Knowing answers wouldn't likely be found there, Joe switched his attention to the more welcoming of the two.

Seth had been coming into the gym for the last few weeks, and they'd since become friends. Joe liked him, and because they were each interested in one of the petite Burke witches, it turned out they had a lot in common.

Joe and Seth were pretty comparable in height, but that's where any physical similarities ended. Where Joe and Anna's brothers were lean and muscled, Seth was built like a power lifter. The proportions of his torso were staggering. Joe could work out from now until doomsday and never hope to gain half the mass this man came by naturally.

"Hey, Seth. You got a minute?" Joe asked when the other man looked up.

"Yeah, what do you need?"

"Is there something going on? Anna just left my gym. She's not acting like herself—she's distracted and edgy."

"Why didn't you ask *her*?" Evan sat back in his chair and eyed Joe with a tinge of mockery.

Joe met Evan's gaze. He ignored the question and instead asked one of his own. "Is she in danger?" When Evan only stared him down, he swung back to Seth. "Has he come back? Is he after her?" He didn't need to say the name for the two men to understand.

"We're not sure," Seth told him as his partner threw him a dirty look. He continued in spite of it. "Something *is* going on; we're just not sure what that entails yet."

"Tell me."

"If she wanted you to know, she would have told you herself." Evan leaned forward and rested his arms on the desk.

Joe didn't have time for this shit. He rounded on Evan. "You need to get your panties out of a bunch and recognize that I'm not going anywhere." Joe set his hands flat on Evan's desk and leaned in. His complete focus centered on the man in front of him. "And if you can't get over yourself long enough to help me ensure Anna is safe, then you need to get the fuck out of the way and let me do it myself."

Evan was gearing up to lay into him—Joe could see it in the black eyes drilling holes through him. But before Anna's brother could let it loose, Seth interrupted.

"He's right, Evan. We all want to keep the girls safe. The more people we have working towards that goal, the better."

Joe stood straight as Evan seethed for another moment. The detective took a breath and then relaxed back into his seat again.

"Noor's back, but not in the way you might think." Seth filled him in on the rest.

"The beast head—it's the same as the day from the beach?" Anna had told Joe about the battle against the new form Noor had taken. She'd been shaken afterward but not hurt.

"Yeah," Seth acknowledged. "There's no mistaking it."

"What do you think it means?"

"We don't know yet. There's a lot of mystery around this child. Where he came from, who he is, why he's seeing Noor's beast."

Joe zeroed in on only one part of that. "What do you mean *who he is*? You have his name."

"We have *a* name." Evan joined the conversation. "We ran it through every database we have, but there's no male child of that approximate age with that name listed on any birth record."

Joe's brows came together as possibilities raced through his mind. He settled on the most obvious. "Someone's protecting him."

Evan nodded. "That's our take."

"How do we find out who? And why?" Joe asked.

"We keep digging." Seth motioned to the computer on his desk.

When Joe left a few minutes later, he drove straight to the school where Anna worked. He found a space in the lot that gave him a clear view of the entrance and waited.

As he did, he tried to figure out why she hadn't told him about Jacob. Did she not trust him? He'd thought he'd proven his intent to stick around the night they'd all shown him their powers. He thought they'd taken a step closer to where they wanted to be.

Was that what was holding her back? Did she still doubt him? The idea of that possibility stabbed into his chest.

When a loud bell sounded, Joe brought his thoughts back and unfolded himself from his car. He rounded the front to sit on the hood. He watched as children poured out of the building and ran for the buses and cars that would take them home from another day of school.

The flow eventually lessened and still he waited. He saw a pretty older woman walk in alone and minutes later come out with a young boy. His head was bent low and he avoided all of her attempts to touch him. He trailed behind a couple of steps as the woman reached for the rear passenger door of her car.

As she opened it, a few papers caught by a breeze drifted out of her car. She hurriedly snatched at one, but the others—a stapled bundle of three or four—fluttered and tumbled in Joe's direction. He managed to trap it under his foot when they touched down near him. Bending to pick them up, he saw it was a list of supplies needed for a certain blonde's class. He walked the stack back to its owner.

"Here you go." Joe handed over the rogue documents.

"Thank you." She eyed him cautiously before turning to the boy. "Come on, Jacob. We need to get going."

*So this was Jacob.*

"I see you're in Miss Anna's class." Joe bent to Jacob. "She's a good friend of mine."

Jacob didn't acknowledge him in any way, and Joe could tell that the woman was nervous by his presence.

"Well, it was nice meeting you." Joe moved off a little way as she helped Jacob into the car and buckled him in. After firmly closing the door, she spun to walk around the front end of the car. As she did, Jacob raised his head. He stared through the window…right at Joe.

Dark brown eyes met his for the amount of time it took a heart to beat. And in that split second, Joe felt like he'd been weighed and measured.

Jacob's head dropped back down at the same time the woman with him slid behind the wheel. She'd missed the entire exchange.

Joe's gaze followed the vehicle's path. His head turned to track it until it drove out of sight.

"What are you doing here?"

The abrupt question pulled his attention back around. Anna stood directly in front of him.

"I just met Jacob."

If she were surprised by him knowing that name, she gave no indication.

"It feels like he's seeing right into your soul when he looks at you."

"Wait. What?" *That* surprised her. "He made eye contact?"

"Yeah." Joe explained how the incident had happened.

"Did he say anything to the woman with him, or do anything else?"

"No. Just stared at me for a couple of beats and then put his head back down. She didn't see any of it."

Knowing that she, of all people, would understand, he tried to explain what he'd felt. "It was almost like he was seeing into me—judging me somehow."

"That's interesting," she muttered, thinking it over. She seemed to suddenly remember. "You never did tell me why you're here."

"If Noor's back, I'm not letting you out of my sight."

"We're back to this? I thought I told you I don't need a babysitter." Some of the earlier hostility returned to her eyes. "And how do you even know about Jacob?" Anna stopped and answered her own question. "Seth."

She crossed her arms over her chest and regarded him with puzzlement. "You and he seem to be getting pretty close. I've heard you talk about stuff like a couple of old women. But instead of gossiping in the back yard or over a drink, you do it surrounded by dumbbells and weights."

She sent him a scathing look before turning to walk away. "I'll thank you not to discuss my life behind my back."

He wasn't going to let her march out of his life like this. She'd crossed a line this morning, and he wasn't letting her retreat back over it.

Joe reached out and hooked her arm. "Anna, stop."

Anna swung back around, and her blue eyes sparked. "Let me go."

"No."

She quirked an elegant blonde brow at him, her mouth set in a defiant line.

Reading the barely-veiled threat in her heated gaze, he leaned in closer. "Just in case you're planning to kick my ass, don't forget it was *me* who showed you all of those moves."

He let out a resigned sigh and tried again. "We need to talk. Can we please go somewhere to discuss this?"

Anna pointedly looked down to where he still held her arm. He loosened his grip and let his hand fall.

Why her family still thought of her as weak he'd never understand. She held strong and fierce against his request.

"Please." His hushed voice was weighted with his need to make things right between them.

She finally relented. "You can follow me to my place. No one will be there. My father surprised Aria with a studio he built so she can work on her sculptures. She spends a lot of her time there now. And, as you'll know because you and Seth are such *close* friends, he won't be home for a while."

He ignored the dig. "I'll be right behind you."

When they pulled up into her driveway a few minutes later, she exited her car and, not waiting for him, walked through her front door, leaving it open behind her.

He followed her in and closed the door, taking in the cozy living room. It smelled like her.

"Do you want something to drink?"

Joe was kind of surprised she'd offered. "Beer if you have it. Thanks."

He made himself comfortable on the couch while she went into the kitchen. He heard the refrigerator open and close. When she came back a minute later, she was holding a brown bottle and a clear wine glass half-full of red wine.

Anna handed him the bottle and sat down next to him. "What did you want to talk about?"

Joe felt frustration welling up. Even though she'd been irritated with him all day, after what had happened that morning, he hadn't given up hope that they could finally be together. Instead, it looked like she was still distancing herself.

"I get it. You don't trust me," he stated baldly.

By the widening of her lids, his comment wasn't what she'd expected. Good. She needed to have her eyes opened to a few things. And he was determined to do exactly that.

"Otherwise, you wouldn't still be censoring what you share with me. I only talked to Seth because I couldn't figure out what you wanted. I told him I'd wait for you to be ready, that I wouldn't push you. I wanted you to trust me with who you are, with *what* you are." Joe held her gaze. "Well, I'm done. I'm not waiting around anymore."

His last words caused her to flinch as if she'd been struck, and her expressive blue eyes dimmed. Her body seemed to brace for something. Joe was perplexed over her reaction but continued on.

"So this is me pushing you." He took a breath and laid it out. "I want you, Anna. So badly I'm slowly going out of my mind. I want to share everything with you. The good, the bad, the natural. And even the supernatural."

Joe watched as several emotions washed over Anna's exquisite face. Relief was first and foremost. That gave way to wonderment and then cautious hope. Moisture gathered in her eyes and made the icy blue shimmer like gems. That, added to the way the tension drained out of her body, and Joe suddenly knew what she'd been protecting herself against.

Heartbreak. She'd expected him to walk away from her because of the things that made her different.

What the hell kind of man did she think he was? What kind

of douchebags had she dated before him?

Determined to prove to her that he wasn't like whomever had come before him, he prepared to bare his soul.

"See for yourself. You're an empath. Use that to look into my mind, into my heart. I don't ever want you to doubt me. If that's the only way you'll feel sure, then do it."

Anna gasped and shook her head. She'd withdrawn again. "I can't. You don't know…"

"I know what I feel for you, Anna. If you can't trust what I say, then listen to my heart."

She was still moving her head from side to side. Joe reached out and took the wine glass from her trembling fingers. He set both of their drinks on the table and then took her hands in his. He let his gaze sink deeply into hers.

"I trust you. With everything I am and everything I have, I trust you." Joe let the truth of his conviction shine through. "Look. Feel it." Anna was absolutely still for a moment and then nodded ever so slightly.

He didn't know what to expect from what was about to happen, but in the end, it didn't feel like anything. She held his gaze, and as they stared at one another, something slowly changed in her.

She lost the rigidity that had returned to her limbs and features. Her body softened again and eased. A smile ticked up the corners of her mouth and gradually spread over her face to include those glorious eyes.

Her hands slid from his and rose to lie gently on either side of his face. When she leaned in to kiss him softly, he reached out and pulled her in close to his body.

"Thank God," he moaned at the feel of her. "I've wanted to do this for so long." He trailed his lips down her neck.

She pulled back just enough to look up into his face. "Me too."

Her admission made his heart trip over itself. Joe leaned

into her until she was lying on her back underneath him. She instantly opened her thighs to make room for him.

Using one callused hand, he smoothed the fine hairs back away from her face. He fixed his eyes on her perfect features and took in everything about her.

From the china-like look and feel of her skin, so completely opposite of his own, to the way the delicate elements of her face combined into a picture that took his breath away.

"So beautiful." He couldn't stop the words from slipping out. Joe lowered his head and sank into her waiting mouth.

All thought left his mind, other than the woman beneath him. His hands roamed freely over her deceptively soft, pliant body. He knew firsthand the strength that lay under the silky skin, as he'd had a part in molding and shaping it.

Supporting his weight on his right arm, Joe slid his left hand down to her hip and back up. On the return journey, he slipped it under the hem of her shirt and up her ribcage. He didn't stop until he found the firm roundness of her breast.

Even through the material of her bra, he could feel the pebbled nub of her nipple. Slowly, he rolled it under his thumb. She moaned deep in her throat at the touch. The sound of her pleasure made his blood run hotter, and a need like he'd never known demanded he taste her more fully. He deepened the kiss, his hunger for her building into a frenzy.

Breathing as if he'd just gone five rounds, Joe ripped his mouth from hers. He jerked her shirt up until it bunched above her heaving chest. Only nude-colored lace covered her now, and he impatiently pushed that aside so that her pert breasts were free and bare.

He took a moment to marvel at the soft, rounded mounds before he bent and sucked one taut, puckered nipple between his lips.

Anna gasped and arched her back, pushing herself more ardently into the heat of his mouth. Joe suckled again and released it to blow hot breath over it. Anna mewled and her hands came up to grip the back of his head.

Completely lost in his need to devour her, Joe switched to the other and gave it a hard flick of his tongue before taking it between his teeth. Applying firm pressure, he took the bite to the brink where pleasure met pain before backing off to rain tender kisses over it.

Anna was writhing against him. The demanding upward thrust of her hips nearly made him lose control, but he was determined to take her higher than she'd ever been.

"Again," she panted out. "Again."

Taking the first in hand again, Joe repeated the love bite. Listening to Anna's cues, he took it even further before kissing away the sting.

Adrift in the throes of passion, Anna widened her legs to let Joe settle more fully against her core. Unable to stop himself, Joe pressed his erection hard against her. Even through his denim and her slacks, he could feel the heat of her arousal.

He ground himself into her over and over, wishing there weren't so many layers between them.

"Oh God, oh God." Anna reached down, grabbed his ass, and pulled him closer. "I need... I want..."

"I know exactly what you want." His first time with Anna would not be on a cramped couch. He wanted room to take her the rest of the way over the edge. Joe planted a foot on the floor and wrapped one arm around Anna's back. He locked down into her dreamy, half-closed eyes.

"Hold on to me."

~~~

Anna couldn't do anything *but* hold on. What he'd done to her had left her shaky and tingling all over.

She'd dated a few guys, but none had made her feel like
~~~

Joe did. He was rough and insistent, and had already driven her arousal further than she'd ever been before. His intensity should have scared her, but she couldn't bring herself to care. Not only was she not afraid—she wanted *more*.

She never would have guessed she'd like it rough. But something about his not-so-tender embraces made her crave his touch in ways she hadn't thought possible.

When she locked her arms and legs around him, he levered himself up to his feet. She scraped her teeth along his neck, biting down on his shoulder as he crossed the room. He groaned into her hair, and with his big, strong hands keeping her center firmly wedged against the ridge of his shaft, he made every step he took a study in sweet torture.

"Where?" he growled.

After a moment to reorient herself, she pointed to the room on the right. "There."

Joe wasted no time in getting her inside and closing the door behind them. Once locked away, he let her legs slide down the length of his. She didn't think her own would hold her weight, but he gave her a moment to steady before he began to strip away her clothes.

When she was fully naked, his eyes raked over every inch of her. At any other time, she may have felt uneasy. Although he'd seen her in tight shorts and a sports bra countless times, no one had ever seen her like *this*. But the hunger in his molten gaze evaporated any insecurities she might have had. Watching his muscles bunch and his jaw clench, she could see he wanted her every bit as much as she wanted him.

"Perfect. Absolutely fucking perfect."

He stepped in close and claimed her mouth once again, finally breaking away to run his tongue over every inch of her shoulders. Open-mouthed kisses left a fiery trail over her chest where he bit and suckled, and her breathing rasped in and out unevenly.

Dropping to his knees, Joe laved over her stomach and into the indentation of her navel.

The muscles in her belly quivered with every stroke of his tongue and nip of his teeth. Her heart thrashed wildly in her chest, and her knees threatened to give way. She braced her hands on his shoulders for balance as he set out to steal even that.

Reaching her hips, she felt his lips skim to the right, planting kisses along her hipbone and into the curve of softness between it and her mound. She shuddered as he brushed against the trimmed V of hair he found there.

Anticipating more of the same, Anna was surprised when his touch disappeared. She glanced down to find his gaze focused on the mark that tied her to the element of water.

Nestled low on the left side of her abdomen was a circle about four inches in diameter. Within that ring were six curved lines—three branching towards the center on either side, flowing in waves like the water she communed with. Joe traced the entire shape with his finger before placing his mouth dead center and kissing it.

Her whole body trembled at the unexpected tenderness. Cupping his face in her hands, she bent and kissed him gently on the lips. When she rose, she pulled him with her. Needing to touch him, she fumbled hurriedly at his clothes, anxious to join his with hers in a pile on the floor.

Her hands, finally having found what they sought, slid over his smooth skin and kneaded the strained muscles underneath. She kissed and tasted, using her teeth to tug and pull, and when her fingernails raked across the ridges and valleys of his midsection, his breath caught and his abs rippled.

She wasn't the only one who liked it rough.

Joe reached past her, and in one big sweep, threw the covers back and off the bed. He lowered her gently, following her descent, and their bodies finally met, skin to skin.

She loved the weight of him on top of her, his masculine heat warming her as his hard body pressed firmly into her softness. Her entire world narrowed down to his face, his body, his scent.

With one knee, he spread her thighs and fit himself between them, pushing his hips against hers and hinting at what his possession would feel like. Her hips arched up automatically, a primal need to fuse his body with hers.

Before her next breath, the pressure was gone and he was sliding down her body. He rained hot, wet kisses along the path he followed south. When he finally reached her center, she was beyond any measure of reserve or control. She closed her eyes, held her breath, and waited desperately for what she hoped he would do next.

"Anna," he whispered. "Look at me."

It took her a moment, but finally his words registered, and her lashes fluttered open. Her blue eyes found his golden ones, and as he held her captive in his gaze, his mouth closed over her swollen nub.

Her orgasm slammed into her so hard, she could do nothing but hope she survived it. Joe didn't relent, his tongue keeping rhythm as wave after wave rolled over her.

Her mind was reeling, and as her body continued to convulse, he slid two fingers inside her. Her second orgasm shot through her, his fingers curling in time with his mouth, her entire core spasming around him.

When the tremors began to subside, Joe climbed back up her body, positioned himself above her, and thrust deep.

Still panting, Anna gasped at the sudden combination of pain and pleasure. The quick sting of losing her virginity was swiftly forgotten as the bliss of being filled to bursting took her over.

He immediately stilled, his face a mask of confusion and concern. She smiled devilishly and rocked her hips up, clenching around him from the inside.

Apparently satisfied, Joe pushed into her again as his mouth came down on hers, moaning against her lips. She wrapped her legs around him, pulled him even closer, and met each thrust with one of her own. As the speed increased and the urgency built, she felt herself climbing once more.

And just as she crested that peak again, they found their release together.

# 4

It was fully dark when Anna woke. She was stretched out on top of a solid and very warm male body. It took her brain a minute to focus and remember what had happened. A smile curved her lips.

Anna didn't recall falling asleep. The last thing she remembered was drifting as she'd come back to herself after the…what was it…third or fourth orgasm.

She took stock of her body now and felt a few twinges, but they only brought her happiness. Joe had done more than rock her world. He'd completely destroyed it, in a decidedly delicious way. Now she knew why Aria wore that dreamy grin most of the time.

She didn't regret her choice to wait for the right man; she was just glad she'd finally found him. In Joe.

Turning her head enough to bury her nose in his chest, she breathed deeply, taking his scent deep into herself to hold and cherish.

"You okay?" His low, husky voice vibrated near her ear.

"Perfect." She smiled.

"I didn't know…" His words trailed off, but she knew he understood the significance of their union.

"And I didn't say anything. It wasn't a big secret; it just never came up." She rested her chin on her hands and grinned up into his sleepy amber eyes. "And by the time it did, I was kind of busy."

"I would have done things differently if I'd known." Worry tinged their light brown depths.

Anna was quick to reassure him. "I wouldn't have wanted you to do anything differently. I loved every minute.'

She snuggled closer into him and just enjoyed knowing this man was finally hers. She idly drew random designs on his chest and abdomen with her fingertip, following the natural taper of his physique as she learned the planes of his body.

"Mmm, that feels so good," Joe's voice rumbled above her head. "I think I've become addicted to you. Those hands are amazing." He paused for a beat. "Can I ask you something?"

"Anything," she answered immediately, still trailing her hand over him.

"What's it like?"

"Touching you? *Amazing*." Anna smiled.

A short laugh escaped his lips. "Good to know. But I was asking about your magic."

She giggled. "I know." He'd let her see into his mind; it was only fair that she give him a glimpse into hers. "The empath part has been a little harder to deal with than the elemental," she admitted. "There was a long time that it overwhelmed me, and I needed my family to shield me. But I've worked my ass off to build a solid barrier around my mind, so that I could stand on my own and fend for myself."

"And it's such a fine ass too." Joe gave it a light slap and she laughed.

"Well, I'm glad you like it."

"How do you do the water thing? Do you need a source, or can you make it yourself?"

She shifted until she was sitting on her knees beside him and then raised her hand to look at it, front and back.

"I don't need to make it; there's moisture all around us. In the air, the ground— it's everywhere." Anna summoned her magic from within. She swirled her fingers around and had water dancing on their tips.

"That is so freaking cool." Joe reached out his hand and touched the droplets.

Anna aligned her hand with his, palm to palm, and set the water to dancing over and through their spread fingers.

"It feels like silk."

Answering an unnamed need, Anna wound the beads of water down and around Joe's arm to snake over his shoulder and onto his chest. With a small motion of her hand, she had it trailing over his skin as her fingers had only moments ago. The trickle dripped down his torso, across his stomach, and around his navel.

The sensuous play drew a groan from deep within him. "Anna."

She let the water travel lower, fondling him until his golden eyes darkened with arousal and his manhood grew and pulsed. Her own desire bloomed, so she recalled her magic and the water dispersed, returning from whence it came. Once gone, Anna rose up, threw one leg over his waist, and straddled him.

His hands came up to steady her hips as she leaned down to kiss his full, sexy lips. The short black hairs of the goatee that framed his mouth brushed against her face, which she'd quickly learned to appreciate the night before.

As they kissed, one of his hands swept around to reach underneath her. His abdominal muscles bunched, and she felt the head of his shaft at her entrance. When his hand returned to her waist, he guided her down as his hips came up.

She broke the kiss to gasp as her tender flesh gave way.

"Too much?" Joe's gaze was full of need, but she could still read the concern behind the heat.

"No." Anna straightened and settled fully onto him.

She took a moment to adjust to the new angle and sensations this position brought. At his urging, she raised and lowered her body onto his, finding the rhythm that quickly had them panting in contentment a few minutes later.

Collapsed on his chest, Anna felt her stomach growl. She tried to ignore it, but she hadn't eaten since breakfast, and it was well after midnight.

Joe laughed underneath her. "Are we raiding the kitchen now?"

"Definitely yes. I'm starving."

Anna rose and slid into her robe as Joe pulled on his jeans. Together they went to look for food. She'd just pulled the door of the fridge open when she felt a stirring in her mind.

*"Finally came up for air, huh?"*

She could feel Aria's laugh. *"Are you home?"*

*"Yeah, we have been for some time. Saw Joe's truck in the driveway but no sign of either of you. Figured you were a little occupied."*

Anna felt herself flush at the thought. *"You could say that."*

*"That good, huh?"* Aria's mind teased before turning serious. *"Are you okay?"*

Anna sent soothing thoughts. *"Couldn't be better."*

*"I'm happy for you, sis. I'll let you get back to your man, and I'll see you in the morning. Love you."*

*"I love you too."* Anna was smiling when she swung around with bowls of leftovers in her hands.

As they sat at the table eating, Joe asked her about Jacob. "What do you think his story is?"

Anna looked directly into his eyes before answering. "First, I want to tell you I wasn't deliberately keeping anything from you. I just had so much going on in my mind, it consumed me. I'm sorry you thought I didn't trust you."

"It was just a misunderstanding. But one good thing came out of it." Joe gave her a smug grin. "You kissed me."

"I did, didn't I?" Anna sent him a sassy glance.

"One I'll never forget." Mischief danced in his eyes and the corner of his mouth quirked. "You're pretty hot when you're mad."

"Is that a fact?" Anna laughed and took a bite of her spaghetti. Bringing the conversation back around, she continued. "Anyway, as far as Jacob goes, I wish I knew. He's so scared, I can't see past the fear to get to what's really going on. I have to figure out a way to get through to him and find out why he's seeing Noor's beast."

"Why would Noor go after a child?" Joe asked, clearly disturbed by the idea.

"We don't know that he is," Anna reminded him. "The fear I sense isn't an ongoing kind of thing. It feels more like something he was exposed to at some point recently, and it's still haunting him."

Joe ate a few more bites of steak. She knew there was something he was contemplating but let him work out how he wanted to approach it.

He pushed a hunk of meat around his plate before finally lifting his eyes to her. "Do you think he's like you? Like your family?"

"A witch?" she asked for clarification.

He nodded. "Yeah. Do you think he has powers like you guys? And that's how he's able to see this monster?"

"I guess it could be a possibility, but I just don't know. And we won't until I can get him to open up and talk to me."

They discussed Jacob until the food was gone and the dishes washed. Joe wiped his hands on a dish towel and watched her. She knew he was waiting for her to make the next move.

Anna figured she had two options. Send him on his way or invite him to stay. When she looked inside, there really was no decision to be made.

"Let's go back to bed."

His amber eyes deepened in color as he set aside the towel and took her into his arms. She looked up into his handsome face, her gaze tracking over his closely-cropped black hair, wide forehead, and straight black brows, down his strong nose, to his full, sensuous lips surrounded by neatly-trimmed, soft bristles.

She knew from previous conversations that he came from a mixed heritage, and the combination of black and white had come together to form this insanely gorgeous man. Strong, ropy muscle wrapped in milk-chocolate skin so smooth, she just wanted to lick and nibble all over it.

And now she had the liberty to do exactly that. She took his hand in hers and pulled him back into her bedroom.

~~~

When Anna opened her eyes again, the sun was winning its battle against the dark. She rolled, looking for Joe's warmth, and found only cool sheets.

Her brain still hadn't fully registered the fact he was gone before he stepped back into the bedroom in nothing but a towel. When he saw she was just waking up, he came to her and leaned in, placing one hand on either side of her head.

As he lowered to her and Anna realized he was going to kiss her, she said a quick chant in her head and sent silent thanks to her dorky brothers.

Once Evan and Ethan had become teenagers and discovered girls, they'd invented a little spell they'd bragged about to her and Aria—one that would cure even the most repellent bad breath. At the time, she'd thought they were idiots. But now she was glad she'd paid attention as Joe's lips found hers and planted a kiss more effective than any caffeine had ever been.

"Good morning," she greeted when he finally released her mouth. He tasted of toothpaste and smelled of her soap.

"I hope you don't mind," he murmured before rising, "but I used your shower and toothbrush."
~~~

Anna pushed herself up to a seated position and swept her hair back off her face. "No, not at all. What time is it?" She looked around for her cell, but he answered before she could locate it.

"A little after six." He folded one leg underneath him and sat on the edge of the bed facing her. With his eyes and a fingertip, he traced her bare collarbone down to the top of the sheet she had wrapped around her breasts. "I hated to leave this bed, but I need to get to the gym. I have a meeting this morning." His gaze rose to meet hers. "Will I see you there later?"

Anna leaned forward and licked across his bottom lip. "You missed a little toothpaste," she taunted, knowing how that would torment him.

Joe's pupils dilated as he drew in a deep breath. "You are so dangerous."

His words, spoken in that hushed, tension-fraught way, combined with the barely-restrained control in his heated glare, brought her all manner of pleasure.

"If there weren't someone meeting me at six-thirty," his face and body were tight with his fierce need, "I'd show you what I do to tempting little witches."

Anna cocked her head with an innocent look. "Promise?"

She couldn't help it. She found she loved the intimacy of teasing him like this.

Joe shifted his position, undoubtedly to accommodate his growing arousal. He watched her with such intensity she thought he'd throw the towel aside and take her right then. But instead, he closed those molten-gold eyes and gave his head a shake.

"Give me strength."

He inhaled deeply and then stood up and backed away. His hand came up as if to warn her off. "I can do this. You just have to stay there."

Anna saw the pained humor in his tortured and smoldering

stare. "Sit and be still, and don't say anything else."

Anna opened her mouth to speak, but he halted her with a quick point of his finger.

"Ah." A sharp, abrupt sound. "No. Quiet."

She grinned wickedly at his antics but held silent. Instead, she watched his every move as he found his clothes and laid them out. Anna had to bite the inside of her cheek to keep from laughing when he sent her a brief glance, frowned, and then fought to pull his underwear on one-handed without removing the towel.

When his naughty bits were fully covered, he finally dropped the flimsy barrier, and Anna took the opportunity to drink him in, admiring every visible square inch of his mouth-watering form.

He turned and caught her study. "Damn it, close your eyes."

"But—"

He stopped her with a stern look this time. "You're not helping at all. Close those sexy eyes, or I'll never get out of here."

Anna huffed out an aggrieved sigh but did as he asked. A short time later, he gave her a short, hard kiss and left. When she heard her bedroom door shut, she fell back onto her pillows and laughed until her sides hurt. Oh, this was going to be so much fun. She never would have guessed she could have this much power over someone so big and tough.

Still reveling in her newfound advantage, she got up and headed for the shower. Every time she thought of how Joe had acted that morning, she chuckled.

Half an hour later and dressed in her workout gear, Anna walked into the kitchen to see Aria and Seth locked in a heated kiss.

"Oops, sorry." Anna backed up a couple of steps.

Seth reluctantly released her sister and turned to Anna. "This is your house. You should be able to get something to eat without us in the way." He glanced at Aria and then back to Anna. "Which brings up something we wanted to talk to you about."

"What's that?" Anna asked, pouring herself a cup of coffee.

"I know when you bought this house, you didn't count on your sister and me moving in," Seth said. "I guess I just wanted to make sure you knew it wouldn't be forever. We would have given you back your privacy before now, but it's too dangerous for you to be here by yourself. With Noor and the prophecy term coming up, none of us can be too careful."

Seth and Aria had come from completely different directions to find each other. Aria had run away to Ohio when the quads were eighteen and had stayed there for the next six years. Until their big bad, Edrick Noor, had awakened and forced her to return home. When she'd first arrived, she'd stayed with their parents. But eventually she'd moved to Anna's to be closer to her twin and reestablish the bond they shared.

Seth Lawson, once known only as Law, had been an undercover officer for a specialized task force whose goal it was to infiltrate motorcycle gangs to take them down from the inside. His last assignment had brought him to Daytona Beach, and here he'd decided to stay.

In large part due to her sister. They'd met and fallen in love, despite everything that had stood between them. Seth had eventually given up the cloak and dagger and traded it in for a detective job as Evan's partner on the Daytona Beach police force. With nowhere else to go, Aria and Seth had both ended up living with her.

Which was fine. She loved having her twin close again.

But Anna could see their dilemma. They were in love and wanted to start building their lives together. She could completely understand. And although her relationship with Joe was still very new, if it headed in the direction she hoped, then there could potentially be four grown adults living under the same roof.

Her modest little home just hadn't been built for that.

However, because she and her siblings were slated to face off against a force bent on their destruction, they had targets on their backs. If any one of them died, Edrick Noor would have free reign on this world and wreak unimaginable havoc.

He'd tried multiple times already to pick them off one by one and had been thwarted at every turn. As time went on, he would inevitably grow stronger, and his attempts would only become more formidable.

"I understand, and I agree. We all have to be vigilant to stay safe," Anna admitted. "But don't worry about staying here. We have time to figure this all out." She grinned. "Even if we have to start hanging a tie on the front door."

"Let's hope it doesn't come to that." Seth chuckled and turned to Aria. "Are you ready to go, Pixie?"

Anna swallowed the rest of her coffee and rinsed out her mug. "What are your plans for today?" she asked her sister.

"I'm headed to Mom and Dad's again. I have some work to do, and then I want to hit the internet again. I'm determined to find out how and where Noor got his power. Dark magic, a deal with the devil—whatever it was, I think if we can find that, we'll know better how to defeat him."

"Well, I wish you luck. I think we're due for a little good news." Anna gave Aria a hug and a kiss on the cheek and then did the same with Seth. "I'd better go too. I'll see you both later."

Joe was waiting for her when she reached the gym, and he wasted no time in getting started. She'd barely worked up a sweat though when she made a rather pleasant discovery.

Since she and Joe had become intimate, their workout had taken on a whole new dimension. As he grabbed her from behind, his hot breath washed over the bare skin at the back of her neck. Delightful shivers coursed through her with his body locked tight against hers. She tingled in the most interesting places.

When she employed a move that threw him to the floor and had her straddling his hips, arousal slid lava-hot along her veins to settle in her core, which was in direct contact with the growing evidence of his own desire.

They barely made it through without tearing each other's clothes off, and by the time they finally called it quits, they were both sweaty and on edge. Anna would have liked to find a private place to relieve the pressure, but he was slammed with training sessions today. So it would have to wait. She was still flushed with a simmering need when she left him to return home to shower.

As her system leveled out and the time neared for her to see Jacob again, thoughts of the troubled child pushed everything else aside. Her mind was so focused on trying to find the key to reaching him that the whole drive to the school was a blur.

One thing she did know was that her first stop had to be the principal's office. Jacob had been in her class a little over a week now, and she hadn't made near as much progress as she'd hoped. She needed to see if Mrs. Steeple knew anything more about Jacob's history that she hadn't already shared.

She knocked on the doorjamb to get the older woman's attention.

"Anna," she greeted with a smile when she looked up. "Come in and have a seat. What can I do for you?"

Anna sat. "I wanted to talk to you about Jacob Murphy."

Mrs. Steeple's open expression became hooded and reserved. Anna could only take that to mean there was more to the story than what she'd been told.

"You said you put him in my class for a reason," Anna reminded her. "I know it's only been a week since you brought him to me, but he's just as withdrawn and unresponsive now as he was then. I didn't expect miracles, but I'd at least hoped for some kind of sign that I was getting through to him. Something traumatic must have happened to cause Jacob to retreat to this extent. If I'm going to have any success with him, I need more information." Anna leaned forward in her chair. "Is there *anything* about his past that you can tell me?"

The principal was quiet as she considered Anna's words.

Finally, she relented. "The specifics are closely safeguarded, but I do know that he's in something similar to the witness protection program. He was brought in from out-of-state to further conceal his identity. As far as his current condition goes, I was only told that he and his mother were attacked prior to his placement within the foster care system. She was killed, and he was left for dead."

# 5

Anna gasped and brought her hand up to her heart, which was aching over what this small innocent boy had suffered. "Who would do that?"

"I don't know."

"What about his father? Was he there?"

Mrs. Steeple shook her head. "I don't know."

Anna had so many more questions but gleaned that they'd all be met with the same response. She carefully formed one final inquiry.

"Would you be opposed to me speaking with his caretaker? I want to work with him on an individual basis."

"I don't foresee a problem with that," Mrs. Steeple allowed. "But be prepared if he starts responding. I get the feeling that the authorities overseeing his case are chomping at the bit to learn what he knows."

"Thank you. I'll keep that in mind." Anna rose and made her way through the halls to her own classroom. She had fifteen minutes before the children began to arrive. Mrs. Pier, with Jacob, was always the last to show up.

Anna stood in the doorway and greeted each student, waiting for any sign of the dark-haired boy that tore at her heart.

Finally, she saw him. As he and his guardian neared, Anna angled her body to slow their approach.

"Good morning, Jacob," Anna said cheerily. "Please go find

your seat. I'd like to speak with Mrs. Pier for a moment."

Both women watched as he shuffled sullenly to his desk and sat down. Anna turned to the other woman. "I spoke with the principal briefly this morning about Jacob," she prefaced. "I'd like to spend more time working one-on-one with him. If there's any chance of breaking through to him, I think it's going to be privately, away from the other kids. Would it be possible for him to come early or stay after school?"

Before the foster mom could voice her apprehension, Anna spoke again. "Mrs. Steeple shared with me what little she knows. I realize he could still be in danger, but if I'm able to make any progress at all, you will be the first call I make. I want to keep him safe as much as you do."

Mrs. Pier shook her head. "Unfortunately, that decision isn't mine to make. I'll need to make some calls. If it's approved, it'll have to be before class. I just don't have the time in the afternoons."

Anna felt a ray of hope. "Yes, that can be arranged. Thank you."

"Give me your number. I'll call you as soon as I know."

She hurried to her desk to jot her cell number down and gave it to the other woman. Once she was gone, Anna stepped into her room and got her lessons underway.

When there was an hour left of class, Anna let them have a special treat and allowed the kids to have a small snack. As they ate quietly at their tables, she looked through the work the children had done earlier.

She suddenly became aware of someone watching her. Without looking up, she lowered her shields a fraction to ascertain whether it was a threat. She knew immediately who it was and raised her attention to Jacob.

He was staring directly at her.

It was so out of character for him, she slowly she set her pen aside and went to him. His big brown eyes solemnly followed her progress until she squatted down next to him.

"Did you need something, sweetheart?" She kept her voice soft and light.

He said nothing, continuing to watch her. She lessened the barriers around her mind further to try to gauge what he was feeling.

His eyes widened and his breathing became short and choppy. His renewed fear swamped her.

*Can he feel me in his mind?*

"Shhh, it's okay," she soothed gently. "No one is going to hurt you. I only want to help."

It took a few minutes, but Jacob slowly settled under her calm reassurances. Even though he was only six years old, Anna thought it best to be as truthful as she could with him. "I know you're frightened of something, Jacob, and I'd like to talk with you about it. Would that be okay? I think I can make it better. I've asked Ms. Pier if she can bring you in early tomorrow. Would you like that? I promise you'll be safe with me. I know a little about keeping the monsters away."

His focus never wavered, so Anna kept talking. She took a shot at her theory. "I don't know how, but I think you felt it when I checked on you." She paused a moment. "I didn't mean to scare you, honey. I promise I'll never do anything to hurt you." She reached out to gently stroke his tiny arm. He didn't pull away.

She made a show of glancing around the room before leaning in. "Can I share a secret with you?" she whispered.

He remained silent, his eyes glued to hers, his expression never changing. But she could feel little sparks of curiosity blooming from deep within him. Pleased, Anna prepared to tell him what she was, in hopes that if he had a connection to the world of the supernatural, he may feel more comfortable speaking to her about it.

She lowered her voice even more. "I'm a witch."

His lids widened almost imperceptibly, but she saw it. And he remained calm. Anna took that as a good sign. Before she could say anything more, the final bell rang. It was time to end the day.

Anna stood and took charge of getting them organized and ready to go. She caught sight of Jacob leaving, but since his foster mother had arrived with the rest of the parents, she didn't get a chance to ask her if she'd heard anything. Anna left soon after, hoping to get a call from her.

She was about halfway home on a long stretch of busy two-lane road, when Noor's beast bounded into the middle of the road right in front of her.

It looked the same as it had that night on the beach. Extremely large—ten feet tall at least—grotesquely bulging muscles, and the exact head that Jacob had drawn. Its mottled, hair-less black body loomed directly in her path.

Questions flashed through her mind. Was this moment what caused the car accident Aria had seen? Was her very life hanging on the decision she made right here, right now?

Her first instinct was to slam on the brakes. But wouldn't that choice result in other people also being hurt? There were too many innocent bystanders in the cars around her. And obviously none of them could see the monstrosity blocking the way ahead.

She couldn't take the chance of hurting anyone else, and screeching to a halt in the middle of this busy road would definitely do just that. If this was what Aria had seen, Anna would make damned sure it was only her that suffered.

Ignoring the impulse to stop, she did exactly the opposite. She stepped on the gas and aimed directly for the legs of the colossal creature.

Anna braced herself for the impact, but at the last minute, he dissolved into nothingness.

Relief washed over her as she checked her rearview mirror

and laughed out loud. "Ha, that's right! I'm not falling for your pathetic tricks! Fuck you, asshole!"

She heard and felt his rage and knew the next time he showed up, she may not be so lucky.

Changing course, she headed to the one place she always felt safe. A place where she'd trained both her mind and body to deal with whatever obstacles faced her, be they mental or physical.

She drove straight to Knight's Place.

~~~

Joe was sparring with a promising young man in the main ring when he saw Anna walk in. He knew instantly something was wrong.

"Hold up a sec, Tony," Joe told him. "Take five."

Joe discarded his pads, jumped down from the raised platform, and went to her. The closer he got, the more he knew something had happened.

"What is it?"

"Noor."

*What had that fucker done now?* Joe reached out to take her hands in his. They were cold and trembling slightly. Whether out of fear or anger, he couldn't tell. Keeping her hands in his, he turned towards the wooden staircase at the rear of the room. They led up to a living area the previous owner had used. Joe hadn't ever lived there, but he kept the space stocked and available.

Once inside, he crossed to the fridge and got them both a bottle of water. She was pacing in front of the couch when he turned back. He handed her one of the bottles and waited until she took a few sips to steady herself.

When she lowered the bottle, he couldn't hold it in anymore. "Are you okay? What did he do?"
~~~

"I'm fine. I was on my way home from work," she started out haltingly. "His beast-self jumped out in front of my car." The plastic bottle in her hands crinkled as she described the encounter. "I think he was hoping I'd panic and slam on the brakes. There were a lot of other cars on the road, and if I'd done that, it surely would have caused an accident. A bad one."

"What did you do?"

"I sped up." She peeked up at him, and he saw a glint of pride in her glance.

"That's my girl." Joe smoothed her hair back. "What did he do when he saw you wouldn't back down?"

"He ran. He vanished before I could hit him, but he was royally pissed. He raged and howled at me afterward."

He had a pretty clear picture now. His Anna had faced off against something that wanted to kill her, and she'd come out on top. Joe sat down and pulled her with him. He guessed by the trembling he'd felt in her hands that the adrenaline from her brush with Noor was fading. Her next words confirmed his theory.

"I was fine during," she said when they'd sat for a couple of minutes. "And even afterward. It was only when I pulled into your parking lot that I started to shake."

"That's the way you hope it happens." Joe kissed the top of her head. "It means you kept your head, you kept thinking. You didn't let the fear immobilize you. And then when you got to a safe place, you allowed yourself to deal with it."

They settled into the couch a little deeper. She was quiet a long time before she spoke.

"I need to call my family and let them know what happened."

She made a move to sit up but Joe held her. "Not yet."

His little bad-ass may have recovered from her near-miss, but he sure as hell hadn't. Knowing that Noor had only shown himself because Anna had been alone infuriated him. Because of the threat JD had posed to the girls, both had made efforts to spend their days surrounded by people. The only exception was Anna's drive to and from the gym and school.

He would see to it that changed. The gym was easy. If they were spending their nights together the way he hoped, she'd have no reason to travel by herself. But getting to and from work might pose a problem, especially if Anna disagreed.

"I don't think you should be alone anymore. I know, at least when you're home, Aria and Seth are with you. The school is always full of people, and even here there's plenty of protection. But when you're in your car, you're fair game. I don't think it's a good idea to leave yourself vulnerable after he's already used that time to try and hurt you."

He released her when she sat forward. She turned to look back at him. "I agree. But what do you suggest?"

"Move in with me," Joe blurted out, shocking even himself.

Anna went still and eyed him warily. "What?"

"Move in with me." The second time wasn't so jarring. The words flowed easier, and he could hear the truth in them as he spoke; he *wanted* it to happen.

"Joe, I don't...we haven't..." Anna stuttered.

"It would solve all of our problems," he reasoned. "Aria and Seth could stay at your place. You'd be with me, and I could drive you to and from school. You'd never have to worry about being caught in a situation like today."

"So you want me to live with you out of convenience?" She stood and looked down at him in puzzlement, her sculpted brows knitted together.

"Hell no," he barked out as he rose to jerk her body into his. "I want you to live with me, because I can't stand being away from you for more than a minute. I want to fall asleep each night with you in my arms and wake up next to you every morning. And all those long hours in between...I want to fill those with you."

He kissed her and then went on. "I realize you don't want

to hear this, but it would also make me feel better knowing that I'm around to protect you. I know you can take care of yourself—you've proven that time and time again. But I can't help it. It's just the way I'm built."

The corners of her sexy mouth ticked up. "My knight. Aria once teased me about that, but I don't mind. Only because you don't view me as fragile or delicate. You respect my ability to live my own life. I also know that when you say *protect*, you mean to stand beside me instead of in front of me."

"Maybe just a *little* in front of," he qualified with a smirk. "But all the rest, you're exactly right."

Her cell phone rang before Anna could say anything more. "I need to get that." She spun around to where she'd left her purse and dug her phone out.

Joe waited silently as she answered.

"Hello?"

Recognition and excitement lit her face. "Yes, Mrs. Pier. What did you find out?"

Anna's gaze found his and she worried her lip with her teeth as she listened to the other side of the conversation.

"That's wonderful. Thank you so much." Anna's smile beamed. "I promise I'll keep you informed of his progress. Thank you again. Bye."

Anna hung up and gripped her phone in both hands.

"Good news?" Joe asked her.

"I got the okay to meet one-on-one with Jacob every day before class."

Anna walked into his arms and rested her cheek against his chest. "I'm so relieved. I want to help him so badly, Joe. Something about him is calling to me, and until I can figure out what it is, I can't help but feel like he's not safe."

Joe tucked a finger under her chin and raised her face up so she was looking at him. "You're going to figure this out. And I'll help in any way I can." He lowered his head and kissed her.

When the kiss ended, Anna reached up and brushed his face with her hand. "With so much going on right now, would you mind if we postpone the topic of me moving in?" Her eyes pleaded with him to understand.

He did. The idea may have taken root quickly for him, but if Anna needed more time to make that decision, he'd give her that.

*To a point*, he promised himself.

"That's fine. Why don't you call in the troops?" He gave her one more smacking kiss and then stepped back. "Just tell them all to come here." Joe gestured around as he crossed to the kitchen area. "This apartment, with its open floor plan, has a lot more room than your house. And Dos Pablos down the block will deliver." He rummaged in a drawer for the take-out menu. "As long as everyone likes Mexican."

Anna nodded. "Order lots. My brothers can put away some food."

She was looking around the rest of the apartment when he finally hung up from ordering just about everything on the damned menu. Considering what he alone could eat, then multiplying that by the size of her family, he just hoped he'd gotten enough.

"I remember you telling me this was up here," she called from across the room, "but I guess I never thought it would be this big." Anna looked around the partition wall that separated the bedroom from the rest.

It was set up like a warehouse loft—one large space. The only actual four-sided room in the whole place was the bathroom. Brett Knight, the guy Joe had bought the gym from, used to live up there, and that was apparently his only concession to privacy. The bed was situated in the far corner, cordoned off by a five-foot wall between it and the living area.

"Do you rent it out?"

Joe glanced around. "No, not really. I've let a couple of

friends crash here for a night, but nothing permanent. Other than that it sits empty."

"It's a great apartment," she commented as a knock sounded on the door.

Joe opened it to find Evan. "Seth went to get Aria, but they'll be here shortly." He held up a large grocery sack. "I brought beer."

"Awesome. Kitchen's right over there." Joe gestured behind him. "Food should be here soon."

It seemed to Joe that Evan seemed to be making an effort to lose the attitude. Maybe what he'd said had sunk in and Evan was going to ease up.

It hadn't been Joe's intention to sneak around behind their backs; that's just the way it had worked out, since Anna had never told her family what she was doing. She'd come to his gym when he'd offered a free self-defense class a year ago. She'd stayed and surpassed even his estimate of how far she'd go with it.

Her brothers hadn't been happy to learn of her training, but by that point it was way too late. And Joe was hooked.

Another series of knocks sounded as Aria, Seth, and finally Ethan showed up.

He was a little surprised by Ethan's appearance. Joe wasn't as familiar with Ethan as he was Evan, but where Evan presented an air of cool confidence, Ethan looked pensive and reserved in comparison. The others didn't seem to notice anything unusual, so Joe just shrugged it off.

Before closing the door, he took a look around the facility down below. It was close to five now and only a few of the die-hards remained. Including Jay, his sixteen-year-old assistant, who Joe knew would lock up when the last finally left.

He closed the door behind Ethan, confident his business was in good hands for the night.

Joe took a seat next to Anna as she filled her siblings in on

Noor's latest ploy.

"I told him I wasn't going to fall for his tricks and to fuck off. I shouted it, actually." Anna smiled and nodded decisively.

"You said fuck?" Evan gaped at his sister. "You never say fuck."

Joe looked on in amusement. In the time he'd known Anna, he'd noticed she wasn't one to use many curse words. Unless her temper got the better of her. Joe grinned to himself as he recalled the few times she'd called him an ass.

"He pissed me off," she said matter-of-factly.

Evan laughed and shook his head. "I guess so."

A quick knock interrupted the conversation.

Joe went to the door and pulled it open to a young kid hefting a fairly large box.

"I'll take that," Joe heard from behind him. When he turned, Evan was there to take the food. Joe nodded and, reaching for his wallet, pulled out several bills and a generous tip. He thanked the driver and closed the door.

Joe turned to see they'd already begun opening various bags and containers. He stepped to the cupboard and pulled out a stack of paper plates and a roll of paper towels before moving swiftly out of the way.

The next few minutes were filled with 'pass that' and 'hey, are you going to eat that' and 'that one has onions, you won't like it'. Joe was fascinated by the interaction between the quads and stood back to just watch Anna and her siblings.

Carrying two loaded plates, Seth joined him. He handed one of them to Joe. "If you wait, you're out."

"Thanks," Joe acknowledged with a grin.

Seth nodded at the four Burkes. "It still catches me off guard sometimes when I see all four of them together. That prophecy sure nailed it—two light, two dark."

"Before I met Anna I would never had guessed that that world existed." Joe figured Seth had been in the same place.

Seth nodded and made an affirmative sound around a bite of taco. Once he'd swallowed it down he went on. "I had a little bit of a jump on that. Evan and I went through the police academy together, and I learned what he was then. By the time I found out Aria was Evan's sister, I already knew she was a witch. But yeah—when they explained about the rest, it came as quite a shock."

Joe watched as Anna broke away from their group and came to him. "What are you two doing over here?"

He wrapped his free hand around her waist, pulled her close, and stared down into her crystalline eyes. "Marveling at how lucky we are." He bent his head and kissed her.

"You *are* lucky. Don't forget it." She gave him a cheeky smirk before stepping out of his arms to call them all back to sit down.

Once they were all comfortable, she told them what she'd learned from her principal and how, beginning tomorrow, she'd start working with Jacob before class started.

Joe's phone buzzed in his pocket. A quick check told him it was a text from Jay saying that everyone was gone and that he was locking up. Joe wished him a good night and set his phone aside, just in time to catch Anna's next words.

"And there's something else," Anna admitted. "I think he sensed me reading him today."

"What makes you think that?" Aria set the last of her burrito aside and wiped her hands.

"I lowered my shields to try to scan his emotions, and he got very upset. I think he felt what I was doing, and it scared him."

"*We* feel it when you do it to us," Evan reminded her. "What's to say everyone doesn't sense you to some degree?"

"I wouldn't know," Anna countered. "I don't make a habit of getting into people's minds."

"You read me." Everyone's attention turned to Joe. "I felt absolutely nothing."

"Maybe it's a power thing," Ethan suggested. "If he has

magic too, that could be why he felt you."

"If he does," Seth spoke up, "that could be why Noor is targeting him and his family. Did they have something he wanted? Is that why they were killed?"

"Even with what we know of Noor," Evan cautioned, "we still don't have any proof he murdered the boy's mother and left him for dead. It could have been an incident of domestic abuse taken to the extreme. If the father did it, that could be who they're protecting Jacob from."

"Then why did he draw Noor's beast? He has to be involved somehow. Or maybe that wasn't our beast at all, and we're reading too much into it." Anna's voice was brimming with frustration. "There's just so much we don't know. And we won't know until I can get him to talk to me." Her tone shifted and it filled with sadness. "It tears at my heart to see him so afraid and alone. I just want to pull him into my arms and tell him it's all right."

Joe was startled when he heard the clanking of weights being moved around in the gym. He knew for a fact it should be empty.

Trying not to disrupt the conversation, he rose quietly and went to the door. As he pulled it open, the sound stopped. Stepping through the doorway and onto the small landing, he scanned the entire area. Security lights lit it well enough that he could see into every corner.

There was no sign of anyone down there. He gave it another moment to see if there were any further movement but nothing happened. With a shrug, he turned and walked back into the apartment, nearly bumping into Anna as she approached from behind.

"Something wrong?" she asked.

"No." He ushered her back in. "I thought I heard something, but I must have been mistaken."

As Anna looked past him through the still-open door at his

back, the look on her face stilled his heart.

6

"Anna? What is it?" he demanded and spun to take another look. Maybe he'd missed something. But when his gaze tore around the room below, it was still empty.

"Get away from the door," Anna whispered as she tried to push him behind her.

*What the fuck is going on?* "Anna, what do you see?"

Joe hadn't realized it, but his and Anna's interaction was being watched. And the single word she uttered next set them all into motion.

"Noor."

At that moment, as if the name alone had pissed him off, all hell broke loose.

Joe spun around and saw equipment and weights flying through the air as if an F5 tornado had lifted and flung them. The ropes on the boxing ring stretched and rebounded madly, the steel fencing around the MMA cage bowed and bent, and the sturdy chains suspending the heavy bags were yanked apart as if nothing more than cheap jewelry.

But through it all, Joe never saw what, or who, was causing the damage.

Five people pushed past him. As he was jostled, Evan issued orders. "Joe, you need to stay up here and let us handle this."

"Like hell," Joe argued. "That's my place he's destroying."

He glared up at Evan when the other man spun back and

slapped his hand flat on Joe's chest to stop him. "Can you even see what's down there?" He flung his free hand in the direction of the doorway and then cut Joe off before he could answer. "No, you can't. How are you going to fight something you can't see? And this isn't even your fight, so just stay out of the way."

Joe's temper flared, but Anna side-stepped between them. The look she gave Evan had him shrugging and turning away to join the others. When she brought her pale eyes back to his, they were awash with concern and anxiety.

"Please stay here," she begged. "Evan's right—that beast could kill you, and you'd never even see it coming. Each time he comes back he's stronger, and we don't know yet what he's capable of."

Joe knew all about Noor's animal form and didn't really like the idea of facing off against an invisible assailant. But damn it! He couldn't just let Anna go out there without him.

"I'm sorry," he told her. "But I can't hide up here while you go down there to fight that thing."

"We know what we're doing." She held his gaze firmly and he saw confidence in hers. "This is what we do."

"I know that. And protecting *you* is what *I* do." Joe cupped her cheek. "Don't ask me to stand back and do nothing. It's not in me to let the woman I love walk into danger without me."

Anna's eyes widened as she drew in a sudden, startled breath. She opened her mouth to speak but before the words could come out, Noor began his rampage in earnest, and the six of them took off down the stairs.

As he ran, Joe hoped to God he figured out what he could do to help, because right now, he had no fucking clue. He did have enough sense though to hang back as the others waded in.

The four Burkes spread out facing empty space. And as they did, all sound and destruction instantly ceased. Joe didn't believe for a minute the beast had turned tail and run, so he switched his attention to Anna and the others. Sure enough, they were all staring in the same direction.

Was this some kind of supernatural standoff? Was each side waiting for the other to make a move?

Evan was the first to break the silence. "Thought you'd try to take us on again, huh? You didn't learn the first time?"

As if that were a cue to his siblings, each of them raised their hands and called their power. Joe had seen them do this once before, but not to this extent. What they'd showed him previously was nothing compared to what they were building towards now.

Out of the corner of his eye, Joe caught a flash of movement. He pulled his focus away from Anna and the others in time to see a fifty-pound weight hurling through the air like a deadly Frisbee. It was headed straight for an unaware Evan.

Thinking quickly, Joe took off at a sprint and snatched up a thick rectangular pad meant to absorb kicks and knee strikes. He jammed his hand through the looped handle on the back and clutched it snuggly to his chest. With a giant push from his legs, Joe leapt in front of the missile meant to take out Anna's brother.

The weight struck him dead center, lifted him off his feet, and slammed him to the ground, hard. The pad dissipated the brunt of the force, but it still knocked the breath from his lungs. Still fighting for air, Joe pushed through it and stood, his eyes scouring the gym for any sign of Noor's next move.

He'd found his contribution to this fight. He'd watch over the Burkes so they could deal with this monster without worrying about him coming at them from behind.

Seth joined him, spanning out in the opposite direction to cover more territory and aiding in their outer layer of defense. Joe did a double-take when he realized Seth could actually see the beast. He knew Seth wasn't like Anna and the others, so what did it mean that *he* could see it?

Joe didn't have time to think about that as he swept his

gaze back to Anna and noticed that her mark was glowing. The four siblings were linking up as he'd seen them do before. He felt a shift in the atmosphere as they geared up. He didn't know what would come next, but he hoped whatever they had planned worked.

Obviously Noor felt the same thing because he chose that moment to strike out. With a raging roar, he blasted all of them with some kind of energy wave. It knocked all of them back and onto their asses. They scrambled to get back to their feet, but at the same time, he took to pelting them with whatever was at hand.

Joe and Seth did all they could to protect the Burkes from the multitude of flying objects. Ethan, to Joe's surprise, started hurling things back at the creature with a wave of his arm. He felt the earth beneath his feet rumble and shift, and knew Evan was using his own power to battle this bastard.

The four tried over and over to combine their magic and strike at Noor, but at every turn he would do something to prevent it.

They needed a distraction. Something that would keep the beast busy long enough for them to gather their powers and make their stand.

Even without being able to see what they fought, Joe always had a pretty good idea of its general location. If he could get its attention, maybe that would give them enough time. With a sketchy plan in mind, Joe went for the rack that held the fighting spears and gathered up what he could find.

There had been eight in the wooden stand, but he could only find three.

*Let's hope that's enough.*

He knew how to handle them from his studies of assorted forms of martial arts, but this would be the first time he'd ever brandished one with the intention of hurting his opponent.

He started forward, never slowing his pace. When he

figured he was close enough, Joe shifted his grip and readied the weapon to throw. Hitting an invisible target wouldn't be easy, but hopefully this thing was big enough that he'd hit it somewhere.

He cocked his arm and let it fly and then quickly readied another. It swiftly followed the first. Joe was grabbing the third as the first two sailed through the air to land ineffectually on the floor fifty feet from where he stood.

Had he missed?

Nope, evidently not, Joe thought as he dodged the dumbbell that had flown at his head.

It didn't look as though he'd hit anything, but maybe he had. Or maybe having sharp pointed sticks thrown at him by a measly human just pissed him off. Joe didn't know, nor did he care, as long as it gave Anna and her family time to take him down.

Joe had the last spear in a two-handed grip like a baseball bat. He swung it in all directions hoping he was in the right vicinity to hold Noor off if he were coming for him.

"Seth!" Joe called out. "Give me a hint to where the fucker is."

He did one better. After retrieving one of the other spears, he came to Joe's side.

"You're a crazy motherfucker, you know that?" Seth was smiling, but a look of respect was in his eyes. "There's no way that should have worked. But it did, and I get why you did it."

Joe was surprised when Seth started shouting at the creature and waving his staff.

"Hey! You want me dead? Well, here I am! Come and get me, you sick fuck!"

Fighting blind sucked major balls. Joe only had a split-second to see Seth duck out of the way before something large and stone-like slammed into him and sent Joe airborne like a crumpled scrap of paper.

Before Joe knew what had happened, he was flying. He had a fleeting thought, as the concrete wall was drawing nearer, that this was going to hurt like a bitch.

And he was right.

As his body connected with the immoveable barrier, he felt and heard his shoulder crunch and pop out of socket. His cry of agony never made it past his lips as his head followed and met cinder-block.

And everything went black.

~~~

When Joe surfaced, the first thing he saw was Anna looking down at him. His muddled brain's initial thought was *my angel*.

Then the pain hit and he sucked in a quick breath. "Fuck me." Joe grabbed for his right arm as the throbbing told him exactly what was wrong.

He'd dislocated his shoulder once before, and he would never forget the screaming torture of the injury. And the worst was yet to come when it was reset back into place.

He tried to sit up, but gentle hands held him down. "No, don't move," Anna said in soothing tones.

"Help me up," Joe grunted.

"You could have a concussion," Anna warned. "You need to stay still."

Joe hadn't noticed any pain other than his shoulder but took stock of the rest of himself. Using his good hand, he probed the sore spot on his head and felt a notable gash and the wetness of blood. Yeah, probably a concussion, but that was nothing new. He'd had his brain rattled more than a few times fighting.

Granted, his time in the MMA ring had been a few years ago, but he remembered suffering many such injuries. He knew his body well, and he knew what it could tolerate.

His head didn't concern him. What did was his arm. And
~~~

lying flat on his back was making that infinitely worse.

"Help me up, damn it," he snapped, the pain shortening his temper. He took a beat and tried again. "My head's fine, nothing I haven't had before. My shoulder is dislocated. It needs to be reset."

More hands assisted his move this time, and finally he was on his feet. His head swam briefly but he fought through it.

His gaze took in the group. "Any of you know how to pop this thing back in?" Joe had a sudden thought and glanced around. All looked calm. "Did you send the fugly SOB back to hell?"

"Oh yeah," Evan told him. "And he left here hurting. Enough so that, hopefully, he'll be licking his wounds for quite some time." Evan paused. "Your diversion worked. We were able to best him this time because you guys gave us the time we needed."

"No problem," Joe acknowledged. "Here to serve. Now, can someone please fix my damned arm?"

Aria and the others stayed behind to deal with clean-up while Anna took him to the hospital. It ended up working to his benefit, as he got some really great pain meds out of the deal. Otherwise, he'd have gulped down handfuls of ibuprofen and hoped for the best.

When they exited the ER a couple of hours later, Joe had seven stitches in his head and a sling that held his right arm immobile. Doctor's orders were to keep it that way for a couple of days to give the muscles and tendons time to recover from the injury. Until they did, another dislocation was possible.

The threat worked, and Joe promised he'd wear the sling. If it didn't get in his way, he thought to himself.

He expected Anna to take him back to the gym, but she drove to his place instead.

"I need to get back to clean up before morning," he protested.

"It's done. My family took care of it," Anna assured him. "And tomorrow is soon enough for you to go back to work."

"They couldn't have possibly gotten the whole place put back together in a couple of hours."

Her face was full of mirth when she returned her attention to the road. "You forget who you're talking about. You left three witches there. We mastered that ability a long time ago." Anna laughed. "Our mom would have had a fit knowing we used our powers to straighten our rooms, but it was so much faster that way, and there was so much more fun to be had."

When she turned onto his road, a thought occurred to him. "How do you know where I live?"

"I know people," she teased. "Their names are Internet and Search."

"Smart ass," Joe muttered, making her grin wider.

Anna pulled into his driveway and turned off her car. When she didn't make a move to exit, Joe knew there was something on her mind. He angled his body sideways in the seat and watched her. All traces of humor were gone, and it finally dawned on him that it had all been an act to cover her true feelings. If his brain hadn't been muddled from being knocked around and then numbed out by pain pills, he'd have realized that sooner.

"Anna," he probed softly.

She was silent for another couple of beats and then whispered brokenly, "Why did you do that?"

It didn't take a genius to know what she meant. "Anna, look at me."

On a sigh, Anna slowly brought her head around. The misery Joe saw in her eyes was nearly his undoing. He hated that he'd been the one to put it there, but if he were ever in the same situation again, he wouldn't hesitate to do the exact same thing if it helped to keep her alive.

He captured her gaze in his. "I can't offer much of anything to this war. I'm not a witch, I don't have magic to wield, and I'm at a huge disadvantage because I can't see a lot of what we'll be dealing with."

She opened her mouth to speak, but he went on. "But what I do have is a particular skill-set and an overwhelming need to protect you. To that end, I *will* do whatever it takes to make sure you are safe and have everything you need to win this battle."

His eyes bore into hers. "And tonight, what you needed was time. Time so that you and your family could rally and do what *you* needed to do."

"But you don't understand. What you did shouldn't have worked."

"Seth said that too. What does that mean?"

Anna took a breath. "Whenever we've tried to fight him with anything other than our power, nothing happens. Evan emptied an entire magazine from his 9mm pistol into the beast. With absolutely no effect. Not a mark, not a single scratch. They all passed right through as if nothing were there. Because, technically, there wasn't. It's only a projection that Noor pushes into this world. Only magic and energy have ever done any damage to it."

"The spears didn't look like they hit anything." Joe recalled how they'd arced across the room to land innocuously on the floor.

Anna's face was intent. "That's just the thing. They *did*. Where they passed through his shoulder, there were bloody gashes. They shouldn't have affected him at all."

"Hmm." Joe rubbed his chin, trying to make sense of this new information. "You've said before that every time he shows up, he and his powers have gotten stronger. So maybe that's your answer."

The more Joe thought about it, the more his theory made sense. "As time goes on and the day of the prophecy nears, maybe he's evolving into a fully-dimensional being, one capable of inflicting the most damage on his surroundings."

At her look of horror, he hurried to continue. "But that should also mean that he's able to sustain damage from more than just magic. Conceivably, even common weapons should cause some level of harm."

And if that were the case, Joe was almost looking forward to that day. He was ready to put a serious level of hurt on that motherfucker.

Anna nodded, still obviously unsure. "I guess we'll just have to wait and see, but for now, I'm just glad your plan worked."

Which brought another question back to mind. "How is Seth able to see him?"

Anna smiled. "I don't think he'd mind me telling you. He's come to terms with it. Mostly."

"Come to terms with what?"

"Seth is a descendant of Edrick Noor and his wife Isabel." At his look of shock, she continued. "When she came to my family to escape her husband in the 1500s, they had two small boys. Seth's family came down through one of them."

"Shit." He wasn't sure exactly what he'd expected, but that idea had never even been a blip on his radar. "Does he have magic too?"

Anna shook her head. "Noor wasn't born with power. He acquired it after his wife had left, as a way to seek revenge against all the Burkes for stealing his family away from him. We're still trying to discover how he got it."

"And that magic is how he tossed my gym equipment around and sent me sailing."

Anna's gaze dropped to the sling holding his arm close to his chest. She nodded.

"I'm fine." Joe glanced down and then back at her "It's nothing."

Tears gathered in her turbulent eyes and fell, unchecked, down her cheeks. "But it's *not* nothing. You could have been killed." Her breathing shuddered. "When I saw you hit that wall...You just dropped and were lying on the ground in a heap. I thought you were dead."

A sob caught her off guard and it hurt Joe to hear it. Despite the agony he knew it would cause his busted shoulder, Joe reached across the small confines of the car and pulled her close. She cried softly into his shirt front.

"That didn't happen. I'm fine. I'm right here." He kissed her temple and wherever he could reach to assure her of that.

"Feel me. I'm right here. I'm not going anywhere. I love you." Joe poured his heart into those words.

"Oh Joe, I love you so much." Anna raised her tear-stained face up and pressed her lips to his. They forgot where they were until Anna tried to shift closer to him.

He gasped as white-hot pain branded him and made everything else fall away.

"I'm sorry." Anna distanced herself quickly and held her hands away from him. "I forgot. I'm so sorry."

The throbbing in his shoulder slowly ebbed and Joe took a couple of breaths. "It's okay. Hard to believe, but it slipped my mind too." He sent her a lascivious grin. "I guess kissing you is better than any meds the hospital could have given me."

Laughing, Anna picked up her purse and opened her door. "Come on, let's get you inside." Just before she stood, she looked back at him. "I'll come around and help you."

Joe just shook his head, reached across his body with his left hand, and pulled the door handle. She was still rounding the hood when he pushed it open and rolled out of her little car.

"Damn it, Joe," Anna scolded.

He only smiled at her. "I'm fine, love. I've had worse than this in the ring."

"Well." Anna made a move to take her keys back out of her purse as she turned. "If you're so fine, then I guess I'll head back to my place."

Joe's good hand snaked out and brought her back to him.

Her body flowed gently into his. "Not on your life. You're not leaving me."

Anna relaxed into his grasp, and her curves molded to his hard planes. "Oh, really? You're a little worse for wear right now. Just what do you think you can do about it if I try?"

"This." Joe sealed their mouths together and swept his tongue past the seam of her lips. When he finally released her, she stared up at him with vague, unfocused eyes.

"That's fighting dirty."

"All's fair..." he let the old adage trail off.

"Well, this war is over for the time being, so let's get my knight in...slightly dented armor, inside." She stepped to his good side and walked with him into his house.

# 7

Anna awoke early the next morning to the ringing of her cell phone. She groggily rolled over and found it on the nightstand.

"Hello?" she mumbled.

"You need to meet us at Mom and Dad's as soon as you can." Aria's voice was loud in her ear. The urgency in it blew out all the cobwebs.

"What happened?" Anna bolted upright on the side of the bed and rubbed the sleep from her eyes.

"Mom may have found a clue to where Noor got his power."

"What?" Anna was fully awake and alert now. "How?"

"Get dressed and get to Mom's." Aria hung up before Anna could get any further explanation.

She looked down at the phone in her hand and jumped when a deep voice sounded from behind her.

"What is it?"

Anna had forgotten where she was for a moment. She turned and saw Joe, propped up against the headboard, his left arm stretched up and over his head, watching her.

It took her a moment before she remembered what he was talking about. When she'd turned and taken in his delectable form, the phone call had quickly left her mind. His amber eyes were intently and bone-meltingly focused on her. The dark stubble shadowing the bottom half of his face added an edgy, almost rugged quality that she found sexy as hell.

Her gaze tracked lower, and she was abruptly brought back to reality. The black nylon straps stretching across his hard chest acted as a stark reminder.

Noor.

"Family meeting." She stood and searched around for her clothes. "Aria said we may have found what we were looking for in regards to how Noor got his power."

Joe sat up and shifted around until he was facing her. "And?"

Anna picked up her jeans and pulled them on. "I don't know yet." She pulled Joe's borrowed shirt up and over her head. "But if we can discover where and how he got them, and exactly what he can do," with absent movements she put her bra on and slid into her own shirt, "it might give us a big boost in figuring out how to defeat him."

When she finished buttoning, she stopped and looked over at Joe. He was just sitting in the middle of the bed with a grin on his stunning face.

"What?" Anna asked him.

He crooked his finger at her, motioning her to come to him.

Anna's body temperature shot up a few degrees at the look in his eyes. She placed a knee on the edge of the bed and, as she did, he also rose up to a kneeling position. She made her way across to where he was waiting for her.

He wrapped his good arm around her and pulled her in for a kiss. His lips claimed hers and she was instantly lost.

When he finally released her, they were both breathing heavier.

"Now, that's a better way to start the day," he murmured.

"I agree. I can think of a better one," she smiled at him forlornly, "but I really do have to go."

"I know." Joe gave her another short kiss and backed off the bed. "Give me five and I'll be ready to go with you."

"Joe..." Anna sat back on her heels.

He stopped and pinned her with a stubborn look. "Are we

really going to have this conversation again?"

Anna knew he was right. "No. Let me help you."

By the time they'd gotten him out of the sling, into his clothes, and then strapped back up, there was a light sheen of sweat on his skin. He wasn't in nearly as much pain as last night, but there was still some obvious discomfort, so she made him take a couple of pain pills before leaving his house.

When they got to her parents' place, Anna realized this would be the first time Joe would have an open and active part in a family discussion. She felt a little self-conscious when they walked in, but she should have known better.

Her dad, Paul Daniels, greeted Joe like an old friend. And she guessed they were since he had set them up together.

"Hey Joe, good to see you." Paul glanced at the sling. "I heard you got clipped. This is a pretty nasty mess to walk into."

Joe nodded. "But I wouldn't be anywhere else."

Anna rarely ever thought about the fact that her dad didn't have a lick of magic in him. When he'd met and fallen in love with Mary Burke, he too had taken on uncharted territory.

In a lot of ways, Joe was very similar to her dad. Strong, confident, protective. And, most important of all, secure enough in himself that magic didn't intimidate him.

Anna looked at her father. "Did it ever bother you that your name wouldn't live on?"

He flipped a quick glance at Joe and then looked deep into her eyes. "No. Once I learned of the protection it would give our future children, I knew it was the right thing to do." He leaned in close, kissed her cheek, and whispered in her ear, "And so will he."

She looked at the two men who meant the world to her. Full of emotion, Anna reached up and hugged her dad tight. "You were right about him. Thank you," she whispered back.

"You are so welcome, Anni-girl. I only want you to be happy."

Tears welled up at the pet name he hadn't called her in

years. She held him closer, then kissed his cheek.

Joe saw the moisture when she turned back around and gave her a questioning look. She only smiled at him.

"I'm perfect."

Joe's hand came up to catch a tear that had dropped off her lashes. "Yes, you are."

Her brothers and Seth came out of the kitchen and drew their attention. When Anna saw Ethan, he was chewing on something and there was a glimmer in his eyes she hadn't seen much of lately—humor.

Their mom would have started cooking as soon as she put the call out for them to gather. She never passed up an opportunity to feed her kids, no matter the reason. And as was Ethan's habit since childhood, he'd probably snitched a bite of whatever their mom was cooking. And gotten shooed out because of it.

"Did she kick you out?" Anna smirked at the three men.

"Yes." Evan sent his twin a scathing look. "All because Ethan can't keep his mitts out of the food."

Seth chuckled, apparently not too put out. "That makes us guilty by association." He caught sight of Joe's arm and grimaced. "Sorry about not giving you a little warning. But it happened so fast, I forgot you couldn't see him. How's the arm?"

"It's all good." Joe smiled easily. "I wanted to thank all of you for putting my place back together for me. You didn't have to do that."

"Yeah, we kind of did." Evan crossed to the couch and sat down. "It was our problem that tore it apart. And you gave us the distraction we needed to send him packing."

"Wish I could have nailed that landing though," Joe joked, and Anna had a flash of him striking the wall and falling limply to the floor.

She pushed it away. He wasn't dead; he was right here beside her.

"You've got some pretty nice equipment over there," Evan

said to Joe. "I was thinking about maybe checking it out."

"Yeah, come by any time."

When they started talking workout goals, Anna excused herself and went to join her mother and sister in the kitchen.

Aria was buttering toast, and Mary was scooping heaping piles of fully-loaded scrambled eggs onto a platter.

"What do you need me to do?" Anna asked after giving her mom a quick kiss on the cheek. "There's too much testosterone out there."

Mary laughed. "You can put the juice and milk out." Setting the platter aside, she grabbed a spatula to transfer the fried potatoes to the serving bowl.

Between the three of them, they hauled everything out to the dining room table. Someone, probably her dad, had already brought another chair in for Joe.

"Breakfast's ready," Mary called out.

The men came in and they all took their seats. Food was passed and once everyone filled their plates, Mary got down to why she'd gathered them.

"I've been scouring every book and website I can find for something that would tell me where Noor's powers originated," she began. "Then I came across a link for an obscure site that seemed to specialize in particularly dark and grim magics. What I saw there doesn't bear repeating, but I did find a reference to an old rite—one that's supposed to bestow great power if certain…requirements are met."

"What kind of requirements?" Suspicion laced Evan's question.

"It didn't go into great detail, thank God, but it speaks of five trials, each one darker and more heinous than the last."

"Somehow, I don't think Noor would balk at heinous," Aria said through a grimace.

"So, what or who is on the other end of these tasks?" Ethan's gaze shot around the table. "Who bestows the magic? Where does it come from?"

Paul picked up the explanation. "We searched that whole webpage and couldn't find any specific information. But this gives us another avenue to pursue. If this ritual is out there, then there's got to be a way to find it."

"I think we need to revisit the idea of me luring Noor in to try to get more information out of him." Aria's plan hadn't been met with great enthusiasm. Even though they'd talked about it more than once, no decision was ever made to actually do it.

Anna, along with the rest of the family, didn't like the thought of Aria being subjected to Noor's evilness any more than necessary. He'd already tried to rape her by getting into her mind and attacking her. She'd tried to play it off, but Anna knew it had affected her sister more than she'd let on.

Because of his obsession with her, he'd tormented her off and on for the last few months, coming into her in dreams to show her what he would do to her when he finally had her. He'd even found a way to get to her in her own home and tried to kidnap her, beating her severely in the process.

Noor wanted her for his own and would do anything to make that happen. Including killing anyone in his way.

With that in mind, the family wasn't too eager to see her using herself as bait. And Anna knew deep down that Aria wasn't looking forward to it either.

Anna studied her sister now, and a plan she'd only briefly considered suddenly solidified.

"I think we should do it," Anna surprised everyone by saying. "But with one small alteration. Instead of Aria luring him in, it'll be me."

Variations of "absolutely not" rounded the table. Anna let them argue and wind down before she spoke again.

"I can gauge his emotions," she pointed out. "I'll get him talking, and see if I can get him to slip about some of these questions we have."

"And how would this plan of yours work?" Her dad's eyes sparked with reluctant curiosity. "How would you lure him to you?"

"Dad! Surely you're not okay with this?" Evan's incredulous tone mirrored everyone else's disbelieving gaze.

"I just think we need to hear her out." Paul turned his stern gaze on her brother.

"I wouldn't have to." Anna ignored Evan and addressed her father. "I'd be in Aria's mind."

Paul prompted her to continue. "How?"

Anna sent a grateful smile at her dad for making the others listen instead of just shooting her down point-blank.

"We use the fact that we're identical to fool Noor. Aria would pull me into her mind, like she did when we helped Christine. Then she can hide herself away. He would never know it was me and not her. Then I'll ask him the questions and read him as he spouts off. I should be able to tell if he's feeding me a line of bullshit."

"There's no way to know when he'll slip into her dreams," Evan argued. "How would you know to be there?"

"I've given that some thought." Anna switched her attention to Aria. "Before Seth came back, you dreamed about him, right?"

Aria nodded. "But that's usually when Noor would show up."

"I think that's the answer right there." Anna tried to find the words to tactfully explain her thoughts. "Noor has staked his claim on you, and he hates it when you think about Seth. The first time he came to you was the first night Seth starred in your dreams."

"If I remember correctly," Seth added helpfully, playing along, "that was when we were on the beach, um…talking."

Aria sent him a withering glare but spoke to Anna. "So, you're saying if I have a…*dream* about Seth, Noor will make an appearance."

Anna nodded. "I'm fairly certain."

"I still don't like it," Evan threw out.

"I'm with Evan." Ethan's dark eyes were serious. "I didn't care for the plan when Aria suggested it, and I like it even less now. What will happen when your mind touches his?"

"I have to agree with the boys." Mary sent an apologetic look to Anna. "It's too dangerous for you to be within such close proximity to that magnitude of evil."

Anna had known there would be protests, but she didn't back down. She had to get them to stop viewing her as the frightened, overwhelmed empath she'd been as a child.

"Aria." Anna turned to her sister. "This was your plan. And it'll be your mind. What's your take on it?"

"Like Mom said, I don't like the idea of exposing you to that kind of malevolence voluntarily, but I can see the merit in your plan. It just makes more sense your way. So I say yes."

She sent Aria a silent 'thank you' and turned to her dad.

"If you think you're up for it, then I'll support you"

She looked at Seth next.

He sat back in his chair, holding his hands up in surrender. "Hey, I know better than to go against you and your sister."

Anna's gaze finally landed on Joe. He would be the deciding vote. He'd never seen her as someone who needed protection from the world, but he loved her now. Would that sway his willingness to let her confront a monster?

"Joe, what do you think?"

He reached out and grasped her hand. "I have no doubt you'll succeed at whatever you set your mind to."

"I have one more matter that we all seem to have forgotten," Evan pushed. "What happens when he feels you fishing around in his head? Didn't we, just yesterday, figure out that people with magic could sense you?"

"No. We didn't determine that for certain," Anna reminded him with a frustrated sigh. "But even if he does, I think it's worth the risk to get the answers we need."

It was obvious he planned to argue further, but their father put a quick stop to that. "That's enough. If Anna's sure she can handle it, then we need to trust her."

"So when do you want to put this into action?" Aria sat forward in her seat.

"Let's plan for tomorrow night. That should give me enough time to write the spell and fine-tune our strategy." Anna noted the time. "Right now, I really need to get going. Today's the first day I'm meeting with Jacob before class. I don't want to be late."

"I hope you can get through to him," Aria said as Anna and Joe stood.

"Me too."

Once they were back in the car, Anna turned to Joe. "Thank you for what you said in there. I knew my family would have a hard time agreeing to it."

"What I said is the truth." He held her gaze. "But you have to remember our deal. I'm with you all the way. So while you're coming up with a plan to trick Noor, find a way for me to be nearby, because we stand together."

She leaned across the center console and kissed him gently on the lips. "Thank you."

He smiled and it crinkled the corners of his golden eyes. "You're welcome."

# 8

Half an hour later, after a quick stop by her place, Joe dropped off Anna at the school. He would be back when the day was done to pick her up.

As she was walking in, she happened to glance at a flyer taped on the glass portion of the door leading into the school. It was a reminder for students to turn in all library books before the end of the year.

That brought her up short for a moment before she realized there were only a few weeks left of class before summer break.

She thought about Jacob and felt a physical pain at the thought of not seeing him every day. That would be something she'd have to talk to Mrs. Pier about when she brought him in this morning. She would have to work out a way to continue these sessions even after vacation started.

Anna pulled the door open and walked straight to her classroom. It wasn't five minutes and they were there.

She crossed to Jacob and bent down to greet him. "Good morning, Jacob. I'm really looking forward to our talk today. Will you please go find your seat?"

When he ambled off, Anna turned to his caretaker. "I realize that the end of the year is nearing, but I'm hoping to extend these sessions with him into summer break, if that's possible. I'd hate to lose ground just when we may gain some."

Mrs. Pier nodded. "I don't have a problem with that. Let

me know when you decide on a time and place. Like I said, mornings are better for me."

"I'll keep that in mind. Thank you."

When the foster mom turned and left, Anna went to Jacob. "Why don't we have a seat on the floor in the reading area?"

He followed her to the square patch of carpet in the rear corner of the room. They both sat down and folded their legs.

Jacob raised his head and looked her in the eyes.

Anna was pleased that it seemed to be getting easier for him to make that connection with her.

*Oh baby, we're going to get you through this. I promise.*

"Okay. I'd like to try something today." She waited to see if he acknowledged her statement. "If you can't speak right now, that's perfectly fine. I may have another way to know what's going on. Do you remember the other day? When I checked on you, and you got scared?"

Anna paused. "Well, I'm what's called an empath. Have you ever heard that word before? That means that if I look, I can feel whatever you're feeling. If you're happy, I can feel that too. If you're sad, I can tell. And, most importantly, if you're frightened in any way, I'll know it and protect you."

She let that settle in for a moment. "Do you think it would be all right if I looked to see how you're feeling right now?"

His big brown eyes never wavered from hers. She took that as a yes and lowered her shields enough to read him.

Testing out her hunch, she asked him, "Can you sense me? Is this okay?"

Anna became aware of the ease with which he accepted her into his mind. "Good. That's really good. Now, I'll keep this connection going, and we'll just talk a little. I'll tell you a little about me. And then maybe you can tell me about you."

She sensed his trepidation but moved on. "Well, where should I start?" She made a show of trying to think and got curiosity from him.

Progress.

"I should probably start with my secret, don't you think?"

A touch of pleasure.

"Like I said, I'm a witch and I have magical powers. I also have one sister and two brothers who are also witches. And guess what? We're quadruplets. Do you know what that means?"

Confusion.

"That means we were all born on the same day. Our mom was carrying all four of us in her belly at the same time."

Curiosity again.

"That's crazy, isn't it? Do you have any brothers or sisters?"

Slight shake of his head.

Anna didn't want to bring back any bad memories yet, so she stayed away from asking about his parents.

"Let me tell you, having three of them was a lot of fun. But sometimes, it wasn't so nice. Especially when the boys would pick on me and my sister. Dumb old brothers."

Humor tickled her senses and her heart melted.

Anna spoke of the antics she and her siblings had gotten into for a little bit, just to build a relationship with him and put him more at ease.

"Do you want to know another secret?"

This time there was a small nod.

"Watch this." Anna did as she'd done with Joe and drew water to her and had it dancing between her fingers.

Jacob's eyes widened and she felt his enjoyment. "Hold up your hand."

When he held it out flat, she took it and turned it straight up like a high-five. She pressed her hand to his much smaller one and let the water play around their fingers.

After a few minutes, she let her dear friend float away. "Okay, little man. Turnabout is fair play." Anna laughed when all she got from Jacob was more confusion.

"All that means is, I showed you my secrets, now can you show me one of yours? It doesn't have to be a big one. Maybe just a little one at first."

Concentration as he thought about her request.

Anna heard an increase of noise out in the hall and glanced at the clock. That hour had gone by fast.

"I'll tell you what. It's almost time for class to start. Why don't you decide what you want to share with me, and then tomorrow when we talk again, you can tell me?"

When her first student arrived, Anna showed Jacob back to his seat.

Throughout the day, Anna would catch him watching her and when she did, she'd smile at him.

When drawing time came, he seemed eager to join in. All of his attention was focused on the sheet of paper in front of him. He worked on it the entire time and when she called a halt, he kept coloring.

As she readied the rest of the class to leave, he still drew. She knew his caretaker would be there any minute, so she went to him.

"Jacob, Mrs. Pier will be here soon. Are you about finished?"

He stopped and took a deep breath. Before Anna could ask about the drawing, he picked it up and handed it to her.

He'd drawn a very detailed image of an angel. Soft light glowed behind her and lit her pale hair like a halo. Anna saw her own face looking back at her from the picture in her hand.

"Is this how you see me?"

Jacob gave her a small nod. And she felt peace in him.

"That is so sweet, Jacob. Thank you very much."

Mrs. Pier came in to collect Jacob, and Anna noticed someone behind her. She tensed for a moment until she saw that it was Joe who'd followed her in.

He stood off to the side of the doorway and waited until she'd bid goodbye to Jacob. Anna took a moment to update the caretaker about the step forward Jacob had made with the drawing. She was pleased with the news.

While Anna and Mrs. Pier were talking, Anna saw Jacob look up at Joe and study him for a moment. So far, she and Joe were the only ones he would look at. Anna wondered what he saw in Joe.

Once goodbyes were said, Joe came to her and wrapped his good arm around her.

"How was your day?" He kissed the side of her neck.

Anna smiled. "It was good. Really good. I think Jacob is beginning to trust me. We found a way to communicate this morning."

"He spoke?" Joe pulled his head back and looked into her face.

"No. I explained about being an empath and connected with him that way. But he did give me a couple of small nods and shakes of his head."

"Were you able to ask him what happened?"

"No. I kept it light and fun today. I couldn't bring myself to make him talk about all that just yet."

"I can understand that," Joe agreed. "Are you ready to go?"

"Almost." She grinned and kissed him. Anna took a few steps toward her desk and then spun back to face him. "You know, if you're going to be dropping me off and picking me up, I'd better clear you in the office so they don't give you a hard time."

Anna gathered her belongings and they left her classroom to walk to the office. She introduced Joe to Mrs. Steeple and then Susan, the Administrative Assistant. Anna explained that he'd be a frequent visitor to the school and her class.

Once he was given the all-clear, they drove back to her place. Anna and Aria spent the evening devising a spell for the following night while Joe and Seth kicked back and watched TV. The next day, after their usual morning routine, Joe dropped her off at the door of the school ten minutes before she was due to meet with Jacob again.

When he walked in with Mrs. Pier, he was holding a piece of paper.

"He drew a picture for you last night." The foster mom smiled. Anna could plainly see her excitement, as this was the first time he'd made any improvements that she'd seen. "He worked on it half the night."

Anna looked down to the little boy she was coming to love. "Another picture, that's wonderful! May I see it?"

Jacob held it out to her and when Anna saw what he'd drawn, it took her breath away. She was still gathering her wits when Mrs. Pier bent to her charge. "I'll see you after school, sweetie."

He walked over to the story-time area and sat down. It took Anna another minute to recover and join him. She sat down across from him and looked at his artwork again.

It was clearly a drawing of Joe, as she could see his facial features plainly. The rest of him though, was covered from neck to toe in shiny, silver armor. In his right hand he held a large broadsword aloft.

A knight in shining armor.

Anna looked at Jacob. *How could he have known?*

"This is beautiful. Is this how you see Joe?"

Jacob nodded and there was something else in his gaze.

Establishing the connection again, Anna felt a sense of... something like mystery or secrecy coming from him.

*Secret.*

Suddenly she knew. "Is this your secret, Jacob? Can you see inside of people to their inner selves? Their true selves?"

He nodded a little bigger this time, and she got a full dose of his satisfaction.

Anna thought back to the first drawing he'd done. The man with the beast's head. Had it been like they'd thought and Ncor possessed whoever Jacob had seen? Was this why he refused to make eye contact with anyone? Was he afraid he'd see that monster again?

But why would Noor want to kill this child and his mother?

She hated to do this to him, but the time had come for answers. She set the sketch of Joe aside and reached out to grasp Jacob's small hands in hers. "Jacob, honey, I want to ask you something, and it's not going to be easy," she warned. "But I want you to remember that I'm here and I won't let anyone or anything hurt you. Okay?"

His fear was rising again, but she pushed on. "That first drawing you did. The one of the man with the monster head. Is that the man that hurt you and your mom?"

Brown eyes went round and his breathing picked up.

"Shh, sweetie, it's okay. You're safe. I'm here. He can't get to you."

After a few minutes had gone by and Jacob still hadn't settled, Anna was about to scrap the idea and redirect his thoughts when he reached out and touched the picture of Joe. She felt his desperate need and thought she understood what he wanted.

"He is a good protector. Would you feel better if he were here with you?"

Jacob nodded.

"Okay. I'll call him right now and have him come." She picked up the paper and laid it in his hands. "You hold on to this until he gets here. I'm going to go and get my phone. I'll be right back."

Within seconds, Anna was seated on the floor with Jacob again. She dialed Joe and was relieved when he answered on the first ring.

"Hello?"

"Joe, can you please come back to my classroom? Right now?"

"What's wrong? Has something happened?"

"It's Jacob, but he's fine. I'll explain when you get here."

"I'm on my way."

She disconnected the call and looked at the small boy clutching the image of his knight in shining armor.

A little over five minutes later, Joe strode into her room. Both she and Jacob looked up, and she felt some of his fear abate.

"Can you come and sit with us, please?"

Joe gave her a questioning look but did as she asked. Once he was seated, Jacob surprised them both by crawling over and climbing into Joe's lap.

"Whoa. Okay." Joe's gaze darted to Anna. "What's this all about?"

"We were talking, and Jacob became scared. He thought he would feel better if you were here with him."

"Well, I'm glad he likes me, but why?"

Anna picked up the paper Jacob had dropped. "He drew this last night and gave it to me this morning." She paused so he'd know what she said next was important. "It's how he sees you."

Joe held her gaze for a beat and then studied the image in her hand. He then looked down at the little boy who trusted him to keep him safe.

Anna had to fight back tears when Joe wrapped his good arm around Jacob's middle and held him close. She didn't know if Joe had ever thought about it, but she knew in that moment that he would make a wonderful father.

A sense of calm settled over Jacob, and Anna forced herself to return to what had upset him so badly.

"Is it all right to talk again now? Joe is here, and you know he'll protect you."

Jacob took a breath and nodded. Anna noted that his grip on Joe's arm tightened.

"That man you saw as the monster. Is he the one that hurt you?"

Even though he was swimming in terror again, Jacob nodded.

"Did you always see him that way? Or was that something

new?"

He shook his head then nodded. Anna didn't read confusion from him so it took her a second to figure out he was answering her questions in order.

"Did you know him before the monster was there?"

A nod.

Anna took a shot. "Was that your dad?"

Another yes.

That was enough for today. Anna couldn't subject this child to any more heartache today.

"You were so brave, Jacob." She stroked his cheek with her fingers. "Thank you so much for talking with me. I know it was hard today, but you did an amazing job."

Knowing there would be more rough days ahead, Anna tried to further alleviate his fears. She looked at Joe then back at Jacob. "Would you like for Joe to be here when we do this again?"

She felt his relief first and then saw him indicate yes.

"Well then, how about we ask him if he'd like to join us?"

Jacob leaned his head back to gaze up at Joe.

"If that's what you want, buddy, then I've got your back."

Anna sensed a glimmer of happiness in Jacob for the first time.

"All right, sweetie." She stood. "Go get ready for class, and I'll walk Joe out. We'll just be in the hall if you need anything."

Joe followed her out, and as soon as they cleared the door and were out of sight, Anna broke.

"Oh God, Joe."

He pulled her into his arms and held her.

She couldn't completely lose it in the hallway, so Anna fought back the emotion that threatened to spill over.

When she had control again, she stepped out of Joe's arms. "Noor possessed Jacob's father, murdered his mother, and thinks he killed Jacob. Why? Was it just to kill again?" A thought occurred to her. "What if Ethan was right? Jacob has power. His mom could have too. Is that why he attacked them?"

"I don't know." Joe wiped a stray tear off her cheek. "I think we need to find out who they were. That might help us to understand."

Anna swiped at her face and pushed her hair back. "You're right. We need more information. I'll tell my family and we'll find it." She stared up into his rugged, handsome face. "Thank you so much for dropping everything to come." Anna thought over the events and progress they'd made in the last hour. "You know, I find it fascinating that Jacob sees you as a knight in shining armor when I've called you that so many times."

Joe smiled tenderly. "I wonder how he sees you."

Anna smiled, both proud and a little embarrassed. "As an angel. He drew me yesterday in class."

Joe let out a little laugh. "That makes perfect sense."

Something behind her drew Joe's attention. "I'd better go. It looks like your kids are starting to show up." He gave her a quick kiss. "I'll be back later to pick you up. Love you."

Anna hadn't fully restored her shields, so she felt the truth of his words blast through her system. "Love you, too."

# 9

Joe drove back to the gym. The more his thoughts sorted through what Jacob had suffered, the more pissed off he became. That anyone would purposely hurt that small, innocent child tore him up.

When Jacob had crawled onto his lap, Joe had been lost. And to know that this precious little boy saw him as his protector had pushed Joe over the edge. No one would ever so much as touch a hair on Jacob's head if Joe had anything to say about it.

Now he understood what Anna felt when she'd said there was something about him that called to her. Joe knew he would do whatever it took to make Jacob's life safe and happy. And if that meant he became Jacob's own personal knight, he'd do it. Gladly.

Joe stormed into the gym and went straight for the locker room. He unhooked the sling holding his shoulder and slowly rotated his arm a few times.

There was still pain but nothing he couldn't deal with. Stripping out of his street clothes, he donned a pair of shorts and slid his feet into some tennis shoes.

On his way out of the locker room, he stopped by the equipment cabinet to get a roll of tape for his hands.

He headed straight for the heavy bags. As he stood taping his knuckles, Jay approached.

"Um, what are you doing?" his sixteen-year-old assistant

asked hesitantly.

"What does it look like?" Joe bit out.

"It looks kind of like you're mad as hell, and you're about to take it out on that bag."

"I always knew you were smart." With a rip of tape, Joe switched to wrapping his other hand.

"Should you be doing that? What about your shoulder?"

One last time around and Joe flexed his hands, checking the tightness. "It's fine, Jay. I think I know what my body can handle. Now, if you'll excuse me." He turned and pinned Jay with a look that revealed all of his pent-up frustration and anger. "Unless you want to pad-up and meet me in the ring?"

Jay took two steps back and held up his hands. "No, man. I know what you can do, even when you're *not* pissed." He motioned to the big sand-filled bag hanging from the ceiling. "Have at it."

Joe wasn't so far gone that he'd risk further injury, not when Anna, and now Jacob, needed him. So he tested his shoulder out first with a series of light punches. As it loosened up and felt pretty good, he put more into it and soon he was pummeling the bag.

He should have grabbed gloves, but he'd wanted the quick bite of pain as he hit the target harder and harder, venting all his fury and dismay over what had been done to such a sweet and pure child.

It was a good hour before he finally stopped. When he dropped his arms to his sides, air was heaving in and out of his lungs and sweat covered his entire body. His knuckles stung. Bringing them up, he saw that the once-white tape was dirty and tinged with red. The rough outer layer of material on the bag played hell on the thin tape—shredding it along with the skin beneath.

He headed for the showers to wash away the sweat, the blood, and the remaining temper that rode him. Once he was dressed and a little more in control, he was able to concentrate on his business until it was time to go pick up Anna.

Anxious to see how Jacob had done after he'd left, Joe arrived early and went to Anna's class. He waited outside the door until the bell rang and students started to file out. When all but Jacob had gone, he slipped in.

Big brown eyes met his, and Joe saw a ghost of a smile on Jacob's face.

Movement behind him drew his attention around as Jacob's guardian came in. She went right to Anna.

"How did he do today?" she asked.

"Wonderfully," Anna told her, glancing over at Jacob. "We made some good progress. Between the drawings he's doing and the eye contact he's been making with me, I really think the one-on-one is helping."

"Has he said anything yet?"

Anna brought her focus back to the woman and shook her head. "No. His words are still stuck, but we'll get there.'

"Thank you." She called Jacob over and together they left.

Joe crossed to her. "You didn't tell her that his father was the one."

"But he wasn't, really," Anna reminded him. "Noor took control of him and committed those unspeakable acts."

"What if the bastard suddenly shows up and wants his son back? If the police don't know his father was involved, they could return Jacob to him, not knowing he was still in danger. Noor got to him once…"

"Noor thinks he's dead. There'd be no reason to even look for him." But fear still dimmed Anna's blue eyes. Joe hated that he'd put it there, but these concerns needed to be addressed.

"And if his father does show up…" Anna paused to think. "Well, we'll just cross that bridge if it comes. Let's see what my brother finds out about Jacob's family before we borrow trouble."

Joe didn't want to rely on uncertainties. If Jacob was in danger, he wanted to know immediately. Since tomorrow was Friday, Joe would make sure that Jacob had a way of contacting him if anything were to happen. There was no way Joe was going the whole weekend without knowing he was okay.

"So you got a chance to talk to your family?"

"I texted Evan and explained to him what we learned from Jacob. He's going to fill everyone else in. He also said that he and Seth got assigned to a case and will be working late tonight, so we'll have to wait until tomorrow to ambush Noor."

There was still a lingering sadness in Anna's face. Joe reached up to offer some comfort and she gasped.

"What did you do to your hands?" She inspected one, and then the other. And then as if just realizing his arm wasn't confined, her gaze tracked to his shoulder. "And where is your sling?"

"It's back in my locker." He bit the inside of his cheek to stop the grin that wanted to slip out at her accusatory tone. "My shoulder's fine. I ran it through some routines today and it held up."

"You beat on the heavy bag, didn't you? Pretty severely too, by the looks of these. I remember what it did to my hands the one and only time I hit it without gloves."

Her ice-blue eyes drilled into his, all fear and sadness gone. "What were you thinking?"

Joe's humor vanished. "That I was beating the hell out of Edrick Noor for what he did to that poor kid."

Anna's eyes dropped to his raw and battered knuckles again. "Yeah." She heaved out a sigh at his explanation. "I can understand that. There have been a few times I would have liked to do the same."

"How do we protect him?" It was in Joe's nature to fight, but he didn't know how. Not with this kind of enemy.

"We'll figure it out," Anna promised. "Because there's no

other option."

A few minutes later, Joe was walking her out to his car. When they got to Anna's house, he talked her into packing a few things and staying at his place since their plans for the evening had been postponed. She left a note for her sister telling her where she'd be and to call if Seth or Evan turned up anything at all on Jacob's family. Then they left, stopping off for dinner at an English pub-style restaurant they both liked.

As they ate, Joe's mind was filled with thoughts of Jacob and how to safeguard him. He was afraid there was still a chance Noor would find him. He'd wanted that particular family for a reason, and until they knew what that was Jacob wasn't safe.

Joe was amazed at how quickly this one child had taken over so much of his soul. When Jacob had asked for and found solace within his arms, Joe knew there was nothing he wouldn't do for him.

"You're thinking about Jacob." Anna's words weren't a question.

Joe nodded. "I can't seem to stop. There's this overwhelming urge inside of me to keep him close."

Anna heaved out a breath that seemed to deflate half her body. "Now you understand why I was so distracted after meeting him. "I have that same fear—that if I can't see him and touch him, he'll disappear and I'll lose him."

"Exactly." Joe didn't know what it meant that they both felt this way, but he wouldn't ignore it. "I want to give Jacob my phone number tomorrow. I want him to be able to contact me if he needs me. I don't like him being out of touch overnight—let alone the weekend—and with the end of the school year coming up, I'd feel better knowing he could reach out if he needed to."

"I completely agree." Anna smiled at him. "His foster mother has my number, but you're right—Jacob needs them too."

They finished their meal and arrived at his house shortly after. They spent the evening quietly, each thinking about the boy who had slid into their hearts and changed their lives.

The next day, Joe was as anxious for Jacob to show up as Anna was. As he leaned against her desk, he watched the doorway, waiting for them to arrive.

When Mrs. Pier and Jacob finally stepped in, Joe looked at Anna and they both breathed a sigh of relief. As soon as the caretaker left, they took a seat on the carpet in their usual spot. Jacob sat across from Anna but near enough to Joe that their legs touched.

Joe reached out and ran his hand down the back of Jacob's head. The feel of the short brown hair under his palm was soft and fine.

Jacob looked up at him and gave a slight grin.

Anna pulled their attention when she spoke. "Jacob, do you think you might try to speak today, or would you rather use our connection again?"

Brown eyes met hers and then dropped to his lap. Joe saw him shake his head.

"Hey." Anna waited for Jacob's gaze to rise to hers. "That's perfectly fine." Her voice was reassuring and light. "You've done so well, buddy. We'll just wait until you're ready. And it's not like we can't communicate at all, so take your time."

Jacob's body relaxed. But it didn't stay that way as Anna approached the subject of his family again.

"I'd like to talk a little more about what happened to you."

Joe felt the tension come into Jacob's body. Taking matters into his own hands, he scooped the boy under the arms and pulled him into his lap. He wrapped his arms around him and held him close. He leaned his head down and whispered into his ear. "I've got you. No one will ever hurt you again."

Over the next hour, Anna asked him several different questions, but when she glanced at Joe and shook her head, he understood Jacob hadn't been much help. The closer they got to what actually took place that day, the more he shut down again. Anna called a halt rather than pushing him too far.

Just before Joe left, he took a small card out of his pocket. He'd taken special care to write out his and Anna's cell phone numbers clearly so Jacob would have no problem reading them.

Joe handed Jacob the card and pointed to the top number. "This is my phone number. Anna's is right below it. I want you to keep this with you all the time. If you're ever scared or worried, or you just want to talk to me, call me. Okay?"

Jacob studied the card and then brought his gaze up to Joe. He slowly nodded and slid it into the little pocket on the front of his jeans. As the other children started to arrive, Jacob went to sit at his desk.

Joe looked down at Anna. Her attention was focused on Jacob.

"We have to find out what happened and why." She brought her troubled, pale-blue eyes up to his. "But for now, we have some work to do."

~~~

It was decided the best place to attempt luring Noor into Aria's dream was at their parents' house. All of them would be near if something went wrong.

Anna had spent the afternoon finalizing the spell she and Aria had written that would induce a kind of waking dream. It all still hinged on whether or not Noor made an appearance, but Anna believed if they played it right, he would.

They all gathered at their childhood home to run through the plan.

Anna turned to her sister. "I've made a couple of changes to this spell, but you should still be able to affect your dream so you can control it and have it play out as we need."

"Which is to make Noor jealous enough that he shows up to punish me for cheating on him." Aria smiled, but it resembled
~~~

more of a grimace. "Awesome."

"Once he pops in," Anna continued, "we'll make the switch, and I'll be the one to confront him."

"I don't like the thought of you two going in by yourselves," Evan argued. "I think someone else needs to be with you."

Anna drew breath to explain why that wouldn't work when Evan rushed on. "We could conceal them. Noor would never know anyone else was there."

"We can't take that chance, Evan." Anna appreciated his need to protect them, but there was too much at risk. "If Noor so much as smells a trap, he'll disappear if we're lucky, and try to retaliate if we're not. But either way, we won't get the answers we need."

"I'll go," Seth spoke up. "He won't think twice about seeing me there; if Aria is dreaming about me, it only makes sense that I'd be with her."

Anna was about to decline his offer when she thought again and realized that might actually work.

"Okay." Anna swiftly altered her plan to include Seth. "In that case, I'll leave it to you to pull his attention at the moment we need to make the switch. Once I'm in place, I can work on him."

A few more details were worked out, the spell was adjusted for Seth's added presence, and then they were ready. Anna was going over her spell one last time when Joe asked to speak with her alone.

She led him into the kitchen and hoped he wasn't having second thoughts.

He must have read her uncertainty. "I'm not changing my mind. I don't like that I can't stand with you, but like your brother, I'm glad *someone* will be there to have your back."

Joe lifted his hands and threaded his fingers through the hair on both sides of her face, smoothing it back. He leaned in and kissed her gently on the lips.

"I know you can do this. But please be careful."

Anna slid her hands around his waist and hugged him close. His arms enveloped her and she rested her head on his chest. She listened to the strong, steady beat of his heart for a moment before tipping her head back to see his handsome face.

"Thank you for believing in me. You've made me stronger than I've ever been."

He shook his head. "You're stronger because you believe in yourself."

They kissed once more and then returned to the others. As the hour grew later, the whole group moved into the bedroom that the girls had once shared. Each of them lay on their mattress, and Seth settled into an armchair placed at the foot of Aria's.

Just before she and her sister began to recite the words that would take them into Aria's mind, Anna sat up and looked at her twin.

"Try to remember that I'll be there too. I know you need to be convincing to bait Noor into joining us, but please let's not venture into the TMI realm."

Aria looked over at the man she loved and back to Anna and grinned. "Can't make any promises."

Anna grumbled under her breath, and everyone else laughed.

Then it was time to get serious. She nodded at Aria, reclined back, and cast her spell.

*"Blood to blood. Mind to mind.*
*Journey together into dream time.*
*One for love, one for protection.*
*Three into one, into Aria's projection.*
*Still in control to mold and scheme,*
*As we will, so mote it be."*

Anna felt a shift, and suddenly she was standing on the

beach with Aria and Seth. Looking around, Anna pinned her sister with a smirk.

Aria shrugged. "What? I figured this is where it all started, so maybe he'll be more likely to show up again when things start to…progress."

Anna winked. "Good thinking, sis." Looking down at herself, she added, "But before you guys get this ball rolling, can you change my clothes? You and I need to look the same."

Before she could blink, Anna was dressed exactly like her sister, down to the earrings. "Perfect. Now, let's get me tucked away."

Anna found that as she slipped away, her sight grew hazy but she could still hear. She hadn't counted on that, but it might work out better. At least she wouldn't have to watch her sister's overt displays to lure Noor in.

She heard some whispers from the couple still on the beach. And then, more clearly, their boisterous declarations of love. Aria crooned how she'd never love anyone as much as Seth, and how no one could ever take his place.

They laid it on thick, without going so far as disrobing and getting overly physical. Anna silently thanked them but worried it wouldn't be enough.

Time dragged as they waited for Noor to appear. It was hard for Anna to judge how much time had actually lapsed. It felt like hours, but it could have been only minutes. She was considering telling Seth and Aria to take it up a notch when a new voice finally entered the mix.

"And here we are again."

Anna tried to see but could only make out the fuzzy images of three people standing on the white sand. Two were together— Aria and Seth—and the other was about six feet away from them.

Anna recognized the voice instantly. That same self-important, slightly old-world accented tone she'd heard only once before on the day he'd destroyed his foot-soldier JD, following the discovery of his betrayal.

"You need to stay the hell out of my head!" Aria's mutinous shout drew Anna's attention. She watched as her sister began to separate from Seth and maneuver Noor into position. "I'm never going to let you touch me again."

"You'll have no choice, witch." He turned and tracked Aria as she moved. As hoped, he completely disregarded Seth, seemingly unthreatened by his presence. "We will finish the lesson I was teaching you the last time we met. I'll take you and break you, and then you'll be *all mine*. You've escaped my grasp before, but soon I'll have you under my thumb—and under me."

Anna watched as the blurred figures shifted until Noor was facing only Aria. "I will relish every moment, and there will be nothing you can do to stop me. I will kill everyone you hold dear, and once my body is flesh and blood again, you will be on your knees before me. You will obey me or feel my wrath."

Seth, who'd remained motionless up until now, was finally behind him and, as discussed, drew Noor's attention to him.

"Hey, douchebag! She said no."

As soon as Noor spun to address Seth, Anna materialized beside Aria. And just as quickly, Aria disappeared.

Now that she could get a closer look, she noticed he was dressed as he had been the other times they'd seen him. Black pants with boots, high-collared white shirt, and flowing black knee-length coat. She guessed that must have been the fashion for men in the late 1500's.

His hair was a mousy brown and trimmed short in the back. The top was thin and sparse. He sported a full moustache and beard in the same drab color as his hair. The beard hung down his neck to end at the top of his chest.

"Keep dreaming, jackass. You and me? You'll never get that lucky." Anna spoke from behind Noor, drawing his attention back away from Seth. She adopted her sister's mannerisms and speech pattern easily. "Why do you even keep trying, Noor? We beat you down every time you show up. Why don't you just accept that your wife and kids were better off without you and leave everyone alone? Just give up already. Seriously, I don't know why you bother."

The depth of her knowledge gave him a start. Anna smiled. "That's right. We know who you are. You're just a..." Anna glanced over his shoulder to Seth and then back at Noor. "*douchebag* from the fifteen hundreds. Isabel obviously went on to live a long, happy life without you there to beat on her every day."

Here's where she bluffed, hoping he'd let something slip. "We know everything about you, Edrick Noor. How you completed trials to gain your magic, and we're ready to put you down as soon as your cage opens."

Her barriers already down and her mental channels clear, she felt his shock first and foremost. But then that morphed to disbelief before landing on speculation. When she pushed deeper and tried to read further into his reaction, something strange happened. Anna was able to actually visualize his thoughts. She caught vague images of books. There looked to be ten or twelve of them, almost identical to the journals the Burke witches had been documenting in for centuries.

If there were something in the family records he was worried about, they would have seen it already.

Unless he was thinking of the missing ones her family had been unable to locate.

There was a large chunk of Burke history unaccounted for in the journals her family had been collecting over the years. Her mother had reached out to extended family, but no one knew where they'd gone.

Could those memoirs be the missing link in learning how to destroy him for good?

Anna was still trying to decipher what it meant when his demeanor flipped yet again. Following the quick shift of his emotions almost made her head spin, but Anna forced herself to concentrate so she wouldn't miss anything.

What she sensed in him now was contempt.

"It won't matter what you think you know." Noor sneered at her. "No one can stop me, so anything those old hags left for you will be useless. I'll have my revenge. Your family will die, and mine will live on."

He stepped forward, close enough that Anna could smell the hellfire stench of him. "And when everyone you love is gone and all you have left is me, I'll show you how a *real* man treats his woman."

With a smirk over his shoulder at Seth, Noor faded away.

Anna let out a breath as Aria appeared next to her and Seth came over to stand with them.

"What do you think he meant by something being left to you?" Seth asked.

"I'm pretty sure I already know, but we can discuss it when we get back. We'll need the rest of the family to decide what to do next." Anna looked at Seth. "I'm a little worried at what was in his mind when he said his family will live on. He was almost gloating. Do you think he knows about you?"

"It won't do him a damned bit of good." Seth's jaw was set and his eyes fierce. "My loyalties are *here*."

"He may not need you." Anna thought of her own extended family—all the countless cousins and relatives she had no idea even existed. And realized that in Noor's case, the implications were far more reaching. "He and Isabel had two sons. They had children, and those children grew up and had more. To Noor, he would see them as living heirs—property to be claimed to do his bidding."

Before Seth or Aria could speak, Anna brought this exercise to an end. "Let's get back. The others have to be wondering what's going on."

# 10

When Anna opened her eyes, Joe was there. He was sitting on the edge of the bed watching her.

"Hi." She grinned up at him.

"Hi, yourself." She saw relief flash in his amber eyes.

"How long were we out?"

"Almost two hours."

She nodded as she sat up and looked over at her sister and Seth right beside her.

"Everyone okay?"

"Yeah." Seth's tone was subdued.

"I'm fine," Aria added.

"How about we take this into the den where there's more space?" Mary stepped up to usher them out of the room. "Then the three of you can tell us what happened."

Only a couple of minutes later they were all spread out on the lofty sofa and cushy chairs.

"Okay." Evan leaned forward and braced his elbows on his knees. "Spill."

Anna relayed everything that was said, along with the corresponding information she'd been able to pick up from his mind.

"So you didn't just *feel* that he was uneasy about something?" Evan asked. "You could actually *see* the thoughts in his head?"

Anna nodded. "Right. I'm guessing my powers evolved the

way Aria's did at the moment she needed them."

"This new ability is something you'll need to work on," her mother advised.

"I know." Tapping into people's minds wasn't something she was comfortable with. She knew her mom was right, and that the only way to master this new skill was to practice, but she'd have time for that later. Instead, Anna steered the conversation back to the matter at hand. "If Noor's worried about books, it can't be the ones we have—there's nothing in them that pose a threat to him. He must have been thinking of the journals we're missing."

"If that's the case, then we have a problem." Mary was shaking her head. "I spent *years* contacting family trying to find them, but no one seems to know where they went."

"How many other Burkes are out there?" Joe looked at her. "I guess I assumed it was just you guys."

"No." Mary laughed. "Our line has always been prolific. Burke blood ranges worldwide."

Joe leaned forward in his chair. "I've known Anna for almost a year, and she's never mentioned any of them. Why haven't I heard anything about them before now?"

"That's our fault," Anna broke in, earning a reproving look from her mom.

"It's no one's fault," Mary stated firmly. "This is *our* fight. They all have families and children to protect. Until this is over, they have to think of that."

Mary turned to Joe and continued the explanation. "When news spread that I was carrying quadruplets, Burkes far and wide sent me all the historical family records they had, hoping they would aid in the battle to come. I started to catalog them as they arrived and soon learned there was a large gap in the collected texts. I reached out to other family members, but I was never able to locate them."

"I think now might be a good time to revisit that search,"

Ethan suggested. "We need to find this missing piece of the puzzle. I've got time; I can help you."

Mary nodded at her youngest child. "I'd appreciate it."

"What does it mean for Seth," Aria voiced a concern Anna knew was haunting her, "if Noor knows they carry the same blood?"

Seth reached out and grasped Aria's hand. He held it tightly in both of his. "So what if he knows?" Seth's brown eyes went cold. "Let him come."

~~~

The waiting in between Noor's attacks was always the hardest, but it gave them time to try to hunt down the missing chronicles.

They had the full collection of writings from their ancestors through the 1590s. The memoirs they had didn't pick back up again until a few months prior to the battle to imprison Noor in 1732. The missing records spanned over a hundred and thirty years. There was no telling what specifics had been documented during that time.

Anna played through her brief conversation with Noor. If he were worried about them having those absent books, that must mean they held some pretty damning information about him. Like possibly where his powers came from and how to defeat him. They *had* to get their hands on those journals.

But without knowing which family member, or members, had them last, or even if they were still in Burke hands, they would be virtually impossible to find.

~~~

As May blended into June, they called everyone they could think of and searched for the lost books. Someone would tell them they thought they'd heard that so-and-so had them, only to find they'd run into another dead end.

After much misinformation and wild goose chases that led exactly nowhere, Anna resigned herself to the fact that they were probably gone for good.

On top of that, the end of the school year was suddenly looming in front of her. She worried because Jacob hadn't made any additional progress and still wasn't speaking. Despite working with him every day, she knew no more about the night his mother had died than she had when they'd started.

On the last day of school, she waited until all the other students had left and then went to him.

"Hey, sweetie. I want you to know that this may be the last day you'll come to this class, but you and I will still see each other. I've worked it out with Mrs. Pier, and I'm going to come over to your house every day so we can talk and work on finding your voice."

Jacob's big brown eyes watched her.

"Do you still have the card Joe gave to you? The one with our phone numbers on it?"

Jacob nodded.

"That's good. You keep that with you, and if you ever need anything, you call one of us. Okay?"

Movement caught her attention, and Mrs. Pier stood in the doorway. Anna looked back at Jacob. "I'll see you tomorrow, buddy."

Anna watched them leave and felt like her heart was being ripped out. She was still lost in thought when Joe arrived to take her to her parents' for dinner and a never-ending discussion about Noor.

"How was he today?" Joe gave her a light kiss.

"The same." It saddened her that, other than the progress they'd made a few weeks ago, Jacob still hadn't opened up about what had happened. The trauma of that day was locked up tight inside of him. She'd thought about using her new ability to *see* what was in his mind, but until she'd gained better consistency and control, she'd decided to wait.

After gathering her things, Joe walked her out to the car. Once they were seated and buckled in, Anna couldn't help but share her frustration. "I'm so afraid I'm not going to be able to help him through this, and he'll remain shut away from everyone. Other than us, he still won't meet many people's eyes. He's too afraid of seeing the beast inside of someone again."

Joe reached out and caught her hand in his. He brought it to his lips and kissed it softly. "If Noor or his father come for him, they'll have to get through us to do it."

"We still don't know why Noor even chose them. Or what his plan was." Anna had racked her brain trying to find the answer, but nothing ever made sense. Seth and Evan had been looking into Jacob's past, but so far they'd run into road block after road block. Whoever had put Jacob into protective custody had done their job well.

They drove on, each lost in their own thoughts. Joe kept hold of Anna's hand, and the love in the gesture warmed and calmed her fears.

Joe gave her fingers one more kiss after he pulled into her parents' driveway and parked. They separated long enough to exit the car. Joe grasped her hand again as they walked up the path.

Joe opened the door and held it for her to pass through. Anna immediately felt a rush of excitement in the air. She looked back at Joe. "Something's happened."

She heard voices coming from the kitchen, so that's where she headed first. When she cleared the doorway, she looked around at the expectant faces.

Her parents stood at the island across from where Aria, Seth, and Evan sat.

"What is it?" Anna demanded.

Seth held up a file. "We've got him."

Tears welled in Anna's eyes. *Finally.* "Tell me."

"Shouldn't we wait for Ethan?" Paul asked.

"Wait for me for what?" Ethan responded as he walked in behind them.

Anna refused to be delayed another second. "Tell me," she said more forcefully.

Seth opened the folder and looked over the paperwork. "I had to pull a lot of strings to get this information. When nothing turned up in the police database, we knew we'd have to go straight to the source. Luckily, during my time working undercover, I'd built up a relationship with one of the clerks at the protective agency."

Anna was nearly bouncing off the walls in anticipation, but she kept quiet and waited for Seth to continue.

"Jacob Murphy is actually Jacob Hagen. His father, Kurt Hagen—a real piece of work by the looks of it—is being accused of the murders of his wife Sami Hagen and little Jacob."

Seth flipped one sheet after another. "Evidently, there was a long history of domestic abuse and violence in that house. The responding officers figure Kurt finally just took it too far and killed his wife and son. When they found a pulse in Jacob, they whisked him away to the hospital and then into protective custody. To further safeguard his new identity, they have Jacob Hagen listed as deceased. The father is still at large."

"He sounds like the type Noor would prefer for a new meat suit." Anna's heart hurt for Jacob and his mother. They must have suffered so much at the hands of such a brutal man.

"Sami. Is that short for Samantha?" Anna asked.

Seth backtracked through the file. "No. It says here her first name is Samara."

Instant recognition struck Anna, and as she looked at each of her siblings and parents, she saw that they'd caught it too.

"What is it?" Joe asked, his eyes darting between them all.

"Do you know her?"

"What are the chances?" Ethan turned wide eyes to his brother and sisters. "It's quite an unusual name, but there could be more out there."

"What's going on?" Seth leaned forward. "Who is Samara Hagen?"

Evan slapped his palm to his forehead. "That would explain *so much* about this mess."

"And why Jacob has magic," Anna added, thinking back to the pictures he'd drawn before.

"Oh, God." Mary covered her lips with her hand and looked at her husband. "Could it be her?"

"Could someone please tell me what the *hell* you know about Samara Hagen?" Seth threw down the file, obviously tired of being ignored.

They all finally acknowledged Seth, but it was Aria who spoke. "We have a cousin. A distant one but still a Burke, named Samara."

Joe's eyes narrowed. "I thought you said all babies born into the family carried the name?"

"Most of the time, yes," Mary explained. "But there are some men out there who refuse to give up their own legacy."

"And given his rap sheet," Evan said in disgust, "this Kurt Hagen fits that profile."

Seth was quiet. His gaze tracked from one of them to the next. Anna could almost see the wheels turning as he replayed what he knew, taking it all in and fitting the pieces together.

When it apparently fell into place for him, Seth swore. "Son of a bitch! Does that mean Noor knew they were Burkes?"

"It's a possibility," Anna choked out. As deep as his vendetta went, the Burke name was all it would take to incite his revenge.

"Let's not get ahead of ourselves," Mary cautioned. "There are any number of reasons Noor could have targeted them, but

I don't think it's because they're Burkes. It doesn't make sense that he could just randomly track down and kill members of our family whenever he wanted. Our ancestors wouldn't have left a loophole like that when they locked him away. The whole purpose of caging him was to save and preserve our line until you four could stop him for good."

Mary shook her head. "No. There must be some other explanation for Noor's interest in that family."

Knowing that Jacob was a Burke made Anna want to hold him closer still. He needed his full family line. He needed her and Joe.

Jacob couldn't be left with strangers. He had blood relatives now, and she wanted him. But being a Friday night, there really wasn't much she could do about that just yet.

The whole situation just niggled at her. If it wasn't Burke ancestry that had prompted the attack on Samara and Jacob, then what else could it be?

As dinner was prepared, they all ran through different scenarios, trying to find a motive that would make sense.

Just as they sat down to eat, Joe's cell phone rang, halting any further discussion. Anna watched as he slid it free of his pocket and looked at the display.

Rising, he excused himself from the table. He was at the doorway leading into the kitchen when Anna heard him answer. "Hello?"

Joe stopped in his tracks. When he turned back, all the color had drained from his face. Anna felt a sense of dread settle into her stomach.

"Jacob? Jacob, tell me what's wrong." Joe's eyes tracked back to hers, and when she saw the fear in them, her heart ceased beating.

The room had gone completely still. Anna rose to her feet, ready to act at a moment's notice. All of her concentration was on Joe, waiting for him to tell her what was happening. For a little boy who hadn't talked in months, Anna knew only one thing could have provoked him into speaking. The tears began to fall as sheer panic set in.

"We're coming, Jacob." The words came out in a rush as Joe turned towards the door and motioned them to follow. "Anna and I are coming for you. Don't hang up. I want you to find someplace to hide and don't make a sound."

Evan swiped Jacob's file off the counter and ran to catch up. "What is it?"

Joe covered the mouthpiece with his hand. "All he keeps saying is 'monster,' over and over again." His eyes flashed with banked rage and fear. "Noor found him. How the fuck did he find him?"

Evan's voice was as taut as steel cables. "We'll worry about that later. Just hurry—I've got his address."

The eight of them ran from the house and loaded into whatever vehicles would hold them. Anger had overridden her fear, and Anna jumped into the driver's seat of the last car in the driveway, determined to get to Jacob in time. Ethan tossed her the keys as he and Evan hurried into the back and slammed the doors. Joe climbed into the passenger seat, still clutching the phone to his ear and murmuring reassurances to the frightened child on the other end.

Anna tore off down the road with Seth, Aria, and her parents in the car behind her. The next ten minutes seemed endless as Anna sped to the house where Jacob was—at this very moment—trying to hide from evil.

She just couldn't understand why Noor even wanted him. If her mother was right and he didn't know about the Burke connection, then why was he so set on getting to Jacob? And how had he found him? Even with Evan in the police force, it had taken him weeks to find Jacob. Noor shouldn't have been able to find him at all.

She screeched around the corner and onto his street at the

same time Joe shouted. "Jacob...Jacob!...*Fuck!*" He threw the phone to the floor and slammed his fists into the dash. "Goddamn it!"

Heart in her throat, Anna barely got the words out. "What happened?"

"Jacob screamed...and then the line went dead."

Anna's breath caught, but she pushed all thought from her mind. When she cast a glance at Joe, his features were set and hard.

The tires squealed as she slammed on the brakes in front of Jacob's house. The front door stood wide open, and lying on the floor in full view, was the body of a woman.

Fear nearly choked her, but she grabbed for the door handle and wrenched it open.

They all piled out and ran for the house. Evan and Seth were first through the door, guns drawn.

Evan bent to check for Mrs. Pier's pulse. Anna held her breath until he looked up at them and gave a slight shake of his head.

She was dead.

A noise issued from somewhere towards the back of the house. Anna thought of Jacob being at the hands of such a monster, and instinct had her propelling forward.

Seth grabbed her arm, and with a quick and decisive shake of his head, motioned for her to stop. He let go of her arm and held his hand up in a halt gesture before touching his forefinger to his lips. Seth turned to his partner and sent another signal. Evan nodded and, side by side, they cautiously advanced towards where the sound had come from, guns in a two-handed grip, barrels at the ready.

They'd taken two steps into the hall when they suddenly stopped and backed slowly out. Anna wondered what they'd seen but didn't have long to wait. As the men retreated, another man stepped out and smirked at them. He carried a limp Jacob under one arm.

Anna's heart clenched. *Oh, Jacob.* She tore her eyes away long enough to look up at Joe. His body was stiff, and his golden eyes were like chips of granite, cold and inflexible as he stared at the seemingly lifeless body of the child they'd both come to love.

"Put him down, you son of a bitch." Evan leveled his pistol at the man's head. "And step away."

"And why would I want to do that?" Glassy eyes stared back at them. "I've gone to a lot of trouble to have him."

"Because he's *mine*." Anna's voice was low and deadly. At this moment, she would gladly kill him to protect that child. She stepped up next to her brother but remained well out of firing range.

"He is nothing to you. The blood in his veins makes him mine," Noor taunted with a sneer. "The same way this one is." Noor, through Kurt Hagen's dull grey eyes, looked at Seth with a knowing smirk. "The same way *you* are."

Anna gasped. Jacob, through his father, was a descendant of Noor?

"I may have lost my sons when that faithless bitch ran off, but I have gained *countless* in my absence. I can feel them all now, and the number is extraordinary." Noor's glee and satisfaction pulled Kurt's face into a grotesque depiction of a smile.

"Why do you even want him?" Anna pushed. "You tried to kill him."

"That was unfortunate." She opened her senses and felt truth. He continued on. "When I found a descendant with power, I knew he was to be my heir. When I went to retrieve him, the woman got in my way."

The rapture radiating out of his mind confirmed he'd enjoyed every minute of it. "She was protecting her son, you sick bastard. That's what mothers do. But that still doesn't explain why you hurt him."

"The insolent whelp stood against me to protect that worthless whore. I knocked him out of the way to teach him who was in control. He fell and didn't rise."

He shrugged like it meant nothing. "When I learned he had lived and that he was here, I knew it was meant to be. I've come to collect him. Now."

"He's just a small child. What could you possibly hope to gain by taking him?" Seth demanded.

"He will stand and rule at my side. And once he's completed the trials and has added that power to his own..." Noor threw his head back and howled with laughter. "He will become my greatest weapon."

The thought of that made Anna's stomach threaten to revolt. There was no way in hell she was letting that happen. She took another step forward and felt it when Joe aligned himself with her. Behind them, the rest of her family held the line.

"You'll never make it out of this house," Joe growled, and Anna braced herself to fight alongside him.

Noor was facing a small army fortified with magic and guns. The man-made weapons may or may not cause damage to the monster himself, but they could put the body he inhabited out of commission.

Noor eyed each of them carefully and evidently saw that he had lost this round. With a mighty roar of rage, he shifted his grip on Jacob and lifted him high above his head.

Anna's first thought was that he'd slam Jacob to the floor. But she didn't figure he'd risk killing him—Noor wanted him too badly. But he could still hurt him all over again.

She was about to race forward to snatch him from Noor's hands when he tossed Jacob right into the middle of their group.

Everyone scrambled to catch him, and at the same time Noor blasted a wave of energy throughout the room. It knocked them all back and off balance, but somehow, Joe was able to remain standing to gently capture Jacob in his arms.

When they gathered themselves, Noor with Kurt Hagen, was gone.

Now that Anna knew what Noor's game-plan was, she knew he wouldn't stop coming for Jacob. And that scared her down to the bone. Just the thought of Jacob enduring the rite that Noor had completed to gain his abilities made her sick.

But they'd won tonight, and this poor child was safe.

Joe was still cradling him when big coffee-brown eyes started to flutter open. Anna was right there with Joe to be the first people Jacob saw.

Anna brushed his dark brown hair back. "Hey, sweetie. You're okay. We've got you. The monster's gone."

"Anna," the small boy whispered.

"That's right, baby." Tears clogged Anna's throat at the sound of his voice. "I'm here, and so is Joe. You did really great by calling us. You were so brave."

He nodded and then closed his eyes and burrowed into Joe's chest.

Mary came over and laid her hand on Anna's back. "Let's get him out of here. Evan and Seth can take care of...the rest."

Anna knew her mother didn't want to scare Jacob further by mentioning the body of his foster mother lying on the floor. Anna nodded her agreement and looked at Joe. "Come on. Let's get him home."

# 11

This time Ethan drove his own car, and Anna slid into the backseat with Joe and Jacob. Their parents and Aria followed in the other car. There'd been a concern about leaving Seth and Evan without transportation, but they'd assured them they could get a ride with a fellow officer.

It was a silent trip back to the family home. After both cars were parked, they filed into the house. Joe and Anna sat down on the couch with Jacob still clutched to Joe.

"I'll go put together some food and drinks." Mary smiled. "I think it's going to be a long night. Aria, Ethan—come help your dad and me in the kitchen."

Mary had effectively cleared the room, leaving her and Joe to spend some time with Jacob on their own.

Anna gazed at the remarkable child in Joe's arms. She reached out and glided her hand over his head in a loving caress. He opened his eyes and looked up at her.

"I am so proud of you," she said softly.

"Mrs. Pier." Sadness gathered in Jacob's features. "It killed her."

Anna felt her heart squeeze. One more person who had cared for him was gone, taken by the hand of evil. "I know, sweetie, and I'm so sorry. She was a very nice lady, and she cared for you a great deal."

"It was my dad, but it wasn't. It was like before...when

Momma died." Jacob switched his attention to Joe and then back to her. "Will he come for me again?"

The last thing Anna wanted to do was scare him, but she couldn't lie to him. She nodded slowly. "I'm afraid so."

Naturally, he became upset. "Hey." She spoke soothingly and touched his face. "Joe and I, and the rest of my family, are here now and we'll protect you. You're not alone anymore."

She wondered how much he knew of his lineage on his mother's side. "I don't know if you know this, since everyone at the school calls me Miss Anna, but my full name is Anna Burke. Do you know that name?"

"My mom said we were Burkes," Jacob said hesitantly. "But that I couldn't say anything to anyone, because my dad would get mad."

"I'm glad your mom was able to share that with you. But what you might not know is that Burke is a very old and very powerful name. And it also means we're family. The magic you and I have? That's because we're Burkes. Did your mom ever explain that to you?"

Jacob's head bobbed up and down.

"You have a big family and a lot of relatives now." Anna wanted to make sure he knew he wouldn't have to live in fear. "Powerful witches that will keep the monsters away. Would you like to meet some of them?"

He thought about that for a moment and then looked up at Joe who smiled tenderly at him. "They're pretty cool people, and I'll be right here with you."

The fear and uncertainty eased in Jacob and he turned back to Anna. "I guess."

"I bet my mom has some snacks ready. What do you say we go see?"

Joe set Jacob on his feet, and they each grasped one of his hands as they walked together into the kitchen.

Ethan, her dad, and Aria were seated at the island while her mom bustled about, putting a cold-cut tray together.

They all swung around when the three of them entered.

"Jacob thought he'd like to meet some of his Burke family." Anna kept her voice light when all she wanted to do was cry.

Mary came and kneeled to his level, but he wouldn't look up at her.

Anna squatted down next to him and gently turned him to face her. "I *promise* you, you won't ever see the monster in any Burke." She waited a moment, but he still didn't move. Placing her finger under his chin, she lifted his head until he was looking at her. "It's okay. You can look at them."

Jacob held her gaze for another moment before slowly pivoting his head around to Mary.

She grinned at him. "Hi. I'm Mary, Anna's mom. It's so great to finally meet you. Anna says you're a very special boy, and I can see she was right." Her mom cupped Jacob's cheek and caressed it before pointing over her shoulder. "That man there, that's my husband, Paul."

Paul too crouched down. "Hey there, short-stuff." He shared a wink with Jacob. "Technically, I'm not a Burke. But I did marry one, so I know that they're the best people to have watching over you."

As her mom and dad stood and moved aside, Aria stepped in and knelt down. Jacob took one look at her and then swung around to look up at Anna.

She and her sister grinned at his reaction. "Remember me telling you that I had a twin? That means we look the same. This is my sister, Aria."

"Hi, Jacob." Aria swept her hand over his head and down the side of his face. "I'm so glad you're here. I know we'll be great friends."

"That big guy there," Anna nodded towards Ethan, "is one of our brothers. His name is Ethan, and he has a twin too. Together, we are quadruplets, and we were all born on the same day."

"Hey, buddy." Ethan crouched in front of Jacob and stuck his hand out. He waited for Jacob to grasp it and then gave it a good shake. "Nice to meet you. If you have any questions, you let me know." Ethan gave him a sly grin before leaning in to whisper, "I know a few secrets that we'll keep between us guys."

Jacob's eyes widened as he nodded.

"Don't you pay any attention to him, Jacob." Mary laughed. "The only thing he knows is how to get into trouble. Now," she bent over, "are you hungry? I didn't know what you liked, so I put out a little bit of everything. But, if you're anything like some other Burke boys I know, I'll bet you like ham."

Jacob spoke softly. "Yes, please."

They moved to the dining room, and Jacob sat on Joe's lap as he ate. Everyone kept up happy chatter until an hour later when Seth and Evan finally arrived. Jacob looked from Ethan to Evan.

"Yup, that's my twin brother," Ethan confirmed. "But I'm definitely the cooler one." He gave Jacob a conspiratorial wink.

Evan jumped right into the game without missing a beat. "He is not," he argued as he grabbed stuff to throw a sandwich together. "If he was so cool, could he do this?" Evan wiped one hand on his pants and conjured a giant chocolate chip cookie into it.

Jacob's eyes almost popped, and Anna had to laugh.

"Yeah, well," Ethan argued back, "can you do this?" He held out his hand and had flames dancing on his palm.

Anna loved her family for making sure Jacob didn't have to suffer through the horror of this night.

"No fire in the house, Ethan Burke," Mary scolded. 'How many times have I told you that? And Evan, no cookie before you eat."

Both of them gave her a sheepish look and in unison said,

"Yes, ma'am."

Jacob smiled and then his gaze shot to Seth expectantly.

Seth shook his head and threw up his hands in a shrug. "Sorry, little dude. That's a Burke thing. I'm like Paul. I'm just a normal guy who loves a Burke witch. Kind of like your friend Joe there."

Jacob turned brown eyes up to Joe. Anna slipped into Jacob's mind and felt a sense of comfort and safety.

They talked for a little while more until Anna noticed Jacob going limp in Joe's arms as he fell asleep.

Mary saw it too. "Why don't you guys stay here tonight? I don't think he'll show up again, but better safe than sorry. You can lay him down in the boys' room."

"Thanks, Mom." Anna was feeling the weariness too.

Mary got up to start clearing the mess. When she disappeared into the kitchen, Joe turned to Anna and shook his head. "I don't want to leave him alone."

Anna understood. "We won't. He can have one bed, and we can take the other."

Joe looked skeptical. "Twin beds, I'm guessing? Like yours and Aria's?"

"No." Anna laughed. "My brothers graduated to full-sized beds by the sixth grade."

He sent a covert glance to her mom as she came back for more dishes. "Are you sure? What about your parents?"

She knew he was worried about propriety and thought it was sweet, but she couldn't resist teasing him. She leaned closer and, in a seductive voice, whispered, "What about them?"

He gave her a pained look and she laughed. "With Jacob in the room, I'm pretty sure you don't have anything to worry about." She kissed him. "Come on."

Joe rose and lifted Jacob with him. He followed her out of the dining room, down the hall, and into the room her brothers had shared. This room was as familiar to her as her own had been, but Anna tried to see it through Joe's eyes.

The walls were painted a dark green, and the two full beds took up most of the room. Wood headboards were separated by a small table holding a lamp and a family picture of the six of them. They were all laughing hysterically over a particularly off-color word the photographer had told them to say just before snapping the picture.

The bedding was different now that they'd gotten older. Instead of the two-toned blue comforters, white quilts accented with greens and blues now covered each mattress. Matching curtains hung over the window, and throw rugs had been put down.

Overall, the room hadn't changed much. It still held the heart of two teenage boys. Their mother had left the sports memorabilia and model cars lining the shelves on the walls. Anna had to wonder if the boys' secret stash of candy and comic books was still tucked under the loose baseboard in the corner.

Maybe she'd share that little secret with Jacob.

The nostalgia dissipated when Joe settled Jacob on the bed. Together they got him comfortable, leaving him to sleep in only his t-shirt and underpants. Tucking the blanket snuggly around his little body, they stood over him, watching him until there was a soft knock on the open doorframe. Anna turned to see her mom standing there.

"I thought you could use these." She handed Joe a pair of thin sweat pants and then gave Anna an old pair of pajamas that had been left behind when she'd moved out.

"Thanks, Mom."

Mary crossed to softly lay her lips on Jacob's forehead. Before rising, Anna heard her whisper something over Jacob and smiled. With a kiss for Anna and Joe both, Mary left.

"What did she say?" Joe asked as the door closed behind her.

"A little chant to keep his dreams calm and easy. She used to do the same for Aria and me when our minds were troubled."

"And it works?"

"Yes. He'll be fine tonight." Anna reached up with her free hand and rested it on Joe's chest. He covered it with his and brought it to his lips to kiss her fingers.

"Let's try to get some sleep," Anna suggested and gestured to the door of the shared room behind her. "The bathroom is through there."

"You can have it first." Joe kissed her knuckles again before releasing her hand.

"Okay. I'll only be a couple of minutes."

True to her word, after a change of clothes and a quick brush of her teeth, Anna was back.

"I left a new toothbrush on the counter for you."

"Thanks." Joe gazed down at Jacob one more time and then disappeared into the bathroom.

Anna got into bed. Positioned on her side, her gaze fell on Jacob. She couldn't take her eyes off him. When Joe returned in only the sweat pants, he crawled in behind her and pulled her back into his body.

"I won't give him up," Anna whispered fiercely.

"Anna, what about Samara's immediate family? Her parents?" The reluctance in Joe's voice said he wasn't fond of that idea either. "Wouldn't they want to take him?"

"I've already thought of that." Anna recounted what she knew of that branch of the family. "Samara was an only-child and was raised by her mother. Amelia was in her mid-forties when Samara was born, and her dad passed away when she was really young. The grandparents on both sides had been gone long before that. Before Samara was even out of high school, her mom had begun showing signs of Alzheimer's. Sadly, she passed away a few years later." Anna paused. "The bottom line is that there's no one else."

Joe was quiet and she couldn't see his face to gauge what he was thinking. Did he want to take on a six-year-old boy when they'd only just found each other? That would be a lot for any man to commit to, let alone the other problems she and Jacob brought with them.

"I know we tabled it before," Joe's low voice rumbled in her ear, "but would now be a good time to revisit you moving in with me? Now that we have Jacob, I want us to be a family."

Anna rolled until she was facing him in the almost-dark room. She glided her hand over the side of his face, just as she had Jacob. "Are you sure you want to take us on?"

Amber eyes glowed warm in the moonlight. "You said you won't give him up. And I won't give up either one of you. So it looks like we're in this together." His voice lowered to a whisper. "I love you."

"And I love you."

He kissed her long and deep and then nestled her into his side. Exhaustion took over and they slept, waking once when Jacob crawled from his bed into theirs. They automatically made room for him between them and dozed off again.

When Anna awoke, the sun was shining in through the window. She was startled when she found Jacob gone. She sat up and looked around for him. Joe stirred beside her.

"What's wrong?"

"Where's Jacob?" she asked frantically.

They both jumped out of bed. Joe grabbed his shirt and jerked it over his head as they tore out of the bedroom. They found him in the kitchen with her mom. Anna breathed a sigh of relief at the sight of him sitting at the table, drawing with a bowl of half-eaten cereal at his elbow.

"He's an early riser like me." Mary was standing in front of the sink and grinned over her coffee cup at their disheveled appearance. "We were having a lovely talk, and then he asked if I had any paper and crayons." She glanced at the clock on the microwave. "That was almost two hours ago."

They all knew about Jacob's ability. Anna could see that her mom was curious but hadn't wanted to intrude upon him.

Anna walked over to the table and looked over his shoulder. He'd finished two already and was coloring on another. She picked up the completed pictures.

He'd drawn her mother. Anna didn't know exactly what she was supposed to be, but the lightness and love that radiated off the paper was definitely her mom. She had always been the center of this family, and the love she spread enveloped them all. And Jacob had seen that.

She studied the next one and saw the face of one of her brothers. He was outfitted in brown pants and a crosshatch of something gray hung over his shoulders and chest. Chainmail, maybe? He carried a large and heavy sword. He looked like a warrior in full battle attire.

Knowing her brothers, she would guess this was Evan, but she'd have to ask Jacob to be sure.

When she glanced down to the one Jacob was working on, her heart clenched. This one was definitely Ethan. He was dressed in the full turnout gear of a firefighter. He knelt on one knee and his helmet dangled from one hand. His head was bent forward and where his heavy jacket hung open to reveal his chest, there was a stark white bandage over his heart.

Reining in emotion, she left him to finish and walked the others to her mom.

When Mary saw what was there, she gasped. "Oh, my."

"He nailed you." Anna smiled. "Show that to anyone in the family and they'll agree. You've always been the heart and soul of us."

Anna leaned in and kissed her mom's cheek as she studied the one of Evan.

Mary glanced over at Jacob still working away. "Who is that he's doing now?"

"Ethan. He's not done quite yet." She didn't elaborate; her mother would see it soon enough and know.

Anna turned and got cups for her and Joe and filled them both with coffee. They sat with Jacob while her mom went to show her dad the drawings.

"If we're going to do this, we have some steps to take." Joe took a sip from his mug.

"I know." Anna watched Jacob. She knew the courts wouldn't just hand him over to them. There would be lots of hoops and red tape to navigate.

But no matter what happened, Jacob would not leave her side. She would just have to make sure the system knew she and Joe could provide the best home for this child. Now that Noor had a direct link to anyone with his blood, he could locate him at any time. It just wasn't safe for Jacob to be with anyone other than them.

Mrs. Pier was evidence of that.

Jacob needed the protection of the Burke witches. He needed her. And she needed him.

"I need to find out who's in charge and have a talk with them," Anna decided.

Just then, Mary popped her head back into the kitchen. "Oh, I almost forgot. You might want to think about calling our cousin, Patrick." She grinned at Anna. "You know, the one that just happens to be a family court judge?"

Anna laughed as her mom's face disappeared around the corner again.

# 12

The wheels of the judicial system could move swiftly upon occasion. Joe's head was still swimming at the rate in which things had progressed since Anna had made her phone call a few hours ago.

Given that Patrick was also a witch and familiar with the prophecy, Anna had given her cousin a detailed account of recent events, and he'd granted them emergency custody of Jacob. As a condition of the ruling, they'd be monitored very closely and subject to periodic home checks. He and Anna would have to keep them apprised of any changes in Jacob's state of mind. As much as they could, anyway.

He was still the only witness in the murder of his mother, and the authorities were waiting, not so patiently, for him to regain his ability to speak. They needed what he knew to move forward with their case, which was at a standstill because, as far as they knew, Kurt Hagen was still on the run.

They'd decided not to inform those in charge of Jacob's case that Hagen had made an appearance in Florida. The death of Jacob's foster mother would be attributed to a break-in. Joe knew they were walking a fine line, but the last thing this situation needed was for the police to get involved. They could end up hurt or worse, because the man they were hunting had beyond-human attributes. It wouldn't help any of them to divulge that Jacob's father had been possessed by a five-hundred-year-old psycho at the time of the murder.

The average person just wouldn't understand. Hell, Joe barely understood, and he was neck-deep in the middle of it. But no matter how much he didn't comprehend, he vowed he would do whatever it took to protect Jacob and make him feel safe and secure in his new home. A home he would now share with Joe and Anna.

Joe shook his head at the thought of Anna in his...*their* bedroom, unpacking her clothes and toiletries. He was amazed at the turn his life had taken since she'd walked into it just a year ago. He remembered that day clearly.

After the news had reported incidents of muggings and car-jackings, Joe thought to offer one free self-defense class to the local women. He hoped that by showing them the basics on how to protect themselves, there'd be one less statistic.

When the day of the class arrived, he had a pretty good turnout and was excited to help in any way he could. He was going over some last-minute details before the women arrived when the business line in his office rang. He caught Jay's attention and asked him to finish up the prep and to greet everyone as they came in.

By the time Joe finally hung up, the class was about to start. As he exited his office and crossed the gym floor, he did a quick head count and saw that he had twenty-two students. Not bad.

He introduced himself and had them spread out. He then took them through a series of stretches to get them warmed up and ready.

"I want to thank you all for coming. I hope some of what you'll be learning here today will help you if you're ever in a situation that could be life threatening. The first thing all of you need to know and remember is that fighting hurts. It doesn't matter if you're landing punches or receiving them, it's going to hurt. Accept that, and don't let it stop you from thinking—you might just survive. Your brain is your best defense.

"Now, there're many ways to fight off an attacker—and I'll show you some of those today—but at some point you're going to try to hit him. I'd rather you know the correct way to punch so you can do the most damage. With that in mind," he paused, "I want everyone to hold up your hands and form fists."

He walked back and forth in front of them as arms rose.

"Look at your hands. If your thumb is tucked under your fingers, it's going to get broken if you ever hit someone like that."

Joe held up his own and showed them the correct positioning. "This is what it should look like. And now that we all know that, I'm going to demonstrate some different types of punches for you. The first will be the hook."

He bent and picked up the piece of equipment at his feet and held it high so everyone could see it.

"This is called a clap pad. As you can see, its two pieces laced together along the top edge, and that flows into this long handle. There are two target areas on this particular pad—one on either side."

He turned the pad and handed it to Jay, who held it in both hands, perpendicular to the floor. Joe pivoted so his body faced his assistant. He spread his feet, loosened his knees, and brought his hands up before explaining the hook punch.

"Always keep your guard up. It not only protects your face and throat, but it also allows you the ability to snap out a punch quickly. This strike begins in the hips for maximum power. As you cock your arm back, your hips are going to begin their twist. Your elbow should be at a ninety-degree angle." He did one in slow motion to demonstrate. "You want to follow all the way through."

He straightened up to look over the class. "Now, I'll throw a couple at full-speed to show you how it all looks."

Joe planted his feet, took up his fighting stance, and struck the pad with three solid strikes—right, left, right. The resounding claps were loud enough to startle a few of the women.

"And now you know why it's called a clap pad." Joe grinned and turned back to face the astonished faces of his class. "It was designed that way so you know you're landing the punch correctly. I'm not going to ask you to hit it that hard, as none of you have protective gloves and I don't want you to rip up your knuckles. We're using these just to give you something to aim at."

Joe signaled Jay to hand out the rest of the pads. "Let's partner up. Jay is going to give each pair a pad, and we'll practice our hook punches."

He was glad to see just about all of the women were taking it seriously. He slowly wandered around, making adjustments to his students' forms. As he wound his way through, he spotted her in the back of the room.

She was so petite, yet she had a larger-than-life presence. He somehow sensed that beneath her slight stature, there was a core of pure steel. Everything about her spoke to him  From her pale, white-gold hair and delicate, classic features to the fierceness in her ice-blue eyes as she concentrated.

And then there was her slight but smoking hot body. He was never more thankful for the bagginess of his shorts, as his body responded to the sight of her immediately.

Joe fought to keep his eyes off her all through class and didn't breathe an easy breath until it was over. He was looking forward to the sanctuary of his office when a couple of ladies waylaid him with questions. Joe spoke with them for a short time and was about to sneak off when he heard her soft, clear voice.

"Excuse me, Mr. Conrad?"

Joe had to steady himself before turning to face her. The velvety-smooth way she talked shot straight to his libido. "Yes?"

"I'd like to continue with this." She indicated the gym in general with her hand. "I'd like to learn more. How do I sign up?"

His mind went blank at the thought of having her around all the time. Knowing how his body had reacted to her after one meeting, he didn't think he could withstand constant contact.

But evidently his mouth had other plans. "Just let me know when you'd like to start."

"Right away." Her clear blue eyes held his.

"Ah, yeah. Sure," he stammered out. How the hell was he going to make this work? Women had never attended his gym on a regular basis. It wasn't set up for that. He had to do some quick thinking and planning to fix the problem his hormones had gotten him into.

"Could you come in around nine a.m. tomorrow?" he asked her as his mind still spun. "We'll...ah...figure out a routine."

"Thank you." Joe watched her leave and then took himself to his office to wait for his blood to make it back to his brain so he could think clearly. As he sat there, he saw the paperwork each woman had filled out before class.

He knew he shouldn't, but he couldn't seem to stop his hand from leafing through until he found hers. He knew it was hers because she'd been the smallest there. When he saw she'd listed herself as five foot four, he pulled the sheet out.

Anna Burke. Twenty-three. An eight-year gap to his own thirty-one. Not insurmountable, but it still gave him pause.

Joe pulled himself back to the present and smiled at the memory of the struggle he'd fought after that. He'd had to force himself not to think about her hot little body once she'd become a client. That line shouldn't be crossed.

It hadn't been easy, but he'd done it. Until her sister had come and blown their precarious existence out the window by telling Anna he had feelings for her.

It had taken a little while longer for them to finally come together, to find their rhythm, and then suddenly a traumatized child had fallen into their lives.

But Joe knew he wouldn't change a thing.

Not only did he have the woman he'd wanted from the moment he'd seen her, but he also had a child who looked up to him for protection and love. Joe's heart swelled ever more as he watched Jacob poke around his new bedroom.

Anna came to join them. "So, what do you think?" she asked Jacob. "Is this going to be okay?"

Jacob looked around again, and Joe thought he knew what might make this transition a little easier. He knelt down. "Hey, what do you say to a little shopping? You don't want all this boring grown-up stuff in here." Joe glanced around the room with a wrinkled nose, and it made Jacob smile. "How about we hit some stores and outfit this place any way you want? Maybe some superheroes, or what about that train that talks?"

"That's for babies," Jacob informed him, and Joe had to bite back a laugh. When he looked over at Anna, she too was fighting a grin.

"Oh. Okay then, no talking trains. Would you like to pick out some stuff to make this room your own?"

His little face fell. "What if I have to leave?" The tremor in Jacob's voice had Joe's throat going tight. He sat on the side of the bed and lifted Jacob into his lap. Anna came to kneel in front of them.

"I think I can speak for Anna," Joe told him, "when I say that we want you to stay with us forever."

They both looked at Anna as she smiled and nodded. "Definitely. You're a Burke, Jacob. That means we're already related. But more than that, we'd like for the three of us to be a family."

"We both love you very much, Jacob," Joe added. "But we know you'll always love your mom and miss her. If you ever want to talk about her, we're here. We don't want you to ever forget her. As soon as we can, we'll find a picture of her for you to keep next to your bed."

Anna gave him a minute to absorb that before pushing further. "So what do you say? Would you like to live here with Joe and me?"

Jacob nodded. "Yeah."

"So how about we do like Joe said and make this room yours?" Anna grinned brightly, stood, and held her hand out for him to take. "You know, I have it on pretty good authority that guys need their own space." She drew her brows together as if thinking. "At least, that's what my brothers always told me every time they kicked me out of their room."

Joe laughed and Jacob giggled.

The rest of the day was kind of a double-edged sword. With them, Jacob was opening up and talking more, interacting. But if anyone else was around, his head would droop and he wouldn't make eye contact. Joe knew it was his fear of seeing the monster again.

They reassured him as best they could, and Joe reminded him that he and Anna wouldn't let anything happen to him.

The bedding store went pretty well. It wasn't very busy and Jacob felt comfortable enough to pick out what he wanted. He decided on a set of sheets and blankets where knights were battling dragons. Joe and Anna exchanged bittersweet smiles, knowing Jacob was trying to surround himself with protection, even in sleep.

When he pulled into the parking lot of their next stop, Joe had second thoughts when he saw how many cars were in the parking lot. It was a popular chain toy store, and Joe hadn't given a thought as to how crowded it would be.

Joe looked at Anna. "We don't have to go in."

Anna looked around and thought about it. "No, I think it'll be okay."

She did take a moment once they were out of the car to stop and talk to Jacob.

Kneeling down in front of him, she took his hands in hers.

"Honey, there's going to be a lot of people in this store." His eyes dropped to the asphalt, but Anna lifted his chin with her finger. "Hey. Joe and I are going to be right there with you. You don't have to be afraid. If you see someone or something you don't like, you just let us know, and we'll take care of it."

Anna brushed her hand over his cheek. "I promise. It's going to all right."

Jacob slowly nodded and together they walked into the toy store.

After a rocky start, it ended up being a big hit. Jacob would forget for long stretches and just enjoy himself. There was one stressful moment when they were walking down an aisle, and Jacob just stopped in his tracks. He stared at a man at the other end and then pulled on Joe's hand, trying to back away. Anna saw what had drawn his notice and turned him to face her as she bent to him.

"Do you see something in that man?"

Jacob bobbed his head but didn't speak.

Joe eyed the man with deadly intent.

"Is it the beast?" she asked him.

He relaxed a little when Jacob shook his head.

"But it's something you don't like," Anna clarified.

"He's bad," Jacob whispered.

"Okay, sweetie." Anna picked him up as she stood. She gave Joe a glance before turning in the opposite direction. "Let's go look at the toys in a different aisle."

Joe kept an eye out and made sure the coast stayed clear. They finished their shopping trip with no further incidents and walked out with two big bags of toys Jacob had picked out. He'd continued the medieval theme by choosing toys depicting that era.

Back in the car, Anna turned in her seat and looked from him to Jacob. "Who's hungry?"

Joe played along. "I am. I'm starving." He stretched up to see

Jacob in the rearview mirror. "How about you, buddy?"

"Can we have pizza?"

His hopeful expression told them how much he wanted it.

"I loooove pizza." Anna dragged out the word just to make Jacob grin.

It worked and as Joe pulled out into traffic, Jacob was still smiling.

He drove them to a nearby pizzeria and while they ate, they talked about everything they'd bought.

Joe had had fun throughout the day, but through it all, he had kept a guarded eye out for Kurt Hagen. Jacob was under his protection now, and Joe would be damned before that murderous bastard got anywhere near this child again.

Even once they were behind the closed and locked doors of his home, Joe didn't ease up. As the hour grew later, Joe became even more vigilant. If someone were coming, he'd be ready to defend.

He and Anna put Jacob to bed in his newly-redecorated bedroom and as they stepped out they left the door ajar. If he called out they wanted to be sure to hear him. When Joe looked down into Anna's face, she was watching him intently.

"What?" he asked her.

She took his hand in hers. "Come with me."

Joe let her pull him into the master bedroom across the hall. She guided him right to the foot of the bed and gave him a push to sit down.

He may not have any magical abilities to assist him, but he didn't need them right now to know that her actions had nothing to do with making love. She had something on her mind.

Anna stepped between his thighs and moved in close to his body. She reached out and ran her delicate hands over his closely-cropped hair and rested them at the base of his neck.

"I want him safe too, but we can't stand watch all night,

every night." She rubbed her thumbs over his jaw. "I have a better idea. If you're agreeable to it."

Her touch threatened to rob him of thought.

"What's that?" he finally got out.

"I can put a protection spell on the house that will act as an early warning system. It'll let us know if anyone, or anything, tries to get in."

Joe didn't have a clue as to how that all worked, but he didn't care as long as it did. He brought his hands up to her hips.

"I don't mind at all. Do whatever you can to make this place safe for him."

She leaned down and kissed him before moving off to put the wards in place. While she was busy doing that, Joe checked on Jacob one more time before heading to the kitchen for a beer for himself and a glass of wine for Anna.

He was waiting for her on the couch when she came in.

"All done?" He handed her the flute.

She took a sip. "Mmm, thanks. Sealed up tight. Nothing getting in or out without us knowing."

Joe held his hand out to her and she sat next him, snuggling into his side. He wrapped his arm around her and kissed the hairline at her temple. He let some of the diligence he'd employed all day ease. He knew it wouldn't go away completely until Hagen and Noor were no longer a threat to the child he now thought of as his son. But with the help of this woman in his arms, tonight, he could rest a little easier.

He took a pull on his beer. "We need to figure out how our schedules are going to work now."

"Jacob will still need one-on-one time." Anna swirled the wine in her glass. "We know what happened and why, but he needs to talk it through…deal with it so it doesn't haunt him."

"What will we tell the authorities?" Joe had never dealt with anything like this before.

Anna blew out a breath. "I don't know just yet. It helps that

Evan, Seth, and my cousin Patrick all know the truth, but I don't know what to do about the rest."

Neither did he. "We'll figure it out as it comes, I guess."

They sat in companionable silence for a bit before Anna spoke again. "Jacob's going to need to know what it truly means to be a Burke. From what we've learned about Kurt, I doubt Samara was able to teach him much about his magical heritage. With everything that's happening, I think we should make that a priority. It'll give him more confidence to know he can defend himself if he needs to. And I want that for him. I also want to bring my mom in on it. She's had more experience with teaching magic to little ones than me." She gave a self-deprecating laugh. "My siblings and I weren't the easiest of students, but we all learned eventually."

Joe didn't want either Anna or Jacob out of his sight right now. Even the thought of them going to her parents' set off his unease.

"How about, for the next few days at least, you and Jacob hang out at the gym? We can drive in together, and after our workout, you and he can do your one-on-one upstairs."

She tilted her head back to look up at him. When she smiled softly, he knew she'd guessed what he was doing. "Yeah, we can do that. For a little while."

He leaned his head down and kissed her. "Thank you."

# 13

It was a good plan, but when Joe, Anna, and Jacob walked into the gym the next morning, that's not how it went.

As soon as he opened the door, and even before he flipped the lights on, Joe heard water flowing.

"What the hell?" It sounded like it was coming from the bathroom.

He hit the switch for the lights and took off across the room. When he pushed the door open, he immediately saw the problem. The toilet was overflowing and had been for some time. There was a good two inches of water covering the concrete floor.

"Shit!" He stood in the doorway and leaned all the way in, far enough to jiggle the handle and get the water to stop running. When he turned back, Anna and Jacob were there.

"Need a little help?" she offered.

"No, but thanks. Luckily, the threshold is built up, so it contained all of the water in here." Joe sighed at the thought of what it was going to take to mop this up. "Why don't you two go on upstairs? I'll deal with this."

Anna shook her head and smiled at him. "Joe."

He was so deep in thought about what to do next, it took him a moment to hear her. "Huh? What?"

"Hello? Water witch, here. Remember?"

Joe gave a start and looked at her. She was laughing at him.

It finally dawned on him what she was saying. "Ha! You are, aren't you?"

"Stand back, boys, and let this woman work."

Joe stepped out of her way. She had his and Jacob's full attention.

With just a subtle motion of her hands, Anna had all the water gathered and undulating in midair. Glancing over her shoulder at Jacob, she winked at him.

What she did next had Joe staring in amazement. When he could take his eyes off of her long enough to look down at Jacob, the little boy had the same expression on his face.

Las Vegas water fountains had nothing on his Anna. She put on quite the show before directing it into the waiting sink.

"There." She swung around to face them, brushing her hands together as if dusting them off. All the while, she wore a huge grin on her face. "Nothing to it."

"Nothing to it," Joe repeated, shaking his head before turning to Jacob. "I think someone was showing off. What do you think?"

His big brown eyes stared at Anna. "That was so cool."

Anna's laughing eyes came back to him and Joe fell into them. She did things to his heart that no one else ever had. He stepped close and tugged her into his arms. "That *was* pretty awesome."

He gave her a quick kiss and then sent them on their way. "Unless you know a little something about plumbing, I think the rest is up to me."

Anna shook her head. "Nope. Not a clue."

After another light kiss, they turned and left.

His first order of business was to shut off the water to the commode. Anna had drained all the water out, but unless he shut the valve, he'd have another mess on his hands. Once that was done, he went to call the plumber.

Jay came in as he exited his office, and he put him in charge for the morning. Joe wasn't looking forward to what had to happen now, but it couldn't be helped. The entire bathroom needed to be mopped down and disinfected.

Lamenting what the next little while would entail, he went to the storage room to get the mop, bucket, and bleach cleaner.

An hour later, with every last surface cleaned and sanitized, Joe wiped his forehead on his sleeve and wrestled the now heavy and sloshing mop bucket out of the bathroom. Setting it off to the side of the door, he went back in for the rest of his cleaning supplies. As he came back out again, he looked up and saw a man walk in and scan the room.

"No fucking way." Joe couldn't believe the audacity of this man. Kurt Hagen was standing there, in *his* gym, like he had every right in the world to be there.

What should have tipped his craptastic morning over the edge actually brought Joe a thrill of anticipation. What better way to vent some frustration?

Kurt saw him and sneered. Joe dropped the paper towels and spray bottle to the floor and strode across the room. Jay also started for the new guy, but Joe held up a hand, and his assistant stopped in his tracks.

*Oh no. This one is mine.*

"What the fuck do you think you're doing here?" Joe demanded when they were toe-to-toe. With the mood Joe was in, he didn't care if Noor was along for the ride or not. He was beating some ass today.

Hagen's eyes were clear, so he looked to be alone.

*All the better.*

"I want my son," Kurt stated baldly, as if that should brook no argument.

"And you can go fuck yourself." Joe crossed his arms over his chest.

Kurt copied his stance and tilted his head, mocking him. "And just what the hell is a *janitor* gonna do to stop me?" Kurt leaned forward until he was an inch from Joe's face. "You have no idea what you're up against."

Joe grinned, but it didn't get any further than his own sneering lips. "Oh, you stupid, mouth-breathing, sorry son of a bitch. You have no goddamned clue."

Kurt must have read certain death in Joe's gaze, because he straightened and paused a moment before his bravado kicked back in. He dropped his fisted hands down to his sides. "Give me my boy before I tear your ass apart."

"You must not have heard me the first time. What I said was—Go. Fuck. Yourself. Was that slow enough for you this time, dipshit?" A subtle shift had Joe's weight over the balls of his feet. He kept the deceptively non-threatening pose, knowing he could strike out with split-second accuracy and drop this loser where he stood.

"Listen asshole, I'm not leaving here without that kid." Kurt's eyes flashed and his face flushed with red.

"Yeah. You *are*." Joe's voice stayed even. "And you can do it in one piece, or several. Your choice."

The madder Kurt got, the more a cold calm settled over Joe. He knew this feeling. It was the same one that washed over him right before he stepped into the ring with an opponent.

He may have been out of the game for a while now, but he hadn't lost any of his agility. At thirty-two, he was still in top form. He made damned sure of that. And right now, he was itching to show this jackass a thing or two.

Joe heard all sound behind him slowly fade away. He knew Jay and the other men in the gym had read the tension and stood ready to assist. But Joe wouldn't need it today. He relaxed his arms, and with a small hand gesture, waved them off. He had this.

He *wanted* this.

His full attention rested on Hagen. "You murdered his mom, his caretaker, and nearly killed him too. What in the *hell* makes you think I'd ever hand him over to you?"

"He's mine!" Hagen shouted and pounded his fist on his chest.

"Not anymore, motherfucker. You forfeited that right the first time you ever struck him. And guess what, shithead? I've got legal custody. And there isn't a *damned* thing you can do about it." Joe laughed in his face. "You know, I really should be calling the police right now." He leaned forward and lowered his voice. "But I'd rather deal with you myself."

Kurt backed off a step, his face mottled with rage.

"Aww...what's the matter? Too much of a punk bitch to take on someone more your size? Or do you get off on hitting defenseless women and kids? I'll bet you do, you sick fuck."

Able to read an opponent's body language, Joe could tell Kurt was on the verge of swinging. Even with the law on his side, with Joe's level of training and skill, he'd come out of this better if he weren't the first to make that move. And since he'd have plenty of witnesses to prove it, he pushed Kurt further.

"Come to think of it, you half-witted fucktard," Joe taunted, "it wasn't even *you* that did the deed, was it? You needed someone else's hand up your ass to get the job done. You'd shit your pants if you ever faced someone who could actually fight back. You're nothing but a fucking pussy."

Joe was ready for the fist that flew at his face and let it land. He'd taken harder hits, and this one didn't do much damage. But it lent to any self-defense plea he'd need later.

The punch had snapped his head to the side. He left it there a beat and smiled. As he brought his focus back around to Hagen, he let loose and gave all his rage and hatred free reign.

Using the muscles in his legs, Joe drove a right uppercut deep into Kurt's ribs. He followed with a left hook that broke his cheekbone and had Hagen's head twisting on his shoulders.

Recovering himself, Kurt roared like a wounded animal and came back at Joe with wild, flailing swings that missed by a mile.

Joe didn't miss.

He rained blows over Kurt's face and body, the resulting blood and crushed bones just spurring him forward, giving him back what he'd dished out to others who'd already battled and lost.

The commotion drew the spectators closer, but Joe needed no assistance. With one final strike, Kurt fell to his knees.

Joe grabbed a handful of his shirt and hauled him up. He bent close to Kurt's ear, so he alone would hear what Joe had to say.

"Don't you *ever* come near Jacob again. He's *mine* now, and I *will* kill you the next time I see you."

Joe released him with a shove and let him fall as Jay and five other men closed in on them.

"Everything all right, Joe?" Jay asked, never taking his eyes off the heap of human flesh on the floor.

"Yeah. It's good." Joe didn't spare Kurt a glance as he turned and walked away. "Get him out of here."

Absently inspecting his battered knuckles, Joe went straight to the stairs at the rear of the room. As he took the first step, he looked up and saw Anna and Jacob on the landing above him.

He continued up, but no one said anything until they were behind closed doors.

"Are you okay?" Anna's eyes zeroed in on his face where he'd taken Hagen's punch.

"I'm fine. How long were you out there?"

"A while."

He didn't hear any censure in her voice, but Joe hated that Jacob had witnessed it. He took a breath, walked over, and knelt down in front of him. "I'm sorry you had to see that, Jacob."

"He's a bad man." Jacob was watching him closely.

Joe nodded. "Yes, he is. But I shouldn't have done that. I

should have called the police and let them handle it."

"He came for me." It wasn't a question.

"Yeah. Yeah, he did." It broke Joe's heart how easily Jacob acknowledged and accepted that.

"You stopped him. Just like you stopped the monster."

Joe reached out and took both of Jacob's small hands in his. "I won't let anything or anyone hurt you ever again. I promise."

Jacob thought about that and then launched himself into Joe's arms, burying his face in Joe's neck.

"It's all right, buddy." Joe rubbed his hand up and down Jacob's slight back. "We've got you."

Joe held him until Jacob made the decision to release him. Some of the fear and uncertainty Joe had seen in his big brown eyes had lessened. And when Jacob swung around to the table where Anna had crayons and paper laid out for him, Joe knew the worst was over for now.

Anna grasped Joe's hand and pulled him with her out of Jacob's earshot.

"You really should have called Evan when you saw him here," she said in a low voice.

Joe tried to think of a way to explain why he hadn't done that, but she went on before he could gather the words.

"But I understand all the reasons you didn't." The fierceness he loved about her filled her blue eyes. "If I'd been down there, I probably would have torn him apart too. I'm almost jealous that you got the chance and I didn't."

Joe grinned at the incredible woman in front of him. She was in full momma-bear mode. He wrapped his arms around her waist and drew her into his body.

"I doubt he will, but if he ever has the nerve to show up again, I'll let you have him."

Anna's bright eyes shone and she smiled up at him. "Thank you."

She took a quick peek at Jacob. "You know, I think that

display only reinforced his image of you. His knight in shining armor protected him, and you not only drove the bad guy away, but you beat him down first. To Jacob, his father was someone who couldn't be stopped. He'd hurt them for so long, I'm sure Jacob believed it would never end. What you did down there showed him that wasn't true. You slayed his dragon with your bare hands."

Joe looked down at his red knuckles and thought about the one that posed the largest threat to Jacob. "I'll take on as many as I need to."

<center>~~~</center>

After the excitement of the morning, the rest of the day passed without incident.

Other than when Anna had to call her family and let them know what had happened. Evan hadn't been too happy about missing out on the opportunity to arrest Kurt, but he hadn't yelled about it too much.

The next morning went better and set the routine for the following days. Anna and Joe would take Jacob to the gym with them, and he would watch from the sidelines as they worked out. After a hesitant start, Jacob felt comfortable enough to get to know some of the clients. As word had spread of the incident, the men had become protective of Jacob, and it didn't take long for him to become the gym's special mascot.

He relaxed more and even laughed when Anna flipped Joe one afternoon during training. The move had Joe landing hard, forcing the air from his lungs with a grunt. He sent Jacob a withering look, but the boy only grinned.

As she'd done since they'd adopted this routine, Anna left Jacob with Joe to go up to the apartment and shower. They had it timed so that Jacob would come up just as she was getting dressed, and then they'd talk about his past and what he'd been through. But not on this day.

Today, Anna knew it was time to stop hiding. They'd been camping out at the gym for four days, and though Jacob was making good strides in his recovery, they both needed to get back some freedom.

And she knew exactly how to do that.

When Jacob came in, instead of getting settled for their chat, she took him by the hand and went back downstairs. She set him on the bottom step and asked him to wait there for her. At his nod, Anna went to find Joe. She found him in the ring, prepping the equipment he would need for his next sparring session with an up-and-coming fighter. As soon as he saw her, he knew something was up.

"What's wrong?" Joe set the pads aside and came to her, his amber gaze searching her face.

"Nothing," she assured him. "But I think it's time to stop hiding and start teaching Jacob magic. I know you don't like us to be alone, and we won't be. I was planning to call my mom. She and Aria can come pick us up, and then we'll go back to my parents' house."

She went on before he could argue her plan. "When you're done here, you can pick us up and we'll all go home together. We won't be alone for a minute."

He watched her for a moment and then surprised her by smiling. "I've expected this. I'm actually surprised it lasted as long as it did." Joe reached out and brought her close. "I know you, and I knew this situation would get old fast. And I'm sure Jacob is bored out of his mind." He kissed her. "But thank you for humoring my need to have you both close for this long."

Anna wrapped her arms around his waist, molded her body to his, and gazed up into his stunningly handsome face. "It definitely wasn't a hardship. It gave us all a chance to catch our breath and get used to one another."

"Will you text me when you get to your mom's?"

She loved that he asked rather than told her. "I will." She let Joe get back to work and made her call.

When her mom and sister arrived, Anna and Jacob were ready. She went to Joe and gave him a kiss goodbye. "I'll see you tonight."

A short while later they pulled into her parents' driveway.

After sending a quick text to Joe to let them know they'd arrived safely, the first stop was the kitchen for lunch. Having had four kids—two of them quickly growing boys who were bottomless pits—her mom always seemed to be feeding someone. And now with a new little boy to take care of, her mother was in her element.

Over sandwiches they discussed the plan for the day.

"Jacob," Mary asked, "was your momma able to teach you anything about your magic?"

"No. Daddy said it was nonsense and would get mad if she talked about it."

Her mom's eyes creased in the corners, but she continued. "Did she explain why sometimes you see people differently?"

Jacob nodded as he chewed the last bite of his lunch. "That's when she told me we were Burkes."

"Good." Mary smiled and rubbed his back. "Now, if everyone is finished, how about we take this outside? I've found that when teaching spells and other magic, it's better to be out in the open." Mary narrowed her eyes at Anna. "Sometimes it has a tendency to get away from inexperienced hands."

"For the last time, I didn't mean to flood the living room," Anna groused for Jacob's benefit. "Geesh."

Excitement sparkled in Jacob's brown eyes. "Will I have water magic too?"

Anna laughed. "Probably not, sweetie. But you'll have your own gifts."

He thought about that for a minute. "But you said you were a em…em…"

"Empath," Anna provided. "I am, but I'm also linked to the element of water."

"How?" Jacob's dark brows came together.

How to explain this to one so young? Anna wondered. "Okay, you know that Aria, me, and the boys are quadruplets."

Jacob nodded.

"A long, long, long time ago," Anna began, "one of our Burke ancestors had a vision. In it, she saw the four of us being born with special powers. And when that happened, a really bad guy would wake up after hundreds of years of being locked away. It would be up to the four of us to stop him for good and save all the Burke witches."

She left out the part about him being the same beast who'd worn his dad's face.

"Special powers?" he asked.

"That's right," Anna told him. "I have water. Aria has air."

Jacob's head snapped around to Aria. She raised her hands and directed her element to swirl and dance all around him, mussing his short brown hair.

Jacob's face filled with glee.

"Ethan showed you his fire," Anna continued. "And Evan is connected to the earth." Not sure he would know what that meant, Anna explained, "That means he can make the ground rumble and shake."

When it looked like he'd absorbed that, she went on. "Air, water, earth, and fire are elements, and those powers came to us because we have to fight the evil that woke up. But being Burkes, we also have the power that comes down through the name. I'm an empath, Aria has visions, Evan can conjure— make things appear."

"Like the cookie," Jacob remembered.

"He always did love that one," Mary teased. "He was forever eating those darn cookies. Ruined his dinner every time."

"I would too," Jacob admitted, and they all laughed. "What

about Ethan?"

"He can make things move with his mind. It's called telekinesis," Anna finished.

"But I can only see inside people?" His voice held a note of disappointment.

"Oh, sweetie." Mary gave him a smile filled with many secrets. "You will be able to do so much more than that. With spells and potions, you can do anything. And that's what we'll start teaching you today."

Relief and happiness bloomed over his small features.

"It won't be easy," her mom added, giving him the same speech she'd given them so many times. "It'll take hard work and a lot of practice, but when done right, magic is incredible."

# 14

Clean up was quick, and then the four of them stepped out back. They pulled the deck chairs together and positioned them in a circle, Jacob next to her and across from her mom. As she had with them, Mary started out by guiding him in how to build a shield around his mind. That would give him the freedom he desperately needed—the option to *choose* whether he wanted to see into people or not.

"Shields are different for everyone," Mary started. "You just have to find the one that works best for you. It's going to take time to build it up solid, but we'll get you started."

"I had to work long and hard on mine," Anna shared. "It's not easy feeling what everyone around me feels. Just like it's not easy for you to see a person's true self all the time. To block all those emotions out, I had to make sure my shields were very, very strong. I tried building it out of bricks, steel, wood, and a lot of other things, but nothing kept everything out. I did some research to find out what some of the strongest materials on earth were. I found out that diamonds were on that list. So that's what I decided to make my shield out of. And it worked." She smiled, content. "Have you ever seen a picture of a diamond? You know how they have all those flat sides on them?"

Jacob nodded.

"Well, each one of those reflects the emotions back, and they don't make it into my mind. Unless I want them to, that is."

At six years old he couldn't be expected to build impenetrable fortifications just yet, but this gave him a place to start. They worked on having him build his walls with different materials to see which might work best for him.

Since the attention spans of youngsters weren't very long, after about half an hour, they took a break. Mary guided Jacob down by the water to look for shells and rocks, a pastime she and her siblings used to enjoy for hours.

Anna watched them from where she sat with Aria.

"How's he doing?" Aria asked, taking a sip of her iced tea.

"Surprisingly well, actually." Anna thought about how far he'd come in understanding what had happened to him and why. "He still doesn't want to look too closely at people, which I completely understand, but I think once he builds up his shields, that'll get a lot better."

"I can't imagine what he's gone through. His father sounded bad enough on his own, but then to see Noor's beast inside of him..." Aria shook her head. "And having to watch his mother die. Poor baby. So young, and already so much hardship."

They followed the pair's path along the water's edge and Aria spoke again. "Have you decided what you're going to tell those in charge of the murder case?"

As much as Anna hated lying, she still felt like it was the right thing to do, given the alternative. "I've been buying time by telling them he doesn't remember anything yet. Kurt needs to be punished for what he's done to Jacob and his mother. But now that he's partnered with Noor, the authorities alone can't handle it. It's like JD all over again."

"Well, JD was taken care of, and so will Kurt be. Then Jacob won't have to be afraid anymore."

"Except for Noor and his plan to force Jacob to go through the same trials he did." Anna took a steadying breath.

"We're not going to let that happen," Aria swore as she turned in her seat to face Anna directly. "We're all here to make sure it doesn't."

Anna tried to push her fears aside and concentrate on today. "You're right."

Aria cleared her throat and a sparkle shimmered in her blue eyes. "So how has it been, living with Jacob and Joe?"

Anna appreciated her sister's attempt to lighten the mood again. "A lot easier to adjust to than I thought it would be. On all our parts. Jacob seems to be thriving with me and Joe there. I showed you that picture of Joe he drew. The knight in shining armor." She shook her head. "I'm still amazed at how much that's played into everything."

"You shouldn't be—you know how the world of magic works." Aria grinned. "Are you enjoying the time with your knight?"

Anna felt herself flush. "My chocolate pastry, you mean?"

The reference to one of their inside jokes made both of them laugh.

They talked for a little while longer before their mom brought Jacob back to continue his lessons. This process was repeated one more time before Mary changed it up to avoid him getting frustrated.

"Anna. Will you please go pick us one of those white daisies?" her mom requested.

Anna did as asked, smiling because she knew what was coming next. Jacob would love this.

"You did such a wonderful job on your walls, and I know that was really hard work. But now we're going to move on to something a little more fun." Mary held the flower in front of her, catching Jacob's attention. "I'm going to do a spell, and then I want you to try it, okay?"

Jacob eagerly indicated yes.

Mary winked at him. "Here goes."

*"Never to hurt, never to harm*

*I seek only a simple charm*
*A change of color I ask of thee*
*As I will, so mote it be."*


The delicate white petals changed to a brilliant pink, and Jacob gasped. His stunned eyes darted between her mom and the flower in her hand.

He wriggled in his seat. "I wanna try it."

Anna's heart was melting at his excitement.

"Think about your favorite color and concentrate on the flower." Jacob leaned forward in his seat, intent on following Mary's every word.

"Are you thinking about your color?"

His head bobbed up and down with such fervor, Anna thought he'd bounce himself right out of the chair.

She looked at Aria and they shared an amused grin.

"Now, I'll say the spell one line at a time, and you repeat it after me," her mother instructed.

In her mind, Anna said the simple words with them. As the last line left Jacob's lips, the pink daisy turned bright orange.

He came up out of his chair and leapt around on his feet. "I did it! I did it!" His face broke into the biggest smile Anna had ever seen on him, and tears welled in her eyes. He was beaming with joy and awe.

She so loved this sweet little boy, and seeing magic fresh though his eyes made her think back to a time when she thought anything and everything were possible.

"Joe!" Jacob yelled, startling Anna out of her reverie. She swung around to see that Joe had just stepped out onto the patio.

Jacob took the flower gently out of Mary's hand and ran off to launch himself into Joe's strong arms. He all but shoved the blossom up Joe's nose in his effort to show it to him. "Look! I turned it my favorite color. It was white, then Mary turned it pink, and then I made it orange!"

Joe snatched Jacob's little fist before it made contact with his face. He held it up so he could take a good, long look. "Wow. *You* did that?"

"Uh-huh." Jacob was so proud of himself. "Mary said the spell, and then I said it, and the flower turned orange, because that's the color I was thinking of. I can do that because I'm a Burke, and that means I'm a witch. I was trying to make my walls, but that was hard. This was way more fun."

Anna had never heard him babble before. He was so happy right now, just like every six year old should be. Seeing him like this gave her hope that Jacob would come out of this mess whole, despite the trauma with his father and Noor.

She rose and went to her guys. Joe's arm was still braced under Jacob's butt, holding him high. She wrapped her arms around both and held them. Love swelled in her chest.

Too much excitement was racing through Jacob's sturdy little body, and soon he was squirming to get down. "Can I do it again?" He looked from Anna to her mom. "Can I show Joe?"

"Sure you can," Mary laughed in delight. "Practice makes perfect, after all." She patted her lap. "Come sit here, and I'll help you with the spell again. You'll have to pick a different color this time though."

He ran to her, and as she pulled him up onto her thighs, his face was alight with excitement. "I got one."

"Okay, let's do this."

This time her mom whispered the words into his ear, so his voice was the only one they heard.

*"Never to hurt, never to harm*
*I seek only a simple charm*
*A change of color I ask of thee*
*As I will, so mote it be."*

She saw it brighten to a paler shade, but it was hard for Anna to see what color he'd chosen until he jumped down and ran back to them. Then her breath caught in her throat.

"It's silver. Just like your armor." Jacob held the flower up for Joe to see.

When Anna looked to Joe, his eyes were rich with emotion. He squatted down to the boy beaming up at him.

"That is the best color daisy I have ever seen." Joe's voice was thick and raw. "I'd like to keep this forever." He turned questioning eyes up at her. "Is there any way to preserve this, so it stays just like this always?"

Anna had to clear the lump out of her own throat before she could speak. "Yeah. We can do that."

Aria and their mom joined them. "Why don't we call that a day?" Mary said, bending down to Jacob. "I want you to keep practicing with your walls, and next time we'll work on some more magic."

With the day Jacob had had, he didn't even complain about the homework Mary had given him. "Okay. Can we do the flower thing again?"

"That and so much more." Mary tweaked his nose.

Shortly after that, Anna, Joe, and Jacob left to return home. Jacob talked non-stop while Anna prepared dinner. He filled Joe in on everything he'd learned, even repeating himself a few times. Joe listened to every word Jacob had to say, no matter how many times he'd heard it.

Like her, he was thrilled with the progress Jacob had made today. Anna made a mental note to ask her mom about defensive spells. While learning new magic was always fun and exciting, she wanted Jacob to know how to protect himself if the worst were to happen.

After dinner, while Joe helped Jacob with his shower—because baths were for little kids since he'd found out Joe took showers—Anna reinforced the wards on the house.

When she heard the water shut off, she gathered drinks and snacks and waited for them in the living room. At night, until Jacob's bedtime, they'd all watch TV as a family. She loved this time and looked forward to it every night. She was ready when they joined her on the couch.

As usual, Jacob fell asleep about halfway through the second show. Joe carried him to bed where they both kissed him and tucked him in.

They walked into their bedroom, and Anna crossed to stand near the bed while Joe silently closed the door. He came to her and took her into his arms, sealing his mouth to hers.

She fell into the kiss gladly but reluctantly pulled away, remaining within the circle of his grasp. "I want to try something."

"Really? What?" He had a leer in his eyes that made her laugh.

"Not whatever it is you're thinking about. Get your mind out of the gutter." She playfully slapped at his shoulder. "I need to delve into this new power I seem to have now. I need to get a better handle on it."

"What do you need me to do?"

Just like that. No questions, no qualifications. "All you have to do is think about something. I'll look into your mind and try to *see* what it is, instead of only feeling it."

"No problem. I'm ready."

"Okay. Here we go." She should have been leery about how quickly he'd settled on something, but she dove right in.

Anna felt first his hunger for her. Assuming that was still lingering from what they'd just been doing, she pushed past it.

And ran straight into a scene of him doing amazing and erotic things to her body. Images filled her head in vivid detail…his tongue sliding over the swell of her breast…his fingers grazing up her inner thigh…their sweat-slicked bodies moving together in a sultry, provocative cadence.

She gasped as her core instantly heated and throbbed. "Oh God."

Joe's head slowly descended to her. "You didn't say *what* I was supposed to think about." His lips took hers.

She willingly sank into him, giving him everything she was as they kissed in the beams of moonlight shining through the window.

Anna needed him. She needed to feel his hot, burnished skin pressing against hers. Her hands found the buttons of his shirt and made quick work of them. It fell, already forgotten, to the floor.

She pulled her mouth from his and laid her lips to the center of his chest. The heat of him nearly scorched her, and the wild beating of his heart thrilled her. Opening her mouth, she licked and nipped her way across the wide expanse of his torso, stopping at each of his dark puckered nipples to lave and tease.

He threw his head back, and an animalistic groan rumbled from deep inside of him. His grip became rougher as he squeezed and molded her ass, grinding his erection into her softness.

She fought free of his hold and kissed and licked her way down his center. Dropping to her knees in front of him, her tongue trailed a hot line around his navel and into the thin strip of black hair that led into the waistband of his jeans.

A quick flick and the button closure released. Anna looked up the plane of his body to meet smoldering golden eyes. She grinned seductively as she grasped the small metal tab and slowly eased the zipper down.

Joe sighed as the stiff material fell away, easing the pressure on his engorged shaft. Anna slid her fingers into the elastic band of his briefs and pulled down, both layers sliding over his hips and past his thighs. He stepped out of them and gave them a kick.

His entire gorgeous body was bared for her pleasure. Holding his gaze captured in hers again, Anna reached up and wrapped her hand around the base of his erection and squeezed hard as she knew he liked. Joe's lids lowered as his whole body shuddered.

Leaning forward, she ran her tongue up the underside from where her fist gripped him to the V on the head.

"Oh, fuck." His hips thrust helplessly.

She took him into her mouth and swirled her tongue over him. When he pushed into her, she took all he had to give. She continued to suck and pull until he was at a fevered pitch.

"Enough." He jerked her right up off the floor and into his arms. He caught her under the thighs as her legs encased him. He walked the few steps to the bed, her sensitive core grinding into him with every step. Her first orgasm rolled through her and left her gasping.

He came to a stop beside the bed. Before she realized his intent, he reached behind him, unlocked her legs, and dropped her onto the bed. She'd barely settled when he reached for her shirt, and grasping it in both hands, ripped it down the middle.

Anna gasped at his lack of restraint and reveled in it. Before she could catch her breath, he stripped her out of her pants and panties.

He came to her then, spreading her legs wide with his hard body, and thrust into her aching center.

Anna shot straight to the brink when he filled her to bursting but didn't fall over. Joe held her there, pounding into her first with ferocity and speed, and then slowing to torturous and drawn out. As soon as her body would find and match his pace to drive for completion, he'd switch up the rhythm and it would deny her.

She was out of her mind with need. "Please, please," she begged.

He ignored her plea. Instead, he dropped his mouth to her breasts and took her nipple between his teeth. He bit down until she didn't think she could take any more, and then kissed and licked away the sting before moving to the other to do the same.

Anna's body was not her own. It was his. It belonged to him completely to do with as he wished. She writhed and tried to find something to hold onto as he blew her world apart. She was nothing but a mass of sensitized nerve endings, over-stimulated until she thought she'd break into a million pieces.

Even the walls she'd meticulously built around her mind were shattered in the wake of his love. She was wide open to him and everything he was feeling. It bombarded her and took her into another realm of pleasure.

She drew a strangled breath into her burning lungs to scream as her body finally erupted, but Joe's mouth was there to take it into himself. As her core pulsed and squeezed around him, Joe thrust hard once, twice, and then buried deep, finding his own release.

Stars were still blinking behind Anna's lids when his weight settled onto her. Spent and sweaty they lay, limbs entwined until reason returned.

He rolled to the side, taking her with him. "That was..."

"Yeah." Her still-responsive nipple brushed against his body, and she hummed at the added sensation. "It was."

"I didn't hurt you, did I?" Anna was still open to him and felt his concern at having lost that much control.

She drew her head back so she could look into his eyes. "You didn't hurt me at all. I loved every minute."

He tucked her head beneath his chin. "You destroy every ounce of restraint I possess."

"That's only fair, because you do the same to me."

After a few more minutes, Joe got up to put his briefs back on and handed Anna her sleep shirt. She would have loved nothing more than to lay naked beside him all night, but they had a small child in the house now. She couldn't bear the thought of him coming into their room and finding them both nude.

Once clothed, they snuggled in together again and slept.

# 15

Anna was alone when she opened her eyes to bright sunlight. She could just make out voices and knew Jacob and Joe would be in the kitchen. She stretched and rolled out of bed. Tugging on a pair of leggings, she went to find her boys.

As expected, they were each huddled over bowls of cold cereal. "What are you two up to this morning?"

Anna went directly to the coffee pot and poured herself a mug.

"I was just telling Jacob here that I'll have to drop you and him off at the gym this morning. I have a meeting that just came up."

Anna hadn't known anything about a meeting. She wondered what it was about but didn't ask.

"Well, then." Anna switched her gaze to Jacob. "You can be my workout partner today."

Jacob's eyes expanded to the size of saucers, and he stopped chewing to goggle at her. She had to bite the inside of her cheek to keep from laughing out loud. When she glanced at Joe, he too was barely holding it together.

"Think you can handle that?" she asked Jacob, a laugh still tickling her throat.

He started chewing again slowly, and his chin dipped down and up in a tentative nod. Then his back straightened, he swallowed down his cereal, and nodded more determinedly.

"Good. Eat up and I'll go change." Anna chuckled to herself all the way back to the bedroom.

She didn't have a chance to ask Joe about where he was going before he dropped them off and drove away. Anna put it out of her mind and got down to the business of showing Jacob some moves.

A couple of men stopped what they were doing to watch and cheer Jacob on. That gave Anna an idea, and she asked one of them to help her out. She wanted Jacob to know he had options if he were ever in danger from a large man.

They took a break when the gym cleared out a little as those who liked to work out early finished up and left. Anna and Jacob were sitting on the floor drinking water when a man walked in.

Anna casually glanced up. He was still across the room, but she didn't think she recognized him.

Not knowing where Jay had gotten off to, Anna figured it fell to her to take care of it. Maybe he was looking to join. She could at least take his name and number and have Joe call him back.

Standing, she called out to the stranger. "Hi. Can I help you?"

Jacob's hand grasped hers and squeezed tightly, diverting her attention down to him. When she saw fear in his eyes, she knew.

Lowering her voice, she asked him, "The beast?"

He nodded, never taking his eyes from hers.

"It's okay, sweetie." She turned and bent down in front of him, blocking his view of the man coming toward them. "When I say go," she whispered, "I want you to run upstairs and lock the door. Don't open it again until I come for you. Do you understand?"

At his nod, she stood, holding Jacob behind her as she turned back to face Noor. As he drew closer, she could finally make out the vacant stare of a man possessed.

Anna put out a call to her siblings. *"Guys, I need you. Now. I'm at the gym with Jacob and Joe's not here."*

*"On our way."* Evan's voice, no questions asked.

Aria came in next. *"Be there soon. What's going on?"*

*"New meatsuit,"* she explained. *"He's here."*

*"Fuck."* Ethan joined the conversation. *"Hold on."*

Anna didn't want to have to hurt this man. He was an innocent in this mess. *"Just get here."*

Anna focused all of her attention on the man in front of her and didn't bother to hide the fact that she knew who he was. "What are you doing here, Noor?"

"I want the boy."

"You can't have him." She needed to distract Noor long enough for Jacob to make a run for it.

He threw his head back and laughed. "You think you can stop me?"

"Actually, I do." Anna stood her ground while she drew on her power and pulled water from everywhere around her. "Where's your other puppet? A little too damaged to be of any use?"

She gathered her element and condensed it into an undulating ball directly behind where Noor stood.

"It must suck not to be able to get anything done yourself. To have to count on douchebags you can't rely on."

His face went red in anger, and she figured he was getting ready to strike out at her. She knew she had to beat him to the punch.

Anna chose that moment to hit him with the force of her collected energy. He turned at the last instant, but it still connected with the side of his head, propelling his body forward to land sprawled on the floor.

She shouted behind her to Jacob. "Run!!" She heard his little feet slapping the ground as he ran for the stairs leading up to the apartment, but she never took her eyes from Noor.

Anna didn't give him a chance to recover, but ran forward

and kicked him square in the ribs.

The force of the blow lifted his body. It definitely caused damage, but only to the vessel, not to Noor himself. Before she could back away from his reach, his hand flashed out and grabbed her ankle. He gave it a jerk, and Anna fell back onto her ass. Her training kicked in, and she flowed into moves she'd practiced over and over, gaining her feet again quickly.

Noor had made it to his knees when she struck a second time. She had to keep him off balance so that he couldn't gather power to use against her. She had to buy enough time for her family to get to her.

Anna pivoted on her left foot and struck out with a round-house kick to the side of his head. She was surprised when he crumpled to the floor, unconscious.

She stood back, still in fighting stance as she watched him, but he didn't move. She was still standing guard when Ethan ran in a second later.

He was joined shortly after by Evan, Aria, and Seth.

Evan's face was incredulous as his eyes darted from Anna to the man twice her size on the floor. "Did you kill him?"

"No, I didn't kill him." Anna gave him a dirty look. "I kicked him in the head."

If possible, her brawny brother looked even more perplexed. But she didn't bother to explain he'd been kneeling when it happened.

"It seems Noor is limited by the frailties of the human he inhabits. And he can't control an unconscious mind." That was good to know, but Anna needed to check on Jacob. "Will you guys watch him? I need to make sure Jacob is okay."

"Yeah," Aria said quickly. "Go check on him."

Anna ran for the staircase and took them two at a time. She stopped at the closed door and spoke through it. "Jacob? Sweetie, it's Anna. Can you open the door?"

She heard the lock release and he pulled it open. "Is he

gone?"

Anna stepped in and bent down to take him in her arms. "He won't hurt you. I promise. As long as I'm breathing, no one will ever hurt you again. My family's here. They're watching him. I just wanted to see you."

He hugged her tight, and she felt his little body shaking. "It's okay, baby."

"Anna," Evan called from below. "He's coming around."

Anna held Jacob's upper arms and looked straight into his big brown eyes. "I want you to stay up here until we know what's going on. Okay?"

He nodded.

She kissed his cheek and brushed a hand over his hair. "I'll be right back."

Anna pulled the door closed as she left and headed back down. As she neared, she saw that Evan had cuffed the man on the floor.

He groaned and tried to roll over. "What the hell? What's going on?"

Evan and Seth grabbed his arms and hauled him to his knees. They all saw that his eyes were clear. Noor was gone.

"Where am I?" There was a dark bruise coming up where her foot had connected with the side of his face. Another would be blooming on his ribs, and Anna knew he'd be hurting soon.

"What do you remember?" Seth asked him.

"I left my house this morning to go to work, and then I'm waking up on the floor." He tried to move his hands. "Why am I cuffed? Am I under arrest?"

"No." Evan reached down and unlocked the restraints. "You're not under arrest. It was all a misunderstanding."

"How did I get here?" The man tried to stand but caught his breath. "What the hell happened to me? Why do I feel like I got kicked by a mule?"

"It looks like you've been in a fight." Anna winced but told as close to the truth as she could.

"You might want to go get checked out," Aria suggested.

"Yeah." The man rubbed his head and stumbled out.

As he was leaving, Joe passed him in the doorway. He gave him a curious once-over and then turned to see Anna and all of her siblings standing there.

Alarm immediately washed over his face. "What happened?"

Anna went to him. "We're fine. Noor possessed that man and came for Jacob."

As if saying his name had conjured him, Jacob came running and launched himself into Joe's arms. He obviously hadn't stayed locked away.

"Hey, buddy. Heard you had some excitement." Anna could see Joe was only barely holding on to his temper while Jacob was present.

"A man came in, and I saw the beast in him," Jacob told him. "I ran upstairs like Anna said and locked the door."

"But you didn't stay like you were supposed to," she scolded, and his eyes dropped. She picked up the accounting of the incident, careful to choose her words wisely for small ears. "He wasn't expecting me to take the initiative. I used the element of surprise to keep him occupied until my family could get here and help."

"He was out cold when we got here," Seth supplied dryly and nodded when Joe looked at him.

Joe's gaze swung back to her and he raised one eyebrow. She shrugged.

"Well, I'm glad everyone is okay." He squeezed Jacob tight. "I'm sorry I missed it."

With the emergency past, the others all left, leaving Joe, Anna, and Jacob. Joe looked around the empty gym.

"Where's Jay?"

"I don't know." Now that Joe had called attention to his absence, Anna was worried.

"Here." Joe transferred Jacob to Anna's arms. "I'm going to look around."

Anna and Jacob watched as Joe searched the main floor, bathroom, and office. He gave her a shake of his head, signaling that he wasn't there. Joe strode out the front door and was gone for about five minutes before finally returning.

He was helping Jay to stay upright and walk inside.

There was blood dripping down one side of his face.

*Oh, God.* Noor must have attacked Jay before coming inside. He was lucky to be alive.

They cleaned him up, gave him a few pain pills, and tried to send him home, but Jay refused to go. He insisted on staying to finish out his day as more clients started to make their way inside.

It wasn't until that evening after Jacob had been put to bed that Anna and Joe were able to talk about what had happened. Jacob had stuck close to them, and Anna couldn't blame him. She didn't want him wandering far from her either.

As she and Joe lay in bed that night, she explained what had gone down in his absence.

"Do you think he knew I'd be out today, or was that just a lucky coincidence for him?"

"I don't know." Anna was tucked into his side with her head resting on his shoulder, her hand lazily stroking his chest.

"I had an appointment with my attorney."

That was the last thing Anna expected him to say. Her hand stilled briefly before making herself relax against him.

"You're not going to ask, are you?" There was amusement in his voice.

"It's none of my business." For as close as they'd become, there was still a lot about each other they didn't know.

"It is, though." He turned his head and planted a kiss in her hair. "With everything that's gone on, I wanted to know that you and Jacob would be taken care of."

Anna pushed up and looked into his face. "What does that mean?"

"Things with Noor are going to escalate over the next eight months until your birthday. If something happens to me, you and Jacob will be set."

She sat all the way up and folded her legs in front of her. "Again. What does that mean?"

Joe sat up too and leaned back against the headboard. "I did really well when I was fighting. I didn't need much to live on, and I invested wisely. I have quite a substantial nest egg, and now it'll all go to you and Jacob if I'm not here."

"What?" Shock colored her face. "Why would you do that?"

Joe rolled away from her, reached for the drawer of his bedside table, and pulled something out. When he turned back to her, he held out a small velvet box. "Because I love you, and I want to marry you. And when the time is right, I want both of us to legally adopt Jacob."

Anna sucked in a breath. "Oh, Joe." She couldn't move. She could only stare at his handsome face and the love she saw shining in his eyes.

"You're kind of killing me here." Joe glanced down at the box she had yet to touch and then back to her. "I know we haven't been together very long, but I knew the moment I saw you a year ago that you were it for me. We still have a lot to learn about each other, and now that we have a traumatized child involved...I can understand if you have reservations. But I love you, Anna. You love me, and together we love that little boy in the other room."

He held the box out to her. "Say yes."

Tears flowing unchecked, Anna reached out and cupped his face in both her hands. She leaned in and kissed him on that extraordinary mouth. When she pulled back, she looked deep into his eyes and whispered, "With my whole heart, yes."

His face lit up and he grinned. "Don't you want to see the

ring first?"

She laughed through her tears. "I don't need to. And I don't care that you have a *substantial nest egg*. I'll take you any way I can get you."

"Good to know." Joe opened the box for her, and Anna got her second surprise in as many minutes. The ring was huge and gorgeous, and it took her breath away.

"Oh, Joe. It's beautiful."

He took it out and then lifted her left hand in his. When he slid the ring onto her finger, it fit to perfection. She gazed down at the multifaceted two-carat diamond set it white gold. Channel set into the band were more shimmering stones.

"Jacob told me you had a special relationship with diamonds."

Anna laughed and clutched her hand to her chest. She nodded. "I told him that I use one as the shield in my mind."

"I know. When he told me that, I knew what I had to get you."

She leaned into him and kissed him. "Thank you. I love you."

"I love you."

~~~

Joe hadn't slept well and when the sun finally crested the horizon, he was still staring at the ceiling. Anna was curled up next to him breathing softly. He watched her face as she slept and thought again about what he'd nearly lost yesterday.

He wanted to know how Noor had known he'd be away from the gym yesterday. Joe hadn't told *anyone* what he was doing or where he was going.

Was Noor watching them somehow? He wanted Jacob and would do anything to have him. Did he have spies keeping an eye on them?

Joe wanted to talk to Seth and Evan. If anyone were following them, those two would be more apt to take notice. Unless it was
~~~

done magically somehow. Could Noor do that from his cage?

If this were something the family had already talked about, Joe hadn't heard. He was still playing catch-up on the witch and magic front. And there was still plenty he didn't know.

He decided to give Anna's brother and Seth a call this morning to see if they could meet him and discuss it.

When he talked to Seth a few hours later, Seth told him they'd have some time around one o'clock if Joe wanted to get together then. They made a plan to grab some lunch at a local place and talk.

After their usual morning, Joe dropped Anna and Jacob off at her parents' and went straight to the diner. He was early but chose to use the extra time to lay out his thoughts.

The two men came in a short while later and joined him. Seeing the others arrive, the server made his way to them. Joe held off on his concerns until after they'd all ordered.

"I'm wondering why Noor picked yesterday to make his move on Anna and Jacob," Joe started. "Did he know that I'd be out? Or was it just luck that he showed up on a day I wasn't there?"

"No," Seth answered. "It wasn't a coincidence. I don't know if he has a crystal ball or just a damned window, but somehow he's able to see into this world."

"So, conceivably, he could be watching all of us. All the fucking time."

"Unfortunately, yes," Evan said on a sigh. "Makes you feel warm and cozy, doesn't it?"

The server came back with their drinks and they waited until he'd gone before resuming. In a more serious tone, Evan continued. "Noor gets stronger every day, and we have no idea as his strength grows, how that changes what he can or can't do. Every time he shows up, we just have to hope we'll be able to send him back to his hole. He only needs to take one of us out, and the prophecy will be broken. If that happens and the four of us can't present a united front against him when he's released in February, he'll destroy every Burke he can find and be free to wreak havoc on the world."

Seth cleared his throat. "And just to make this mess even more complicated, I'm pretty sure he's trying to gather an army."

Joe and Evan both shot a stunned look at him.

"How the fuck would you know that?" Evan asked, none too gently.

Seth shrugged. "He invades my dreams, offering *untold power* if I'll join him."

"What the hell is his game?" Evan growled. "He's been trying to kill you for months."

"I know, but evidently this blood-tie between us trumps me trying to take his woman." Seth huffed, obviously just as confused as Joe and Evan were. "He must think I'll be more useful as part of his team than as collateral damage to get to Aria."

They paused when their food was set in front of them.

"What does he need an army for?" Joe was afraid he already knew.

"My first thought would be his bid to end one of you before February," Seth offered. "Each one he can lure to his side is another chance at defeating you. And he needs as many as he can get, because so far we've taken out every one he's sent. Or…he's just fucking crazy, and there's no figuring out why he does anything."

"Why the hell haven't you said anything about this before now?" Evan demanded.

"I wasn't keeping it a secret. We were planning on telling the rest of the family the other day, but a few other things came up," Seth countered. "And it's not like it'll ever happen. He can make as many promises or threats as he wants. The answer will remain the same. I told him to go fuck himself."

Joe shook his head. "And then there are his plans for Jacob. I can admit it scares the shit out of me thinking about what Noor has in store for him. We all heard what your Mom said about those trials. To think he'd make a child go through that—just to turn him into some kind of weapon." His gut clenched. "Is there anything else we can do to protect him? To...I don't know... *shield* him from Noor? Make it so that Noor can't find him?"

"That's probably something we could do," Evan confirmed, and the tension knotted in Joe's body loosened. "But it would mean sending him away. You know Noor is watching all of us. Even if he can't feel Jacob anymore, he'll still know where he is—with you and Anna."

The anxiety gripping Joe's stomach returned at the thought of being separated from the child he loved. That just wasn't an option.

"He's safer where he is, Joe." He read the sincerity in Evan's dark eyes. "I promise you that. You guys won't let anything happen to him. And neither will we."

Joe nodded, trying to take comfort in the fact that Jacob had so many powerful supporters. Anna had told him that in the world of magic, things had a way of happening just the way they were meant to. Jacob finding his way to the safety of *this* family had to be one of those fated events.

Joe thought he should tell Anna's brother about another fated event. He and Evan hadn't gotten along too well in the beginning, but they'd found a workable coexistence. Joe hoped what he said next wouldn't set that back.

He took a deep breath. "I asked Anna to marry me last night."

Evan's gaze tracked slowly to his. Joe couldn't decipher what he saw in the other man's eyes.

"Did you?"

"I did," Joe answered calmly, readying himself for whatever Evan's response would be. He sent a quick glance at Seth to see if help would be there if he needed it. But what he saw in the big man's face didn't give him hope. Seth was sitting back in his chair, amused at the events unfolding in front of him.

Joe turned back to Evan.

"I guess it's too much to ask that she turned you down." Evan's black eyes held a glint of something. Joe looked closer and realized he was yanking his chain.

"She said yes, asshole."

Evan and Seth both laughed. "I was just messing with you," Evan said after catching his breath. "I'd already heard. Anna told Mom, and after what I'm sure was an hour of squealing and other girly noises, she spread the news to the rest of us." Evan extended his hand across the table in a peacemaking gesture. "Welcome to the family, Joe."

Grasping Evan's hand in his, Joe shook it with a relieved chuckle.

"Congrats, dude," Seth added.

Joe relaxed back into his seat and grinned. "Thanks, guys."

Conversation turned to topics a little less serious as they dug into their food. Joe noticed Evan and Seth glancing around the diner and then back at each other. He looked around but didn't see what could have drawn their attention.

Maybe it was a cop thing. Joe shrugged it off and went back to his grilled chicken salad. He forked up a bite and had it almost to his mouth when Seth and Evan's voices quietly but insistently demanded he put it down.

Surprised by their urgency, Joe looked at his food and then back at them. "What the hell?" Was there a hair or something in his salad?

Both men's eyes scanned the interior of the restaurant again. The revolting expressions on their faces had Joe dropping his fork. Joe took in everyone else around him, but no one else was reacting in any way. Only the two men linked to magic.

If they were the only ones who could see what was happening, that could only mean that Noor was involved.

He hated being disadvantaged this way. "It's Noor, isn't it?

What do you see?"

Seth was the first to answer in a hushed voice. "There is a thick black sludge oozing down the walls and over everyone's tables and plates."

Even knowing he wouldn't see it, Joe looked down at his own.

"It's not real, so it wouldn't hurt you," Seth was saying, "but I just couldn't stomach watching you eat it. It's bad enough that everyone else is chowing down on it."

"That bastard." Evan gave his plate a disgusted grimace. "I loved the burgers here. Now I'll never be able to eat one again. That pisses me off to no end."

Joe pushed his lunch away. "Why would he do it?"

"Just to fuck with us." Evan also shoved his meal to the center of the table at the same time his cell sounded from his pocket.

He slid it free and glanced at the face of it.

"Shit." Evan looked to Seth. "We've got a case. Dead body found behind a bar downtown." He returned the phone to his pocket as he rose, pulled his wallet out, and threw some bills onto the table. "Just as well. Lunch was ruined anyway."

Seth followed suit. "Can you let Anna know what happened here?" He tossed a ten on the table. "She'll want to document it since she's been updating the family journals."

"Yeah, no problem," Joe agreed, putting his own money down to cover the salad he'd barely eaten.

# 16

When he knocked on the door of the Burke family home a short time later, Paul was the one to pull it open.

"Hey, Joe." Paul stepped back to allow him entrance and stuck out his hand. "I heard the news. Welcome to the family, son."

Joe shook the older man's hand. "Thanks, Paul. Are they out back?"

"Yeah. I think they're working on defensive spells today."

"Okay." Joe had only taken a few steps when he turned back to Paul. "Can I ask you something?"

"Sure." Paul gestured to the couch. "Have a seat."

Joe sat on the front edge of the cushion. His forearms were braced on his knees as he stared down at his hands. Asking to talk with Paul had been a spontaneous decision. But now that he'd done it, he didn't know where to start. He had so many questions and concerns about this new little family he'd found with Anna.

He decided to start with the one that plagued him the worst and kept him up most nights.

"How do I protect them?" Joe turned his head and searched Paul's face.

Paul's dark blue eyes held his steadily. "That's a question for the ages, isn't it?"

"Evan, Seth, and I were at lunch, and Noor pulled some

shit—" Joe began, but stopped when Paul interrupted. Worry laced his words.

"What did that bastard do now?"

"Nothing big," Joe was quick to assure him. "Just had some black sludge oozing over everything." Joe dropped his attention back down to his hands. "Or at least, that's what Seth and Evan *told* me happened because, unlike them, I couldn't see a goddamned thing."

Joe brought his tortured gaze up again. "How can I hope to keep Jacob and Anna safe if I'm completely blind to what's coming? I couldn't even see the fucking slime that was all over the salad I was eating. The others had to tell me to put it down."

Paul sighed and clasped his hands together, looking straight into Joe's face. "You trust in my daughter, and you do what you can. They told us what you did by drawing Noor's attention away from them that day in your gym. You couldn't see him then, and still you didn't hesitate to throw yourself into the mix."

Joe shook his head. "I knew approximately where he was by where the others were focusing. What happens if I've got Jacob out somewhere and Noor comes? I won't even realize there's a threat in the first place."

"But Jacob will," Paul reminded him.

"Only because they're related," Joe muttered.

"You're right. He has Noor's blood in him. But he has Burke blood in him too." The fierceness in Paul's voice startled Joe, and when he glanced over Paul's eyes were just as intent. "Don't forget that. It saved that child's life and put him on a course to finding you and Anna. They're out there right now, teaching him how to defend himself, so if he's ever in danger again, he'll know what to do."

"He shouldn't have to." The words burst out of Joe as he rose to pace. "Jacob sees me as his knight—his protector—and I can't do a fucking thing to keep him safe." He spun back on

Paul. "Do you have any idea how incompetent that makes me feel? That I can't even stand between him and the bastard that's coming for him?"

"Yes, I do." Paul's stark words brought Joe up short, and shame immediately washed over him. *Shit.*

"I'm sorry, Paul. I know you do. That was the whole reason I wanted to talk with you. I just don't know how you do it."

Paul inhaled and then let it out. "When I met Mary, she took my breath away. I'm sure you're familiar with the sensation. Anyway, within hours of meeting her, I had our whole lives together planned out." Paul gave a little laugh and shook his head.

"Needless to say, that didn't go the way I'd hoped." He stopped. "Well, I shouldn't say that," he corrected. "I got the girl I still love to this day, and we raised four beautiful, amazing children. But the rest..." He paused. "I never could have conceived of what was coming."

"When did she tell you about her, about what she was?" Joe returned to the couch to sit down.

"She told me pretty early on about being a witch. It wasn't until we were married and started thinking about children that she explained about the prophecy. By that time, she'd shown me so many unbelievable things, I never hesitated to take her word on that too."

Paul was silent for a moment. Joe assumed he was thinking back to when he first learned of the future that could be waiting for his children.

"Chances were pretty good that it wouldn't happen to us. Mary said it'd been hundreds of years since the words were spoken and could easily be another hundred before anything actually happened. And so we went ahead with our plans to expand our family."

"Were you scared?" Joe wondered.

"Hell yeah," Paul admitted freely. "The prophecy wasn't

specific about how these babies would come, you see. No one knew if they'd be born to different families, all at once, two at a time, or what. It was specific regarding the time of day they'd come, but not when or how—just that four babies would arrive, two light, two dark, branded with the marks of the elements."

Joe knew those were the words that had sealed Anna's fate.

"When Mary first found out she was pregnant," Paul went on, "we were ecstatic, but that worry was still there. We told ourselves that everything would be fine and we'd have a normal family. We went to the first ultrasound," Paul remembered with a smile, "and they told us there were three. A set of identical twins and a single. Holy shit, that scared me," he laughed. "Not because of the prophecy, but because there were so many…all at once."

"I hear you on that." Even Joe thought it sounded scary.

"Once the shock of that settled in, we thought about the other. Mary immediately started making calls to see if any other women in the family were pregnant. As far as we could tell, none were. And the ones who'd had kids recently said there'd been no symbols. We thought we were in the clear. We'd be having triplets, but they wouldn't be marked. We relaxed, as much as we could, and reveled in the knowledge that our babies were coming.

"With multiples, they watch you more closely than with single births, so a few weeks later, we had another scan. The tech slid the device over Mary's belly for a couple of minutes and then excused herself. When she came back, the doctor was with her. He picked up the wand, checked the babies, then turned to us with a grin and said, 'Well, looks like we miscounted. There are four babies here. That fourth one must have been hiding last time.' He went on to say that they were two sets of identical twins. Mary and I looked at each other, and we both knew in that moment what it meant. But the telling factor would be when they were born."

Joe couldn't imagine the anxiety and stress of waiting that long, knowing what might come to be.

"I looked down at my children after they were all born and wept at what they'd have to face on their own. I didn't know how I was going to prepare them for their futures. What could I offer? But then my very smart and insightful wife told me that while she made them strong witches, I would make them confident and well-adjusted individuals. That it would take what they learned from the both of us to get them through the coming trials. All the magic in the world wouldn't make a difference if they didn't grow to be secure in themselves. And find their own paths.

"So, while you may not think you can offer that boy much, know that he needs you and your strength just as much as he needs what he's getting out there." Paul nodded his head in the direction of the kitchen and back yard.

"If you can do for him," Paul added, "what you did for Anna, that child will be fine."

"I didn't—" Joe denied, but Paul stopped him.

"We did her a great disservice by underestimating her the way we did. We got stuck in seeing her as fragile. It took me a while to know and believe that she needed something different. When I met you that day at the store and got to talking with you, I knew you were it. I see the difference in her now. She's stronger, more confident in who she is. She knows she can take care of herself. And you played a big role in that."

Joe was humbled by Paul's words.

When Anna's father excused himself, Joe moved into the kitchen and watched the four people through the sliding door. As Anna, her mom, and Aria taught Jacob how to be a witch, he thought about everything Paul had told him.

If it were Joe's job to round out Jacob's education, he'd teach him everything he had to give. And as far as all the things that Joe might never see, he would trust in those he loved to see him through.

~~~

As the city of Daytona Beach got ready for the Fourth of July, Anna and her family fought to maintain some semblance of normalcy. More so for Jacob than themselves. With that in mind, they planned their annual family picnic, despite the fact that everyone was on edge because Noor had been suspiciously absent of late.

Seth also said his attempts at recruiting him had ceased recently, and Aria also denied having seen him.

Best case scenario was that he'd finally gotten the message that he wasn't going to get what he wanted from any of them. Worst—he was saving his energy for something bigger. And as past instances had proven, silence from Edrick Noor didn't bode well for anyone. The last time he'd gone unexpectedly MIA, he'd had a hand in killing nine women.

As Independence Day dawned bright and clear, Anna forced all of those thoughts away. Noor would have no place in their lives today. And as she lay wrapped in Joe's warm embrace, she thought again of how lucky she was. Today they would celebrate not only the independence of their country, but also their growing family. Seth and Joe and Jacob were perfect additions into this crazy clan, and Anna loved knowing that she and her sister had found their true mates.

"You're looking awfully smug this morning," Joe's sleepy voice rumbled.

"I'm feeling smug." Anna tipped her head back to grin up at his darkly handsome face. At the same time, her hand skimmed down his body and under the elastic band of his shorts to find another part of him that was coming awake. She stroked a couple of times and had the pleasure of watching his eyes go molten with arousal.
~~~

His mouth was closing in on hers when they both heard little feet hit the floor across the hall. The sound drew closer, and they knew they'd have company any second.

"Rain check," Joe whispered.

"I'll hold you to it." She gave him a sensual squeeze before releasing him.

"It's party day," Jacob announced as he came barreling into the room and up onto the bed with them.

Joe barely had time to protect certain assets before Jacob landed on them. Anna laughed at more than Jacob's enthusiasm and got a disgruntled look from Joe.

"Yes, it is." Anna scooted to the side to make room and gave Jacob her full attention. "So we'd better get up and get a move on. Do you want to help me make a special treat for today?"

Jacob's head bobbed up and down eagerly. "What kind of treat?"

"Have you ever had a No-Bake Cookie?"

"Nuh-uh. What's that?" His big brown eyes were filled with curiosity and his face was alight with adventure.

"Well, it's a chocolate cookie with peanut butter and oatmeal in it."

His little features scrunched up. "Oatmeal? I don't think I like oatmeal."

Anna tweaked his nose. "Oh, trust me, you'll like these." She got up and slipped a robe over her sleep shorts and tank. "And I'll even introduce you to an old family tradition."

"What's that?" He followed her progress by turning in place on the bed.

"Let's get dressed and I'll show you."

"What about Joe?"

"I think we can let him in on it too." Anna winked at Jacob and then turned to head to the bathroom.

She was still grinning when she found both of them in the kitchen, dressed and sitting at the table waiting for her.

Since cookies weren't a good idea for breakfast, Anna made scrambled eggs and toast for the three of them. They chatted about what the day would hold as they ate. When the dishes were cleared away, Anna gathered the ingredients she'd need. Once everything was out on the counter, she called Jacob to her to help.

He jumped up from his chair and was halfway across the room when he spun his head back to Joe. "Aren't you coming?"

"I'll just watch this time and be the taste-tester."

Jacob frowned and looked at Anna. "What's a taste-tester?"

"That just means he wants to get all the reward without all the work," Anna teased.

"Hey now," Joe protested. "Taste-testing is an important job. It's up to us to make sure the food is fit for others to eat."

"I don't know, Jacob." Anna sent him a questioning look. "That sounds like a cop-out. What do you think?"

He gave it serious thought. "You can help next time."

"Deal." Joe nodded and grinned.

"Slacker." Anna's eyes were filled with mirth as she turned to her little helper. "Okay then." Anna held out her hand to Jacob. "Let's do this."

She pulled a stool up to the stove and let him pour the four cups of sugar into the pot. She helped him measure out the cocoa and unwrap the butter. He got a kick out of letting the stick plop into the cocoa, sending a plume of brown dust flying into the air to coat everything nearby. He was still giggling when Anna tried to wipe it off his face.

Once the milk was in, she turned the heat on medium and showed him how to carefully stir it all together until it came to a boil.

"Now that this is bubbling really well, we'll set the timer for two minutes. We'll need to be very cautious after this, because it's extremely hot and we don't want to get burned."

While the chocolate mixture was doing its thing, Anna got

everything else ready. The oats, peanut butter, and vanilla were measured and set aside. She showed Jacob how to lay out sheets of aluminum foil on the table where Joe still sat watching them.

As a last step, she got out two spoons and poured two glasses of milk. Anna set each on the table.

"Jacob, you go join our taste-tester and I'll finish this last bit." When the timer sounded, she took the kettle off the heat, added the last ingredients, and stirred it all together. Carrying it to where her boys were waiting, she recounted a memory from her childhood.

"Evan and Ethan could never wait for the cookies to set up, so it became a thing for them to dig into the gooey treat as soon as it came out of the pan. Be careful though, it'll still be hot."

Joe got right into it as Anna scooped out mounds of chunky goodness. When Jacob saw how it was done, he dug in too and quickly had as much chocolate smeared on his face as he'd gotten into his mouth. The cookies were extremely rich and decadent, so neither of them ate more than the first scoop she'd put down. Even her chowhound brothers could only ever eat two before groaning in overload.

While the rest of the cookies cooled and set, Anna began to clean up the mess.

"Hey." Joe stood and took the spoons and glasses out of her hands. "You go shower. Jacob and I will take care of this."

"Why?" Jacob asked off-handedly as he licked chocolate from his fingers. "Men don't clean."

Anna's gaze snapped to Joe's. This was the first time any indication of Jacob's upbringing had risen to the surface. Living in the same house as Kurt Hagen was bound to leave more than a physical mark, and she wasn't surprised to hear it manifest in such a chauvinistic manner. She could only guess at what else Jacob might have heard. If what Jacob had said was the worst it got, then she'd consider them all very lucky.

Joe set the dirty dishes on the table. He turned back to Jacob and squatted down in front of him. "There's no such thing as men's work or women's work, buddy. We all help out equally. Since Anna cooked breakfast for us and made those yummy cookies, it's only fair that we clean up." Joe leaned in as if to impart something important. "And besides, a gentleman always looks out for his lady. Even if she *can* take care of herself."

Anna thought Joe had handled that perfectly. Jacob really hadn't known what he'd said was wrong, so getting mad or upset wouldn't have helped. Joe's approach had been spot-on. They both knew that Jacob regarded Joe highly, so his gentle nudge was all it took to change Jacob's attitude on the matter.

"We'll take care of that for you, Anna." Jacob sounded like such a little man that it had moisture gathering in her eyes. Joe was going to be such a good dad.

Anna blinked away the tears and smiled. "I appreciate that very much. Thank you."

Jacob beamed up at her.

She bent and placed a kiss on his forehead before moving off down the hall. As the bathroom door closed, she could hear him and Joe talking and laughing.

A couple of hours later, Anna was putting the final touches on the other dishes she'd made. Jacob had asked her countless times if it was time to go yet, and each time, she'd laughed and told him not quite.

When she heard him coming this time, Anna grinned to herself but waited for the words.

"Anna, is it time yet?" He was trying so hard to be patient, and this time she could give him the answer he wanted.

With a last tuck of foil around the bowl, she bent forward and put her hands on her knees.

"It's time."

The look on his face was priceless. All his pent-up energy burst out of him and he raced back into the living room.

"Joe! Joe, we can go now!"

"No way," Anna heard. "Really? Are you sure?"

"Uh-huh, Anna said."

"Well, then." Anna came around the corner in time to see Joe rise from the floor where he'd been trying to occupy Jacob with a game. "We'd better help load the food up and get this party started."

# 17

Anna handed Jacob the plastic container the No-Bakes were in. Should he drop it or tip it around, they would fare better than the other dishes she'd brought. And even if they were broken to bits, no one would mind. They'd still eat them.

Jacob was the first out of the car when they pulled into her parents' driveway. Luckily, her dad had seen them arrive and came to open the door, because one small little boy would have plowed right through it in his excitement.

Her dad was still chuckling when she and Joe made it in. "Looks like someone couldn't wait to get here."

Anna kissed him on the cheek. "I think he's looking forward more to showing Evan and Ethan what he can do with his magic than the fireworks display later."

"Well, you have to keep in mind," a glint lit her dad's dark blue eyes, "your brothers haven't matured much since the age of six. So they're the perfect playmates."

Anna snickered. "I never thought of it that way, but you're right."

The day was filled with food, family, and laughter. Someone, probably one of her brothers, brought out a football. All the guys moved off to play some catch while the food was getting ready.

Anna lowered herself down onto a blanket next to Aria and glanced over at the men. It looked to be Joe, Jacob, and Seth against her dad and brothers in an impromptu game. After the snap, Jacob took off running with the ball, Joe just behind him trying to protect his back.

When it looked like Jacob would be taken down by the Burke defensive line, Joe reached down, picked Jacob up, and tucked him under his arm. Jacob was howling with laughter as he clutched the ball and dangled from Joe's arm, bouncing with every step Joe took.

Joe, with Seth acting as guard now, tried to carry Jacob and the ball past her brothers.

They didn't make it.

Anna giggled as Ethan snatched not only the ball, but Jacob too, right out of Joe's grip and took off running in the opposite direction. Jacob gave another shout of hilarity, but because he was loyal to Joe, he awkwardly chucked the ball back to him.

When Ethan saw what he'd done, he took Jacob to the ground and started tickling him as Joe scored and did a silly victory dance.

Anna loved the ridiculousness of the game and loved her family even more for giving Jacob some happy memories.

After a few more runs, most of the players collapsed, winded and tired, around her and Aria. Anna smiled when Joe laid his head in her lap and then giggled when Jacob dramatically flopped on top of Joe, making him grunt.

"Need something…to drink," Jacob gasped out as if he were dying of thirst. They were seeing more and more of his quirky personality, and Anna's heart swelled.

"I think I have some water here somewhere." Anna started to reach for the cooler and saw Jacob peek up at her from where he still lay on Joe's chest.

"Coke? Please?"

"Well, I don't know…" Anna tried to keep her face blank and not give in to the grin that wanted to emerge at his hopeful expression.

Joe's head tipped back, and she dropped her gaze to his handsome face. "We could share one."

Two sets of eyes begged her, both brown but from different ends of the color spectrum. She couldn't refuse and knew she was lost to both of them.

"Fine." She huffed out with a laugh.

Jacob jumped up, wringing another grunt from Joe.

"Dude." Joe sat up as Jacob ran for the cooler. "Watch the goods, please." Jacob wasn't listening, so Joe turned to Anna and leaned in to whisper in her ear. "I'm going to need them. I'd like to add a few more little Burkes someday."

"Me too," she murmured back, grasping his face in her hands and kissing him.

"Eww, gross," Evan whined, drawing out the vowels and making his voice sound like a little kid's.

"What's gross?" Jacob asked eagerly when he returned with a bright red can.

"They were kissing." Evan made a yuck-face before pointing to Anna and Joe.

"Oh, they always do that." Jacob sounded disappointed that it wasn't something far worse. "But it's way better than the fighting and yelling my mom and dad used to do."

Anna's heart broke at hearing that, and when she looked over at Evan his humor had slipped a little.

"You know what, buddy?" Evan recovered quickly. "You're right. I'll take kissing over arguing any day too."

"Me three," Paul called from where he was manning the grill. He reached out with one hand and grabbed Mary by the waist, pulled her in close, and gave her a huge smacking kiss. Everyone laughed, and the fun and easy day continued.

They all ate until they couldn't move but when dusk approached, the whole family readied themselves to make the short drive to where the city would have its fireworks show. Anna was smiling and thinking about what Jacob's reaction would be to the sparklers she'd tucked away in the car, when suddenly she was sitting behind her desk at the school.

Everything around her was eerily silent until she heard running feet echo down the hall outside her door. She rose and crossed to the entrance. As she glanced out, she saw Jacob just make the corner at the end of the hall.

"Jacob? Honey, what are you doing out here? Class is going to start soon." Anna started down the corridor where she'd last seen him. "Jacob? Where are you?" She made the turn up ahead, just in time to see him dart around another corner.

She sped up and was soon running, trying to catch up with him, her long blonde hair flying out behind her as she went.

"Jacob? Sweetie, you need to stop. Let me find you."

His terrified scream rent the air. "Annnnnnaaaaa!"

"Jacob! Jacob! Where are you? Answer me!" Panic gave her feet wings, and she ran faster than she ever had in her life. She had to find him. Had to save him.

Around her, the school's hallway gave way to dark tunnels, leading her down twists and turns and into dead ends. Her voice echoed back at her as she shouted for Jacob and tried to find him. Anna could still hear his faint cries calling for her, but the sound bouncing off the uneven walls made it impossible to determine the direction of the source. "Anna. Anna." Her breath caught when he wailed plaintively, "Moommmy."

No matter how far she ran, how deep she went into this network of passages, there was no sign of the child she loved. His voice seemed to come from every direction at once, and she didn't know where to search next. She was quickly getting lost in the maze, desperate to find her little boy.

And so she ran.

And the further she went, the more it drained her. She was so tired now, she could barely get her brain to function. Her heart felt like it was fighting to beat in her chest instead of racing from fear and exertion. Her legs felt leaden and grew heavier with every step. Anna pushed through into another passageway and stumbled. She had to grab hold of the wall just to remain standing.

"What is...going on?" She couldn't seem to pull enough oxygen into her lungs to speak.

She forced her legs to carry her a few more faltering steps before they gave out completely. She dropped to the ground and started to crawl. She refused to give up; she had to find her son.

To her dismay, soon even that movement was impossible. Anna barely had enough strength left to drag and lift herself up to prop her back against the wall.

She'd rest, she decided, but just for a minute. As she sat though, instead of regaining energy, what little she had left seemed to fade away.

"Jacob. Joe. I love you both so much," she whispered into the darkness. "I'm sorry."

Anna's eyes closed, and as she fell asleep, her heartbeat slowed and finally ceased altogether.

~~~

Joe was admiring the sway of Anna's hips as she walked in his direction, preparing to leave for the celebration downtown. When she suddenly went completely motionless, he wondered what she was doing. His gaze traveled to her face, and he froze, shocked to find she only stared blankly outward. He watched her for a few more seconds, but a feeling of panic and dread was growing in his gut.

"Anna?" He'd just started towards her when she slowly folded in on herself and fell to the ground. He shouted her name and raced for her at the same time he heard more cries of alarm sounding all around him.

He blocked it all out as he reached her side. He knelt down,
~~~

gathered her into his arms, and pushed her hair back away from her face. "Anna?"

Joe got his first good look at her and gasped.

She looked dead.

"Anna!" He called to her over and over, shaking her frantically, but there was no response. He checked for a pulse but found nothing. She wasn't breathing.

"Oh, God."

*What the fuck was happening?*

Joe looked up for help, and that's when he saw Seth bent over Aria, and Mary and Paul attending to their sons. The other three quads looked to be in the same condition as Anna.

"What the hell is going on?" Joe shouted to the others.

Mary stood and, through her tears, took control. "Noor. Bring them all into the house. Immediately."

Joe lifted Anna into his arms and when he rose, he saw Jacob standing utterly still right behind him. The look on his face ripped Joe's heart in two. He pushed his own fears aside and stayed strong for the little boy who'd lost so much already.

"Jacob. She's going to be fine. I promise." When Jacob didn't move, Joe tried again. "Come on, son. Let's help get everyone in the house. They need us now. Anna needs us."

That seemed to snap Jacob out of it, and he followed behind Joe into the house.

He and Seth laid the women on the living room floor and then ran back out to help bring Evan and Ethan in. It took Joe, Seth, and Paul to heft the oversized men in and settle them next to their sisters.

It nearly killed Joe to see Anna lying there like that. He couldn't imagine what Paul and Mary were going through, seeing all of their children lifeless and vulnerable.

Jacob came to Joe's side and wrapped his arms around Joe's waist. He reached down and lifted him into his arms. Jacob wound himself around Joe's neck and held on as Joe embraced him tightly to offer whatever comfort he could.

Joe turned to Mary for answers. "What's happening to them?"

"I don't know. But to impact all of them at once? It has to be Noor," she repeated, all doubt gone.

"What has he done?" Seth looked lethal. Joe knew Seth's story and got a glimpse of the outlaw he'd been before meeting Aria.

"I'm not sure." Behind her brave façade, Mary sounded distraught.

"You'd better figure it out soon." Seth's chilled brown eyes bore into Mary's. "They're not breathing."

"I know!" she snapped back. "He must have gotten into their minds somehow. His favorite method of torture has been to mess with their dreams. He must have put them into a dream-state to control them."

She looked at each of her children.

"What are you going to do?" Paul asked.

"I'm going in after them." Mary took a steadying breath. "I'll use the same spell Anna used on Aria to enter her dream. He's not getting my children. I'll find them, and I'll drag them back if I have to."

"I'm going when you go after Anna." Joe wasn't taking no for an answer.

Mary didn't argue; she just nodded. "Get comfortable."

Joe sat down on the couch with Jacob still in his arms. He took a moment to speak softly to him. "Hey, buddy." He waited until Jacob raised his head and met his eyes. "We'll get her back. We're going to go get her." Remembering how it had been when Seth had gone into Aria's mind, Joe tried to prepare Jacob as best he could.

"I'm going to go to sleep for a little bit, so don't be scared. When I wake up, Anna will too." Joe couldn't let any doubt enter his mind.

Jacob laid his head back on Joe's shoulder. Joe nodded at Mary and she started the spell.

*"Blood to blood. Mind to mind.*
*Journey together into dream time.*
*One for love, one for protection.*
*Three into one, into Anna's projection*
*Still in control to mold and scheme*
*As we will, so mote it be."*

Joe and Mary materialized into deep shadow. All around them were walls and tunnels. Joe squinted through the darkness and could just make out a form on the floor up ahead.

Joe pointed. "There!"

They took off running and found Anna slumped against the wall.

Falling to his knees beside her, Joe tried to find any sign of life. His hands shook as he searched for a pulse. He shook his head at Mary when they found nothing.

"Give me a little room. I need to look deeper."

Joe kept hold of Anna's hand but backed off and let Mary have whatever space she needed.

She grasped Anna's head in her hands and closed her eyes. Joe didn't know exactly what she was doing, but he knew that if there were anything left of Anna inside, Mary would find it.

"Anna, I know you're still in there," she spoke softly. "Hear me. Hear my voice and find your way to us."

Another few moments passed in silence before Mary spoke again.

"That's it. I'm here, and so is Joe."

Joe split his attention between mother and daughter and waited for any sign that Anna was coming out of it.

"Jacob's fine, honey. We've got him. He's safe and wants you to wake up."

Mary paused as if listening.

"That's not real. Noor is tricking you. I promise Jacob is okay. I need you to wake up now."

Had Noor led Anna to believe that something had happened to Jacob? Was that how he'd lured her here and trapped her into staying?

Joe was still contemplating that when Mary shifted and started issuing orders.

"You need to lift her and follow me."

Joe cautiously slid his arms under Anna's neck and knees and then lifted and curled her into him. As he followed dutifully behind Mary, he couldn't help but ask, "What's wrong with her, and where are we going?"

"From what I was able to get from her, I'm pretty sure we're deep inside Anna's subconscious. We need to get her out of here."

"Can't you just wake us all up?"

"No. We need to back her out of here first, but gently. Being this deep, she's effectively shut her body down, which is why she's not breathing and doesn't have a pulse."

"How is that possible?"

"As witches, we're more in tune with nature and everything in it. Including our bodies and minds. There are some rituals that require us to enter into a meditative state where we look into ourselves. The deeper we go, the more absolute the…sleep, we'll say. In these states, we can control our breathing, our heart-rate, even our brainwaves. She's been led so deep that she has, without realizing it, slowed her entire system until it all just stopped."

Joe looked down at the beautiful woman in his arms.

Mary touched his hand. "If we're going to wake her, we have to get her back to the surface of her mind where her body starts functioning again."

He nodded and with renewed determination, picked up

speed as Mary broke into a run.

They ran for a while before Mary halted to check on her daughter.

"It's working." She smiled. "Her life force is growing stronger."

They took off again until Joe heard a sound he'd been afraid he'd never hear again. Anna's voice.

"Joe."

He immediately stopped and looked down at the slight figure cradled against his chest. He knew he had tears of relief pooling in his eyes, but he didn't care. "I'm here, love. I'm waiting right here."

Black lashes fluttered and separated, revealing pale blue eyes. When they met his, Joe felt love wash over him.

"Where are we?" Anna murmured wearily.

"We'll explain everything," he promised her. "But we need to get out of here first."

He looked to Mary and at her nod, returned his attention to Anna. "It's time to wake up now, my love.

When Joe opened his eyes, he sat up with Jacob still clutched close. He saw Anna starting to stir.

"Jacob," Joe whispered. "Look."

His small head lifted and turned to look down at Anna. When her eyes opened, Joe and Jacob scrambled to get to her.

"Jacob?" Anna gasped and tried to sit up.

"He's fine," Joe promised, lending her a hand to sit. "He's right here."

She reached out and took Jacob into her arms, tears already running down her face.

"What happened?" Anna's blue eyes traveled up to his.

"Noor got to all of you," Joe said quietly.

"All?" Anna looked around and saw her siblings still lying on the floor. "Oh my God."

Joe heard Mary reciting the spell again, this time taking

Seth with her into Aria's mind.

Over the next half-hour, Mary repeated the process over and over, bringing her children back one by one.

To retrieve the boys, Paul went with her. They'd already brought Evan out and were now working on Ethan as the others sat around the living room and talked about where they'd been and what they'd seen.

Evan had just explained about chasing a perp when Anna spoke over her brother's words. "I don't like how long this is taking." Her eyes never left her sleeping parents. "It didn't take nearly this long to pull you two out."

# 18

Joe stood back as the Burke family gathered around to see if they could help.

Another fifteen minutes passed, and still no sign of Mary, Paul, or Ethan waking. Anna and Aria were discussing the logistics of going in when, finally, Mary took a deep breath as she surfaced from the spell-induced slumber.

Her husband quickly followed, but Ethan was a little slower to come around. Mary glanced at her son as she sat upright. She didn't say anything—just sat, holding his gaze.

"What happened?" Anna asked. "Why did it take so long to bring Ethan back?"

Mary said nothing for a moment, and a look passed between mother and son. "He was just harder to reach." Mary smiled, but Joe thought it felt a little forced.

"Paul, honey, could you make some of my special tea?"

Something was off, Joe thought. Mary and Paul were hiding something. But all Paul said was, "I'll be right back."

Evan and Ethan remained on the floor, backs propped against the couch. Seth and Aria sat huddled on one end while Joe, Anna, and Jacob snuggled at the other. Mary was resting in a chair across from them.

The stress and strain of recent events had been too much for Jacob, and he drifted into sleep in the protection of Anna and Joe's embrace.

No one spoke until Paul returned with a tray carrying a flowered teapot and matching cups. He set the tray on the coffee table and poured a cup for each of his kids. He prepared one more and handed it to his wife, taking a seat on the arm of her chair. His hand went to her head to brush along her auburn hair.

Joe understood his need to touch and reassure himself that the woman he loved was safe. Joe wouldn't likely forget anytime soon the sight of Anna lying essentially dead. Those had been the worst moments of his life, and he'd gone through some pretty shitty times. He turned his head into hers and pressed his lips along her temple. He remained there, just breathing her in, until Paul spoke in a low voice so as not to disturb Jacob.

"How did he get to all of you at once? You were there one minute and gone the next.

"His powers must have taken another leap," Evan speculated. "I don't know how he did it, but I was packing the cooler to take with us, and then I was chasing a perp through alleys. The longer I ran, the less I could keep up. It got harder to move, and even to breathe."

"It was Jacob for me," Anna lamented. "I was running through the halls at school, and then they just morphed, suddenly becoming dark tunnels." Anna pressed her hand to her chest over her heart. "I felt it slowing down, but all I could think about was getting to Jacob, so I kept going."

"He was killing you," Mary's voice shook, "using whatever he knew you'd pursue to lure you in. The deeper inside yourselves you went, the more you faded away, and your bodies shut down. Eventually, your hearts just stopped beating."

Joe's nearly did the same at how close he'd come to losing Anna. How close they'd come to losing all of them. He tightened his grip on his little family.

Anna glanced at everyone. "I still can't believe how real it felt. I didn't even question the change in my surroundings." Disbelief tinged her tone. "I just knew that Jacob had been taken, and I had to find him, no matter the cost."

"He sure upped the ante this time." Aria settled deeper into Seth's side. "What if the whole family hadn't been together when it happened? There would have been no saving us."

Joe knew that Noor had invaded Aria's and Seth's minds numerous times. He thought he remembered Anna saying that Ethan had also had dreams about Noor, but he didn't know if anyone had ever said what they'd been about. As far as Joe knew though, this was the first time he'd nearly killed any of them.

He'd come too damned close for Joe's peace of mind. "I thought you all had these super shields in your minds. How did he get in?"

"That's a very good question." Evan's eyes narrowed as he pondered it.

"We've faced off against him enough for him to know he can't come at us head-on while we're awake," Anna hypothesized. "The only way for this plan to have worked was for him to render us asleep first. Once he'd done that, we were fair game."

"But all at the same time?" Paul asked.

"I don't claim to understand it. That's just what makes the most sense," Aria responded, sullen. "We still have no idea what kind of power he has." She looked at her mom. "Have you been able to learn anything more about that ritual he went through?"

"Nothing more than that one small mention. We're still searching for any other information on it. The problem with that type of magic is that it's so dark and malevolent, a good majority of it is kept secret and hidden away among those who would actually use it. It's not well-documented, or even known about, within respectable witching communities. We'll find it; it's just going to take some time."

"Which gives him plenty of opportunity to do this again." Joe kept his tone level, when what he really wanted to do was yell out his frustration. "How do we keep that from happening? There has to be something you can do. He nearly killed all four of you." Joe looked down at his son, asleep in his arms. "And how do we know he hasn't been in Jacob's dreams, lying to him and tempting him too?"

"He hasn't been. I promise you that." Anna turned her face up to his and held his gaze. "Part of what Jacob and I talk about is the possibility of nightmares because of what happened to him. If Noor were getting into Jacob's dreams, he would tell me. He'd be too scared not to."

Her assurances warmed some of the chill in his blood, but Joe would still worry until Noor was out of their lives for good.

"Look, we're all exhausted, and I don't think anyone is in the mood for fireworks." Mary set her teacup aside. "Let's all get a good night's sleep. We can figure out our next move in the morning when we all have clear and refreshed minds."

Everyone agreed and a short while later, Joe and Anna were settling Jacob into his own bed at their home together. They silently gazed down at their little boy. Anna sat on the edge of his bed and reached out to run her hand lightly over his head.

"It's still weird that it never happened," she whispered. "I see him here, sleeping without a care in the world, but my mind is having a hard time believing it."

Joe couldn't imagine the horror she'd suffered in that dream world, thinking their son had been taken. And if she needed reassurance, he'd sit with her in Jacob's room as long as it took.

"Do you want me to bring some blankets in? We can bunk on his floor until you feel more certain."

Anna turned shining eyes up to him. "I love that you'd camp out on the floor for me, but I don't think I need to go to that extreme." She gave a small laugh. "Thank you for making the offer, though."

"Any time. But know that I was planning on making a blanket fort for you. I'm pretty awesome at forts."

"Wow, a blanket fort?" Fun sparkled in her blue eyes. "I'm sorry to be missing that."

He was glad to see a little more of the fear in her expression fade away. He knew firsthand that it wouldn't ever leave them, but right now the sharp edge of it was dulled.

Together they headed to their bedroom. He secured the door behind him and slowly closed the distance between them and laid his lips to hers. The kiss was gentle and seductive and restorative. He drank her in and finally…finally felt his system even out.

She was here and she was okay. He had her back.

With one last lingering kiss, Joe drew in his first clear breath in hours. "Are you sure you're all right?"

"I am." Anna smiled up at him. "Thank you for saving me."

"What other choice did I have? I can't face life without you." He ran his fingers through her hair. "I love you more than you can possibly know."

"I *can* know." She grinned up at him. "And I do. I feel it deep in my soul, and it fills in all the missing pieces I never knew were there. I wasn't looking for you. I wasn't looking for a knight to come riding to my rescue, but you've saved me in so many ways already. Mostly from myself. But you're right here, right where you're supposed to be."

Joe didn't know how he'd ever made it without her. To think he'd survived all this time on this planet, not knowing there was someone like her out there. The last year had given him more than he could have ever dreamed of.

He dipped his head and kissed her again. He slowly walked her backward until the bed bumped the backs of her legs. Joe unhurriedly stripped her out of her clothes. He tasted and loved each patch of skin he revealed.

He set a leisurely and determined pace to show her exactly

how much he needed and wanted her.

Later, as she slept, Joe lay in the dark and watched over her. He didn't think Noor would try his tricks again anytime soon, but it would take some time before Joe rested easily. He'd need to stand guard and make sure Anna didn't slip away from him again.

~~~

After the first couple of hours, Anna hadn't slept much either. She and Joe had just lain awake in drowsy silence, content in each other's presence, occasionally dozing. She'd used that time to do some thinking, and when the sun finally rose, Anna had the beginnings of a plan.

One that could turn the tables on Edrick Noor.

She'd explained her idea to Joe later that morning. He'd listened but had been resistant to trying something so daring and dangerous. After a little more convincing, he had eventually conceded that her proposal made sense.

She just hoped that the rest of her family would see the merit in her idea too. Especially considering that the whole thing hinged on the agreement of one person in particular.

After settling Jacob into the boys' room with a new video gaming system, Anna stood in her parents' living room.

"Hell yeah! Let's do it!" Seth jumped at the chance when Anna laid it out.

She hadn't been sure if Seth would be willing to take advantage of the blood connection he shared with Noor. He'd had a hard time accepting the truth when he first learned he'd descended from Noor and his wife Isabel. Not that she could blame him. It would be a shock to anyone who knew what a sadistic bastard Edrick Noor was.

But she should have known better. Seth wanted Noor stopped as much as the rest of them.
~~~

"Hold on." Aria held her hand up, bringing all conversation to a halt. She held Seth's gaze for a long, pointed moment before turning her attention to Anna. "I agree that if this works, it could be a game changer for sure. But if Noor finds out..." Her words trailed off. Aria gathered herself and went on. "He came far too close to succeeding this time. If he's grown that powerful, I don't want him turning that kind of attention on Seth."

"Pixie," Seth started, but Aria shut him down quick.

"Don't *Pixie* me. We barely survived his last stunt. I'm not taking that chance with you."

"I'm with Aria," Ethan added. "I think our focus needs to be on finding a way to stop him, not get into his head."

"We *will* work on that, but before we do, I think this is too great an opportunity to pass up. We've all wondered what the significance of this connection is between Seth and Noor. Whatever he's doing to locate his blood relatives could be the answer we've been looking for. I think we need to see if, through Seth, we can trace it back to the source." She paused. "Can you imagine what we could learn by being inside Noor's head?"

"I hear what you're saying, but I really don't think it's a good idea for us to go traipsing through his mind," Ethan reiterated.

Anna narrowed her eyes at her brother. "Why are you so against this, Ethan? Don't you think I can handle it?"

Before he could answer, their mother interrupted. "I'm sure that's not the case, sweetie. I think all Aria and Ethan are trying to say is to be careful. Make sure that in your haste to turn this around on Noor, you're not jumping in with both feet and ignoring the danger this could bring down on all of you. Noor is unpredictable on a good day. The lengths he'd go to if he found out what you're doing could be catastrophic."

Anna wasn't convinced that's what her youngest brother had meant, but without looking she couldn't be sure. Since she wouldn't do that without his permission, she had to let it go.

"I'm not discounting that, Mom. But if this works out the way I hope, Noor will never know we were even there."

"Explain." Evan leaned forward in his seat.

Anna detailed her plan.

"And when are you wanting to put this plan into action?" Aria asked.

"Why not right now?" Seth answered before Anna could respond. "We're all here. Let's do it. After the energy he expended yesterday taking you all down, he might be easier to get to right now."

"He has a point," Evan agreed.

"All right." Anna nodded decisively. "Now, it is."

They moved to the floor. Seth sat in the middle of a circle created by the four of them.

"You'll have to open yourself up to let us into your mind," Anna reminded Seth. "Take a deep breath, hold it, and as you let it out, concentrate on that air leaving your body. Try not to think of anything else. Clear your mind, and picture a door opening."

His head bobbed once and he did as she'd instructed. As he exhaled, he closed his eyes. Anna probed his mind but found it still locked down tight. She'd bumped into this specific obstacle before.

When she'd first met Seth, she hadn't trusted the rough outlaw he'd been back then, and she'd tried to read him—to gauge his intentions towards her sister and find out exactly who he was. She'd found this—an impenetrable wall.

What she hadn't known at the time was that he'd been an undercover cop, working to bring down the very biker gang he belonged to. His line of work had been one that required him to hide most of his true self away.

Seth's life had depended on his ability to build compartments between Seth Lawson, the law-abiding-citizen, and Law, the hardened criminal.

Those shields he'd built wouldn't be easy to overcome.

"Just breathe. In and out." Anna kept her voice gentle and even, and tried to help him open up. "Picture that door. Your hand is on the knob. Now see yourself turning it. Open the door and breathe."

She'd been afraid of this very thing when she'd originally come up with her plan. Anna had counted on the fact that because he'd shed his Law persona, his mind would be more permeable. She'd hoped between that, and guiding him into a relaxed and receptive state, she'd be able to get through.

But that wasn't the case. He still guarded himself staunchly against intrusion. Anna looked at each of her siblings and shook her head. It wasn't working. The protection Seth had built around his mind was still resolutely in place.

Neither Evan nor Ethan had a power that would enable them to look into someone's mind. Once the link was established, they could follow her or Aria in, but by the nature of their powers, they couldn't establish the connection themselves.

That left only her or Aria. Anna's gaze caught her sister's. *"You try."*

Aria nodded.

Anna had led him into a light, trance-like state. Aria, keeping her voice low, took over seamlessly without disruption.

"Seth. It's Aria now. Can you still see the door?"

"Yeah. I've tried to open it, but I can't."

"That's okay. Don't force it. Look around it. Is there light coming in anywhere? Maybe along the edges?"

"No. It's sealed tight."

Anna understood what Aria was trying to do. If there were even the slightest sliver, they could work on making it bigger until they had a way in.

Aria worked with him for a while longer, but they eventually decided to call it quits. The walls in Seth's mind were just too ingrained into who he was. It would take time and a lot of practice before he could start tearing them down.

"I'm sorry." Seth ran his hands up through his short brown hair in frustration. "I don't understand. If this wall I have is so strong, how is Noor even getting in? Is it the blood link?"

Anna patted him on the shoulder. "You've had to keep your mind locked away for so long, it's just second-nature to you now. And after trying to get through it myself, I can only guess that Noor is somehow able to reach you because of the connection between the two of you."

"So there's no way I can help lead you to him."

"It's still possible," Mary countered. "But it'll just take some time."

"Time we don't have." Seth stood and stalked a few paces away.

As Anna pushed herself off the floor to take a seat by Joe on the couch, text alerts split the silence. Evan and Seth both grabbed for their phones.

Anna watched as they read the message and then looked at each other grimly. Whatever had happened was bad.

"We've got to go." Evan was already on the move, and Seth was right behind him.

"What do you think that was about?" Anna asked no one in particular when they were gone.

"There have been a few murders that have them worried," Aria explained as she too rose from the floor. "By their expressions, I'd say there's been another one."

"A few?" Mary gasped in dismay. "How many have there been?"

Aria took a seat in a nearby chair. "If this is the same as the others, it makes three."

"How do they know it's the same person?" Joe asked as he leaned forward.

"Seth said the way they were killed is very distinctive, but that's all he'd say." Aria shook her head. "And I really don't want to know any more than that."

Anna hated to ask, but after what he'd done the last time, she had to know. "Is it Noor?"

"They're not ruling it out, but all the victims have been men. That doesn't really fit his MO. He always seems to go for women."

"If we're done here," Ethan spoke for the first time as he stood, "I'm going to go. I've got some stuff I need to do."

Anna saw concern flood into her mom's eyes as she watched her other son leave.

"What is it?" Anna's question drew Aria and Joe's attention. "What's going on with Ethan?"

Mary stared at the door for a moment before bringing her focus back around to Anna. "I'm worried about him. He's very troubled."

"About what?" Aria rose from the chair to sit on the couch, closer to their mother.

Mary looked to her husband before turning back to them. "Yesterday, when all of you were attacked, we almost didn't get him back."

Anna felt the shock on her face. "What?"

"When we found him deep inside his mind, he was with Honor."

Anna and Aria both gasped.

"Honor? What does that mean?" Joe asked.

Anna turned towards Joe on the sofa. "Honor Andrews. She and Ethan were high school sweethearts. They met in the seventh grade, fell instantly in love, and were inseparable from then on." Anna's fingers twisted together in her lap as sadness washed over her anew. "They dated all through high school and into college afterwards. She was going to school while still living at home, but she and Ethan were making plans to get their own place together."

Anna paused and looked at her mother before continuing.

"Late one night about four years ago, there was a fire in her parents' house." She met Joe's eyes again. "Ethan was here at the time. When he found out, he raced over there, but it was too late. None of them survived." Anna swallowed hard. "He blames himself."

Confusion flickered over Joe's face. "Why? It doesn't sound like he had anything to do with it."

Mary cleared her throat. "Ethan's element is fire. He tried to control the blaze, but it was beyond what he could handle. He thinks if he'd been stronger—if he'd practiced harder—he could have saved her."

"And then Noor fucks with his head and uses her to lure Ethan to his death." The loathing in Joe's voice was clear.

Mary nodded and resumed her previous account. "When Paul and I finally found him inside his subconscious, they were in the middle of a hedge-lined maze. He was on the ground, much like I'd found the rest of you, with his head cradled in Honor's lap. I could tell they'd been strolling deeper and deeper into the maze until he'd collapsed. I tried to reach him like I did with all of you, but he fought me. He didn't want to leave her."

Anna felt her heart clench. She'd never truly understood what Ethan had gone through when Honor died. With Joe and Jacob in her life now, she had a much better idea of how a loss like that could rip your world apart and leave you feeling hollow. Just the thought of losing either of them made her physically ill. She reached out and grasped Joe's hand in hers. What would she do? What would she give to have them back? Would she risk it all for only a moment with them again?

The answer was a resounding yes.

That had a horrifying thought surfacing in her mind.

"Did Ethan ever tell anyone what his dreams were about when Noor first started stirring? We all felt something." Anna looked around the room. "I sensed his hate, Aria had visions, Evan felt Noor rumbling against the earth, and Ethan said he had dreams."

She looked to her mom. "But I don't recall him ever saying what they were."

Mary shook her head. "No. He never did."

Aria picked up her train of thought. "You don't think Noor has been tormenting Ethan with dreams of Honor all this time, do you?" Tears choked off Aria's words. "That has to be the worst kind of living hell. Why hasn't he said anything?"

Finality rang in Anna's voice. "Because he has her back." She thought about her own reaction when she posed this question to herself. "Imagine if something happened to Seth," she looked at her mom, "or to Dad...Wouldn't you do whatever it took to be with them, even if only in a dream?" She gripped Joe's hand tighter. "Without question, I would."

Anna could see the sorrow settling over each one of them. And when they all parted ways shortly afterward, they separated with heavy hearts and a new worry to add to their growing list.

# 19

Another week passed, and on a clear and balmy July night Anna stood with her siblings. They were here to work their magic again. They'd been coming together for months and still hadn't found what they would need to finally defeat Noor for good.

The prophecy said 'four into one,' but no one knew exactly what that meant. The theory was that they'd have to combine their magic in some way, but they had yet to figure out the method.

Each time they worked as a group, they called to their elements, but as far as combining those into one—that's where they had a problem.

It had only been since Aria returned a few months ago that their abilities had seemed to elevate to another level. Growing up, they'd called the corners countless times. But it'd never felt anything like it did now. The elements brought with them a surge of energy that flooded their systems and took them higher than anything else they'd known before.

The first indication that things had changed were in the marks themselves. The always-innocuous symbols had begun to burn and sting, as if power were actually blazing within each one.

That had quickly progressed to them glowing with subtle color. When she'd felt the shift, Anna had glanced down at her lower stomach to find her water birthmark emitting a soft blue luminescence. Aria's air had radiated green on her shoulder blade, Evan's earth symbol had gleamed a yellowish-brown high up on his left arm, and the right side of Ethan's chest had flared red where his mark of fire lay.

The next time they'd come together, their call had carried a wave of intensity so strong, it had manifested itself into raging storms. Each of them had been engulfed in a cyclone of their own signature element. It had swirled around them and caught them up in a tempest that had left them giddy and flying high.

But their magic hadn't progressed any further since that day, no matter how many times they'd tried. And combining those storms had proven difficult at best.

Tonight they were at Knight's Place after hours. Joe, Seth, and Jacob waited off to the side and watched as they took up their positions.

Anna and Aria were across from each other, and Evan and Ethan stood at the other points. As first-born, Aria began her call to air.

*"Still and calm or a raging storm*
*We are as one, from the day I was born*
*I am Air and Air is me*
*As I will, so mote it be."*

Energy filled the room, and Anna looked forward to adding her own magic to the mix. She made her call next.

*"From the heavens above to the oceans below*
*Together always as you ebb and flow*
*I am Water and Water is me*
*As I will, so mote it be."*

Anna felt the rush of water rising in answer and let it fill her up.

Beside her, Evan brought forth the earth.

*"Sand and soil, dirt and stone*
*Neither you nor I shall stand alone*
*I am Earth and Earth is me*
*As I will, so mote it be."*

And finally, Ethan summoned his fire.

*"Smoke, spark, ember, flame*
*You and I forever the same*
*I am Fire and Fire is me*
*As I will, so mote it be."*

They all took a moment to revel in that first breathtaking surge. Anna threw her head back as her soul came alive. Her blood sang and her body hummed. She couldn't contain the delighted laughter that bubbled out of her as she let it take her over.

A quick glance at those around her confirmed they too were reveling in the magic they'd invoked.

Reluctantly, they pulled it in. They were here to find the secret that still eluded them. The key to taking Noor out.

As one, they continued the ritual.

*"We call to our elements for protection and grace*
*Gather now in this blessed place*
*Grant us your strength and your power*
*On this night and in this hour."*

"All right," Evan said when he'd reined in his abilities enough to take control, "let's do this."

Each raised their arms and lifted their storm high above

them. They all pushed them to the center of their circle, but there they stayed. Four twisting, turning masses of elemental energy.

"Anna," Jacob called.

"I'll be right there, sweetie," she called back. "Let us work on this a little longer." She tried to force her water funnel into the fray. Only to see it bounce off the rest and stay stubbornly divided.

"Anna," he repeated.

"Just a minute, baby." Anna's mind was racing, trying to find a way to merge energies so obviously repellent of each other.

"I think you need to hear what he has to say, Anna," Joe interrupted this time.

She looked at her brothers and sister. "Give me a second." They lowered their arms and released their power with silent thanks.

Anna walked over to where Jacob sat with Joe and Seth. "What is it, love?"

Jacob's deep brown eyes gazed up at her. "You and Aria are the same."

She blinked in confusion. "Yes, I know. We're twins."

"No," he stressed. "When you have your magic. You're the same."

She squatted down to his level, wanting to understand. "But I'm water, and she's air. That's not the same."

"I know. But you look the same on the inside."

Anna searched Jacob's face as she considered what that meant. She and Aria were identical twins. Essentially the same person. Would their elements merge because of that fact? It was worth a try.

She leaned forward and gave him a smacking kiss on the cheek. "You are so smart. I love you so much." She reached up and kissed Joe too. Just because.

He smiled at her as she turned back to where her siblings

were waiting. "Aria, I want to try something. Jacob said you and I look the same on the inside when we're wielding our elements. I want to try to merge just yours and mine."

Aria cocked her head. "You really think that'll work?"

"We won't know until we try."

When they moved back into position, Anna looked at Aria and nodded. "Here goes."

The elemental magic returned, but like magnets of the same polarity, the two streams just bumped against each other and refused to merge. Anna felt disappointment but insisted on trying again. There had to be something to what Jacob had seen.

She reached out and grasped Aria's hands. And felt an instant shift.

Connections. Maybe it was all about connections.

Anna closed her eyes and sent her thoughts to Aria. *"Open. All the way."*

As soon as that link was made, it seemed as though everything clicked into place. Anna could feel her sister's mind, their thoughts aligning until only a centralized awareness remained. As their souls came together, so did their magic. When their minds and spirits were completely and totally one, air and water fused.

Each now had access to every thought, every feeling, every memory in the other. Aria's clairvoyance and Anna's empathy were shared by both of them. This was the complete and total merging of two individuals. They were one.

If either had held back anything at all, the union wouldn't have worked. But because they freely gave everything they had to the other, they'd found the secret to bringing the forces of their elements together.

Above them, what had once been air and water was now a churning, bubbling hurricane. Only full, communal cooperation could influence and control this new energy.

They'd done it.

Holding the connection, Anna and Aria opened their eyes and laughed in perfect unison.

"Someone want to tell the rest of the class how you did that?" Evan stood off to the side with Ethan. They both wore expressions of shock and amazement.

When Anna and her sister turned, they moved in synchrony. They each let go of one hand but held tightly to the other.

"It's not just about merging your power." Anna and Aria's voices, integrated just as their souls were, spoke in harmony.

"That is so weird," they heard Seth mutter.

Together they continued the explanation. "*We* had to merge. Jacob saw that we looked the same inside. Even though our elements are different, a complete alignment of our beings allowed our powers to convene. You and Ethan should be able to do it too."

"Can you stop that now?" Ethan grimaced with a small chuckle. "It's giving me the willies hearing you talk like that."

Facing each other again, Anna and Aria slowly separated their minds. As they did, everything connecting them divided. Their elements split apart, and when they were each back to themselves again, they sent thanks to their dear friends and stood looking at each other.

"Okay," Aria grinned. "Wow."

"Yeah." Anna was in awe. "That was incredible."

Evan turned to his twin. "You ready to try this?"

Anna thought she caught a glimpse of hesitation in their brother, but she dismissed it when Ethan nodded. "Yeah, let's do it."

They did as the girls had done, grasping hands and closing their eyes. But before they could really get started, Evan and Seth's phones sounded.

"Shit," Evan muttered as he pulled it out. After glancing down at the screen, his eyes clicked to Seth. "We gotta go."

"We need to close our circle first," Anna reminded him.

Evan nodded, and the four of them returned to their positions.

*"A circle cast for a favor asked*
*Closed now that the need has passed*
*Our thanks and blessings be to thee*
*As we will, so mote it be."*

"Another one?" Aria asked of Seth when they'd finished.

"No, this is something else." He gave her a quick kiss. "I don't know how late I'll be."

"That's fine, go. I'll hang out with Anna and Joe."

As Evan and Seth started out, the telephone in Joe's office rang. Instead of letting it go to voicemail, Joe jogged across the room and through the doorway to grab it.

"Hey," Aria drew her attention. "Since we have a minute, were you able to talk to your friend and get those scraps for me?"

Anna nodded. "They're upstairs. Come on up and I'll get them for you." She turned to her brother. "Ethan, will you stay here with Jacob while we run upstairs?"

"No problem." Ethan grinned down at Jacob. "We'll be fine."

Anna and Aria wound their way through the gym, chatting excitedly about their most recent accomplishment. About midway up, Anna looked down to where Ethan and Jacob were already wrestling around and smiled.

Opening the door, they stepped through and closed it behind them. Anna went to the bed where she'd stored the box of materials Aria had asked for. She was always looking for new, unusual items to add to her wind sculptures.

When Aria had left home at eighteen, she'd traveled around for a bit before landing in a small town in Ohio. She'd been hiding from not only the prophecy that had foretold of their birth and the evil they were destined to face, but also from herself.

Anna had understood completely. It had taken her longer than eighteen years, but she herself had eventually rebelled against the tight constraints of their lives too. That's when she'd taken her own life in hand and started working out and learning to defend and protect herself. That's when she'd met Joe.

Aria hadn't had a Joe in Ohio. She'd had herself and her blooming talent for metalwork. She'd expanded that into using any items she could get her hands on, and she'd created the most extraordinary pieces of wind art Anna had ever seen.

They were garnering the attention of serious collectors and pulling in staggering sales.

Aria had had to take a leave from her art when, on the morning of their twenty-fourth birthdays, Noor had started making his presence known. Aria finally had to admit that everything the prophecy had predicted was true and beginning to come to fruition.

Coming back hadn't been easy for her, but she'd done it because the alternative was to let a monster loose on the world. And that was something none of them would allow.

A lot had happened in the last few months that spoke of Noor's willingness to destroy anything good. And there would be still more to come until he was put down for good. In an attempt to maintain some kind of balance during that time, Aria had been drawing and designing new sculptures.

With an unerring insightfulness, their father had given his daughter exactly what she'd needed. He'd built Aria a studio where she could plan and build and weld to her heart's content.

Now that she had somewhere to work, Aria was trying to garner some supplies. When she'd asked Anna for help in finding odds and ends that she could use, Anna had started gathering what she could and stored it here until Aria could get over to pick it up.

Aria was so excited, she sat right down on the bed and began going through it all. She took out each one and looked it over before setting it aside. Anna could almost see the wheels turning in Aria's mind with ideas of what she could do with the pieces.

Anna lost track of time as she and Ari talked and discussed the possibilities of what was in the box. When she heard the door open, she glanced over and saw Joe walking towards them.

"Hi, honey. I was just showing Ari her box of goodies."

"I see that." Joe came over and looked through everything spread out on the bed. "Just looks like junk to me." He laughed at the haughty look Aria gave him.

He took a quick look around the apartment. "I expected to see Ethan and Jacob up here."

"We left them downstairs when we came up." A warning went off in Anna's stomach. "They're not down there?"

"No, I just came through. I didn't see them."

"What about the bathroom?" Anna tried desperately to stay calm and come up with an explanation. "Or outside?"

"I'll go check." As Joe ran out and down the stairs headed for the front door, the girls sprinted after him, searching the rest of the gym. He met back up with them in less than a minute. "They're not out there. And Ethan's car is still in the parking lot."

"They're nowhere in the gym." Anna pushed her thoughts out to her brother. *"Ethan, where are you?"* When she got no response, she tried again. *"Why would you leave with Jacob and not tell us? Ethan! Damn it! Answer me!"*

She waited but there was still nothing. She pulled her cell out of her pocket and called him. It rang and rang and then went to voicemail. She left him the same message but with a little more bite to her words.

Aria was disconnecting a call she'd made at the same time. "Mom and Dad haven't heard from them. I checked in with

Evan, and he said the same thing."

"Where could they have gone?" Anna's heart was pounding in her chest like a kick drum. She looked at Joe, begging him to tell her it was going to be okay. She couldn't stand the idea of Noor having them.

Then a worse thought snuck in and took root. She looked at Aria and Joe, remembering the conversation they'd had with their mother about how far they would go to have a loved one back. "You don't think Ethan...?"

Joe took her into his arms. "No. Don't go there." But the fact that he knew what she'd been thinking said his thoughts had gone there too. His next words were strained. "Ethan wouldn't do anything to hurt Jacob. He loves him. There has to be another explanation."

Anna wanted to believe that, but her doubts were pushing harder. "Then why can't I reach him?"

"I don't know," Joe admitted. "But we'll find them both."

As Joe held her, Anna's mind raced. All the uncertainties and questions she'd had about Ethan rushed at her. Would he risk Jacob's safety if Noor had promised him Honor? Anna wouldn't have thought so, but Ethan had been so distant and quiet lately.

No one knew what he was going through because he wouldn't let anyone in.

"No." Anna forcibly drove all those fears away. He was her brother, damn it! Her quad-mate. There's no way he'd hurt her this way. "Ethan wouldn't betray us. It doesn't matter if Noor is making promises or not. Ethan didn't cause this."

There had to be another reason. Whoever had taken Jacob must have somehow over-powered Ethan and taken him too. He must be unconscious, and that's why she couldn't reach him telepathically. She'd take heart in the fact that wherever they were, they were together, and Ethan would be there to protect Jacob.

She pulled herself together. "Okay. How do we find them?"

"We go to Mom's." Aria spoke before Joe could answer. "Everything we could need is there. We'll use all the magic available to us to bring them back."

Anna felt hope deep in her heart. She looked up at Joe and he nodded. "Okay. Let's go."

The three of them took off running towards the door. Just as they'd almost reached it, Jacob came tearing into the gym. There were huge tears streaming down his face, tracking through dirt and blood.

# 20

"Jacob!" Anna ran to him and scooped him up into her arms. She kissed every inch of his face she could reach. Joe was right there to hold them both while Aria stood back and let them check him over.

"They took him." Jacob was sobbing as he fought against her hold, and Anna finally registered what he was saying.

"Who took him, sweetie?" Aria stepped forward, brushing at the wetness on her own cheeks.

"I don't know. Men." His words were interspersed with hiccups from crying. "They came to the door. We thought they wanted in to work out." He wiped at the snot that mixed with the blood on his face. "Ethan was gonna tell them we were closed, but they hit him real hard and he fell. I should have stayed back like he told me, but I didn't." Jacob started to cry even harder. "I tried to scream but another one grabbed me. He held my face really tight."

Anna could see the red marks on his little cheeks from rough fingers. She let her anger simmer as she helped guide him through the rest. "What happened after that?"

"They put us in a van and started to drive away. I was crying. I thought Ethan was dead, but he woke up. He woke up and then he looked at the door and it was opening. I was so scared because we were still moving."

His breathing was gasping in and out as he fought through

the tears to tell them. "When the bad guys heard the door open, they stopped really fast. Ethan pushed me out," he hiccupped again. "He pushed me out and told me to run." Jacob sobbed. "I did what he said, but he didn't come with me. He was supposed to come with me."

"Shh," Anna soothed him. "It's okay. You did the right thing by running away. You were brave and strong and did exactly right. We'll find Ethan, I promise."

Anna hugged him close again and silently thanked her brother for saving her son. She also sent an apology for doubting him and thinking he could have had a part in this.

"We have to find him," Jacob argued and pushed out of Anna's arms.

"We will, buddy." Joe bent to him. "Let's take a look at you first." Joe hooked a finger under Jacob's chin and lifted it. "How did you hurt your chin?"

"When Ethan pushed me out, I fell. I hit my face on the road, and one of the men caught me again." Jacob's eyes swung to Anna. "But I used a spell. I used magic to make him let me go, and I ran all the way back here."

"You did so good, Jacob." Anna hugged him again. "I'm so proud of you."

"I'll go get the first-aid kit." Joe went to one of the cabinets and came back with a big white box with a red cross on the top.

He did what he could for the cut on Jacob's chin and the scrape on his knee where the denim had torn away. They also found that his palms were abraded and seeping blood from when he'd hit the concrete.

While Joe was attending to Jacob, Anna called her mom to give her an update. She agreed that they all needed to meet up at her house to begin the hunt for Ethan.

Once Jacob was cleaned up, they jumped into Joe's SUV and flew to her parents' house.

They were waiting when Anna, Joe, Aria, and Jacob came

through the door. Mary reached down and lifted Jacob into her arms and held him tight. "I'm so glad you're okay."

"I did like you told me. I did the spell and got away, but Ethan didn't come. He was supposed to come too." Jacob's emotion-clogged voice had Anna's eyes stinging.

"That's okay, short-stuff," Paul said encouragingly. "Ethan is going to be all right."

Jacob looked right at Paul. "Because he's a witch too? Because he has fire and can move things with his mind?"

"That's right," Paul agreed. "Plus, he's smart and tough like you. He'll be okay."

With Jacob still in her arms, Mary spoke to the rest of them. "I've already started gathering the ingredients we'll need for a couple of different spells we can try." She guided them back to the room where all their stores were kept. They followed without comment.

Anna stepped into warmth and familiarity and took in the tools her mom had set out to find Ethan.

"Come on, buddy." Joe took Jacob from Mary. "Let's give these Burke witches some room to work their magic."

Jacob looked from Mary to the table and back. "Can I help? I'm a Burke witch. I want to help. I can do magic too."

"Oh, baby." Anna choked on the knot in her throat. "I don't think—"

"I think that's a wonderful idea," Mary interrupted. "I would love your help."

Anna sent her mom a look. It asked 'are you sure?' Jacob was already suffering because of what had happened. Anna didn't want him to endure more disappointment if the spells didn't work.

"The more witches, the better," her mother confirmed. "Come stand next to me, and I'll show you what to do."

Joe set Jacob down and he immediately went to Mary's side. His head barely reached the top of the table, so Anna's dad got a small stepstool for him to stand on. Anna remembered it as one of the four that she and her siblings had used when they were learning magic.

Anna caught her mom's eye. "What's first?"

Her mom didn't get a chance to respond as Aria gasped and braced her hands on the table. Everything stopped as Anna and Mary went to her.

Aria's eyes were tightly closed as she watched the vision only she could see.

"What is it, Ari?" Anna coaxed.

"Ethan. He's tied to a chair."

Their mom made a little sound of distress but Anna didn't let up. This connection was an unexpected boon, and they needed as much information as they could get before the link severed.

"Is he okay?"

"He's been beaten. His face is bruised and bloodied. I think he's unconscious."

"What about where they are?" Anna guided, even though her heart was tearing apart in her chest. "Is it a house? A building of some kind?"

"Concrete floor," Aria shared. "Block wall. Windows are set high, and they're small. It could be a basement."

"Okay, good. Is there anything else you can tell us about where he is? Can you see anything out the window?"

Aria shook her head. "No. It's too dark." Then she slumped as the vision released her. "I'm sorry. That's all there was."

Anna went to her twin and gave her a hug. "It's okay. It's more than we had. Thank you."

"He's hurt?" Jacob's big brown eyes searched Aria's face for more answers.

She crouched down to him. "A few bruises and a little blood—kind of like you." Aria touched his chin gently. "But you're okay, and Ethan will be too."

"I want to try scrying for him." There was moisture in Mary's eyes, but she held it in and bent to her task.

As much for her as for him, she asked Jacob to help her finish putting the herbs in the bowl. Once that was done, she picked up an oblong white crystal that hung from a long piece of leather lacing and added that to the same bowl. Anna knew that, along with the herbs and crystal, there would be something of Ethan's to aid in focusing the spell.

Just then they heard voices from out in the living room, and Anna guessed that Evan and Seth had arrived. Sure enough, a few seconds later, they appeared in the doorway.

"What are we doing to find him?" Evan asked as he entered. He looked down at the tabletop and nodded. "Scrying. That's good."

"And Aria had a vision." As Mary finished readying the spell, Anna filled them in on what their sister had seen.

"They b…" Evan's words halted when he saw the little boy next to his mother.

Anna could feel his rage and torment at knowing his twin was in pain.

"Do we even know how they did this?" Seth asked.

"Jacob said men came and lured them to the front door and knocked Ethan out," Joe answered, his anger barely bottled. "Ethan came to long enough to get Jacob out, but he wasn't able to follow."

"Ari, get the map, please," Mary instructed.

"Use the city map," Evan turned to add.

"You think they're still in the area?" Paul stepped closer. "Wouldn't they have gotten as far away as possible?"

Evan consulted his watch. "It hasn't been that long since he was taken. If they've had time to get to their hideout and work him over, they couldn't have driven very far. So, yeah—they're still close by."

Aria brought over the map of Daytona Beach  and laid it out on the table.

Thinking of Jacob, Mary quickly jotted down the spell they would use so he could join in.

They took up positions around the table as Mary pulled the crystal from the bowl. She held it by the very end of the cord and let the weight of it hang free. She extended her arm so the point of the pendulum was mere inches off the center of the map.

The five Burke witches recited the spell that would direct the magic to find Ethan.

*"On the wind we send this rhyme.*
*Point us to what we need to find.*
*Reveal to us so that we may see.*
*As we will, so mote it be."*

The pendant began to sway and move, traveling over the city in ever widening circles. Suddenly, it all but jumped out of Mary's grasp and slammed to the table. As one, they leaned forward to see where it hit.

Scrying was an extremely useful tool but Anna wished, especially in this case, that it was more exact. It wasn't like doing an internet search. It couldn't pinpoint an address, but it would get them close enough that they should be able to find it once they were near.

"I know that area. It's about fifteen minutes away," Evan said hurriedly.

"Your dad and I will stay here with Jacob," Mary offered. "The rest of you go get my son and bring him home."

They used Joe's SUV so they would all fit. With Evan's guidance, in less than the time he'd estimated, they arrived at a neighborhood left unfinished mid-construction.

At Seth's urging, Joe slowed and came to a stop about a hundred yards from the first structure. He shut the engine off, and all that could be heard in the silence that followed was the ticking of the cooling motor.

Anna saw that up ahead were five partially-finished homes, two on the right and three on the left. Each of them was completely dark and seemingly abandoned. There were no outward signs of any inhabitants.

Looking around, Joe swiveled his finger outward. "What is this place?"

"The developer ran out of money," Evan said. "It's sat here for almost a year. We've had to roust kids and homeless out of here plenty. If that spell hit its mark, looks like someone else found a use for it."

"How do we figure out which one Ethan is being held in?" Joe asked.

"We go in on foot and," Evan glanced back at her, "I'm hoping as we get closer, Anna will be able to sense them. We know Noor's been recruiting soldiers. That has to be who came for Jacob and Ethan, and I can bet, right now, they're scared shitless. They fucked up big time. Noor wanted Jacob, and he only got Ethan instead. If Noor's in there, I'm sure his rage is howling loud and clear at being denied what he wants, yet again."

Anna thought it was a good plan and she was ready. "All right, let's go."

The five of them exited the truck. Since Joe had parked on the right side of the road, that's where they started. As they slowly made their way close to the first house, Anna opened her senses and searched.

She didn't feel anything close by, but there was…something just out of reach. She took the lead and followed her instincts—crossing to the left side of the street when the signal became stronger in that direction.

They were skirting by the first house when Anna locked on to the emotions coming from the inhabitants of the next one. Along with the waves of panic that were pouring out of the structure, she also sensed a combination of rage, fear, and a good dose of resentment.

When she stopped and knelt down, all the others did the same. Joe positioned himself close behind her. Open the way she was, she could feel everything he felt. She could also read the mixed bag of emotions coming from the rest of her family.

She worked to block them out and narrow in on the men in the house. Closing her eyes, she let more through her multi-faceted diamond. They needed to know how many were in there and whether or not Noor was in attendance.

As had happened in the dream when she'd pushed her talent, images now accompanied what she picked up from the men. They all had one common element. Noor. He was in there.

"Noor's in there," she whispered to the others. "And I can read at least three more." She pushed harder but couldn't tell if she'd gotten them all. "There could be others, but I just can't tell."

"That's fine. It gives us something to work with." Evan came forward to kneel next to her. Seth followed him.

"You three stay here," Evan said in a hushed tone. "Seth and I will scout around. Figure out our best plan of action.'

He didn't give them a chance to argue. He and Seth ran, crouched forward, towards the house she'd indicated.

She, Aria, and Joe held silent and waited for the other two to return. Anna tried not to think about what her brother could be enduring at Noor's hand. None of them had been able to reach out to him telepathically. Anna had to hope that he was only unconscious; she refused to let her mind consider anything else. They needed to find him and bring him home.

Two dark shadows glided towards them across the bare lawns. "Here they come." Anna notched her chin in their direction.

"What did you see?" Anna asked Evan as soon as he was close enough.

"They chose the one that was the most completed. Plywood covers the entire outside. Only the doors have been cut in and hung; a single wood door on the front and a sliding glass one on the back. We'll split up and breach both at the same time. Joe and Anna will come with me around back, and Seth and Ari will go in the front."

"In Aria's vision, she said it looked like Ethan was in a basement," Anna reminded him.

"I saw the windows, but they've been blacked out. We didn't see any entrance from the outside, so we'll have to locate that once we're in. We'll clear the upper floor first and then take below."

"Everyone ready?" Seth asked, and when they all nodded, they split up and went their separate directions.

Anna and Joe followed Evan to the back of the house. He halted them to the side of the glass.

*"Aria, you guys in position?"* he asked her telepathically.

*"Yes. Seth said we're ready on your signal."*

*"Let's do this quietly, guys. Go."* Evan grabbed the handle and pushed. The large panel slid open without a sound. Evidently they didn't feel they needed the added security of locks.

Anna and Joe were close behind as he slipped into the house. Once inside, they saw that though the supports were up throughout the house, none of the drywall had been installed. They had a clear, unobstructed view through the wood studs of the whole interior.

A quick scan showed them the stairs to the basement were just off what would have been the kitchen area.

They gathered together, and in a voice that was barely above a whisper, Evan laid out the rest of the plan. "Seth and I will go first. Be ready for anything."

Anna pulled on her magic to have at hand for whatever they'd find down there. She felt the energy around her gather and knew Evan and Aria were just as prepared.

Her brother and Seth descended the steps at a quick pace to surprise whoever may be waiting. Their guns were drawn and aimed as they hit the concrete at the bottom. Anna heard Evan shout out orders.

"Step away from him and back up against the fucking wall!"

As Anna, Joe, and Aria followed, she looked for Ethan. He was secured to a chair across the long, dim room. His head was slumped forward and he wasn't moving.

Anna glanced around and saw five men in total. Four had done as Evan instructed and stood with their backs against the wall. Seth was covering them with his pistol.

The fifth man stood behind Ethan's chair. It was Noor, wearing Kurt Hagen's body. He was partially shielded by her brother's large form.

"Back away from him, motherfucker." Evan made his threat more menacing by raising his gun and pointing it directly at Noor's head.

He only laughed and grabbed a handful of Ethan's hair to jerk his head up. "Oh, I don't think so." Noor brought his other hand up to reveal a deadly-looking knife. As he laid it against Ethan's throat, it caught a glint of light off the single glass bulb dangling from the ceiling.

Anna got her first look at the damage they'd done to her brother. Both of his eyes were swollen shut, and they were covered in blood from the cuts to both brows. His lips were busted open in several places, and on his left cheek there was a gash that looked severe enough to expose the bone. His nose had been broken and had bled enough to leave a gruesome trail of blood down over his mouth and onto his chin. From there it had dripped and ran further, saturating the front of his shirt with bright red.

And those were only the injuries she could see. Her stomach threatened to revolt at the thought of what other tortures he'd suffered.

Noor studied their reactions to what he'd done, taking in each of them in turn and smiling at what he saw.

"The sadness and grief in all of you is thrilling, but it's not quite enough. Not nearly enough to make up for what's been taken from me." His dull grey eyes narrowed as his hand tightened on the knife, pressing it further into Ethan's neck. "I'm curious. Would you all be so sentimental if you knew what I knew about your dear Ethan here? If you knew that, even now," he glanced down at the unconscious man seated in front of him and sneered, "he begged me for what only I can give him?"

"What the hell are you rambling about?" Evan challenged, never wavering with his aim.

Anna could guess what, or rather who, Noor was referring to. Honor. She glanced at Aria who stood beside her and saw her knowledge of it too.

Noor caught their exchange and chuckled. "Ah, it seems your sisters know what I'm talking about."

Helpless to stop them, doubts about Ethan's actions started to creep back into Anna's mind.

"Either of you want to fill me in?" Evan demanded without taking his eyes off Noor. "What's he done to our brother?"

"Oh, he's done it all to himself." Noor returned his gaze to Evan and sneered in triumph. "He's quite the little addict you know. I just supplied his drug of choice. And he kept coming back for more."

Evan raised his gun higher. Anna saw his finger was now on the trigger, ready to pull it back.

"It's Honor," Anna told Evan in a rush before he could shoot. She didn't doubt her brother's marksmanship skills in the least. What she didn't trust was Noor. She wouldn't put it past him to somehow route the bullets to hit Ethan instead. "We're pretty sure Noor's been taunting him with Honor in his dreams."

"What?" Evan spared her a swift look and then turned to

stare at his twin in shock.

Anna watched a change overtake him as what she'd said sunk in. His black eyes slid slowly back to Noor, and Anna could see the rage glittering within them.

Evan's words were like shards of ice as they hurled from his mouth. "Get the fuck out of his head."

"Oh, I'm having too much fun to give *that* up." Fully aware that taking out his puppet was the worst damage Evan could do, Noor was completely unconcerned that there was a gun trained on him. He actually had the gall to shrug. "Why don't I slit his throat right now, and you can just watch him bleed out?"

He pressed the razor-sharp edge further into Ethan's neck, and Anna saw the blood well up and trail obscenely down his neck.

Neither of these men would give in, and Anna knew she had to do something. She moved her hand the few scant inches that separated hers from Aria's. They had a secret weapon, and if it would send him back to the pits of hell and keep him there for a while, Anna was all for using it.

Taking a deep breath, she mind-sent just one word.

*"Link."*

# 21

She felt her sister flow into her mind. The connection was easier and smoother this time. They united within seconds. Each had called to their element before entering this place and they merged them now, holding the tempest they created just outside of the physical world.

When the time came to strike, they would hit Noor with everything they had.

Together, they sent Evan a heads-up. *"We've got Noor."*

It startled him, but he caught himself quickly. *"Ethan's right—that is freaky."* He paused and they wondered if he'd fight them on this. They sensed his decision the moment he made it. *"Make sure you kick his ass all the way back to his fucking cage."*

*"Consider it done. Keep the others off of us."*

*"Can do."* When Evan raised his hands up in surrender and backed away, Noor's eyes went round in surprise.

She and Aria stepped forward.

His head tilted in curiosity until he saw how they were joined and sneered. His focus landed on Aria. "Do you always do everything together? That might be something to consider when I finally make you mine."

They ignored his comments and took another step forward. "This is your only warning. Back away from our brother."

Their words came out as one voice. The creep factor Ethan

and Evan had mentioned wasn't lost on Noor either.

"What are you doing? Why are you talking like that?"

Anna and Aria raised their free hands and brought forth their power. When Noor realized what they were now capable of, he slapped back at them with the force of his anger and fear. They felt the strike but withstood it. When he realized it did nothing to them, he redoubled his efforts and struck out again, this time taking down the whole room.

It rocked them back, but they stood strong against his power. They heard grunts from behind them as the men were knocked off their feet in the wake of Noor's energy. The clatter of metal told them that whatever weapons they'd had were torn from their hands. Noor took advantage and shouted to his men.

"Get them!"

All hell broke loose at the other end of the room, but they didn't spare it a glance. They knew the men could take care of themselves. That confidence let them focus their attention entirely on Noor.

He tried to take them down with another magical blast—this one stronger still. When the blow landed, they tasted their own blood as they now shared even injuries, but it didn't sweep them away as it had the others. They stood proud and strong against the best he had to give.

The sounds of all-out war filled the basement. The men fought with fists and physical might while Anna and Aria battled Edrick Noor with magic and energy.

They raised their free hands again, watching as an enormous cache of elemental power took shape in front of them. They sent it careening into Noor, propelling him back away from Ethan and into the wall. As the head of Kurt Hagen smashed into it, the knife fell from his hand and skidded across the floor out of reach.

They felt it as Noor switched it up and attempted to attack their minds. Presumably, to render them asleep and vulnerable to his dream power, but the combination of Anna's diamond shield and Aria's solid steel wall let nothing of his magic through. They returned the favor by spearing their minds straight into his.

With Aria's clairvoyance and Anna's empathy, they knew his next move as quickly as he thought it. They anticipated each one and countered it with one of their own. They knew even their combined magic wasn't strong enough to kill him yet, but they could keep him busy until he'd depleted whatever stores of power he still had.

When they felt him weakening, they let loose the full brunt of their magic. Their storm of joined elemental energy tore through him with such ferocity it ejected the snapping, snarling beast right out of Hagen's body.

It towered over them and howled out its rage. They hit him again, and the howl was quickly replaced by a scream of true agony as their tempest enveloped him, slashing at him mercilessly.

The creature suddenly dropped to its knees, head hanging low, its sides heaving. It shook once and then slowly became a man, battered and broken.

Now *they* stood towering over him. "Take your sorry ass back to hell and stay there."

Noor could do nothing but glare up with a look of utter loathing before fading into nothingness.

As one, Anna and Aria turned. They saw their men standing over the four others lying unconscious on the floor.

Kurt Hagen was nowhere to be seen. He'd escaped in all the commotion.

Seth approached Aria. "Hey, Pixie. You still in there?"

They smiled and released the connection between them as Anna and Aria returned to themselves.

"I'm here." Aria reached up to run her hand over the bruise forming on Seth's cheekbone. "Looks like you took a hit," she teased.

Seth's thumb wiped at the blood on the corner of Aria's mouth. "So did you."

Aria looked over at Anna. "One of us did."

Joe came and folded Anna into his arms. She relaxed into his embrace, and when they separated he dabbed at the same drip on her own mouth. "You don't know which of you was hurt?"

They both shook their heads. "No."

A soft moan sounded from behind them and they all turned and rushed to Ethan. As he was regaining consciousness, Aria and Seth untied his hands and feet. Anna knelt in front of him and cupped his face in her hands. She gently lifted his head.

"Ethan? Can you hear me?"

"Jacob," he mumbled through distended and bloodied lips.

"Jacob is fine; he's with Mom and Dad. You got him back to us. You saved him."

He tried to open his eyes, but they were swollen shut and crusted with dried blood.

"What happened?" he asked.

"Shh, don't try to talk." Aria rubbed her hand over his head. "Noor's men beat the shit out of you."

His words were distorted, but Anna could still make them out. "Yeah, they did most of that in the van when Jacob ran." Pain filled his words. "Stomped on me good before I passed out. Think they busted a few ribs."

"Okay, we'll get you taken care of. Mom and Dad are waiting. We can talk about everything else once we get you home."

"No." Evan's tone was sharp and direct from where he still stood over Noor's men.

Anna recognized that tone. She knew her brother well. He was hurting and angry. If it had simply been Noor boasting about what Ethan had done, Evan could have ignored it, chalking it up to lies intended to inflict pain. But to have his own sisters confirm it—that made it impossible to dismiss.

And now he had to deal with what must, to him, feel like betrayal. His own brother, his twin, had broken his trust with the choices he'd made. So until he was ready, he was covering that up and falling back on his police training and procedure.

"We're doing this by the book. This is a crime scene, and we have to call it in. Ethan will be transported to the hospital by ambulance. Statements will be taken, and these four will become guests of the Daytona Beach PD."

"And how are you going to explain all this?" Aria took a few steps back towards Evan.

"I'll stick as close to the truth as possible. The official report will state that Kurt Hagen, along with these four, found and attempted to kidnap Jacob. Ethan was there, saw what was happening, and tried to stop them. When Jacob successfully escaped, they took Ethan in retaliation. They'll be charged with kidnapping and assault, at the very least."

Evan turned away to make the calls. He had yet to approach his twin.

"He sounds pissed off," Ethan murmured to Anna.

She sighed. "We're all a little pissed at you, Ethan. But Evan—I think he's more hurt than anything. Why didn't you tell us about the dreams?"

His breathing hitched and he bowed his head. "I couldn't lose her again."

Anna heard the raw torment in his voice. She wasn't sure of exactly what had happened, but he was her brother. And he had risked his own life to make sure Jacob had gotten free. She owed him that much. "Let's just get you better, and then we can all sit down and talk."

"Anna." His limited gaze was intensely focused on hers. "I would *never* endanger your son. Tell me you believe me."

"I want to, Ethan. I really do." That was the best she could do at the moment.

He nodded, but her uncertainty seemed to have broken him.

She didn't have a chance to say anything more, because they all heard the sirens drawing near. Soon the house was swarming with police and EMS.

Anna stepped back and let them do their jobs. She was comforted that she happened to know one of the paramedics. He was the father of one of her students.

"Hey, Greg."

"Hey, Anna." He touched her arm gently. "Don't worry, we'll take good care of him."

"Thank you."

Anna watched as they knelt on either side of the chair and assessed her brother's condition and injuries.

"Sir, can you hear me?" Greg asked Ethan as he looked at all the damage done to his face. He ripped open some gauze pads and applied pressure to the cut on Ethan's cheek that was still bleeding.

"Yeah." Ethan winced and tried to raise his head.

"Try not to move," Greg cautioned. "Can you tell us what happened to you?"

While Greg was tending to the lacerations and getting information from Ethan, his partner was checking his vitals.

"Airway is open and clear."

Greg acknowledged that with a quick nod.

"Got beat up. Kicked in the ribs," Ethan rasped out.

After noting that down, Greg asked him, "How much pain are you in right now?"

"Breathing is labored," the other medic stated.

"Hurt everywhere. Mostly my ribs."

"All right. We'll get you something for the pain." Greg reached into his kit and pulled out a clear bag of fluids and a long line of tubing.

They were thorough in the care they gave Ethan. Before she knew it, they had an IV started and had him strapped to a backboard to transport him up the stairs and out to the waiting ambulance.

Evan and Seth rode with him to take his statement. The rest of them followed in Joe's truck. Anna called her parents on the way to let them know they were headed to the hospital. She made sure to stress that physically he was going to be fine.

Mentally, they'd have to wait and see.

They'd only been there a short time when Anna saw her mom and dad arrive with Jacob. Anna immediately went to her son and pulled him into her arms as her parents went to check on Ethan's status.

"Nana Mary said Ethan was okay?" Jacob asked in confirmation, concern and worry marring his young face.

Nana Mary, huh? Anna liked it, and she was sure her mom did too. "Yes, he got beat up some, but he's going to be okay."

"Can I see him?" His big brown eyes bore into hers.

"In a little while, sweetie," she dodged. Ethan looked bad enough that she didn't want his appearance to scare Jacob. "The doctors are fixing him up right now."

They ended up admitting him to monitor him the rest of the night. Her parents refused to leave him but told everyone else to go and get some rest.

Anna and Joe took Jacob home and tucked him into his bed. When they fell into their own a short time later, they lay wrapped in each other's arms.

"What's going to happen now?" Joe asked her.

"I don't know. We'll probably have to give it a couple of days to let Ethan recover a bit. Then we'll all need to sit down and discuss it."

Joe fell silent, and Anna could sense there was something he was trying to work through. She waited, and when he finally spoke his voice held a hard edge.

"Did he make a deal with that fucker and then get cold feet?"

Her own thoughts had gone down similar lines too, but she didn't want to believe that of her brother. "God, I hope not."

Anna shifted against Joe's side. "Let's not think about any of that tonight. Our son is safe and asleep in the next room. We're here, together. Let's just take heart in that and be grateful."

She brought his hand up and rubbed her thumb over the bruises on his knuckles. Bringing it to her lips, she slowly kissed the first one.

"I seem to have developed an affinity for watching you beat the hell out of bad guys." She settled her lips over the next. "I wish I could have caught a glimpse of you tonight."

"It was over pretty quick." Temper still sharpened his tone, but her actions were dulling the edge.

Her mouth trailed over red and swollen skin. "I'm thinking you must've looked pretty damned hot." She tipped her head back and grinned at him.

More of the hardness in his features softened as humor and arousal slipped into his golden eyes. "I don't know about that."

She rolled on top of him. Her knees straddled his hips and her hands pressed into the mattress on either side of his head. Her hair rained down around them like a curtain. Anna ran her lips up the side of his neck, grazing it with her teeth. "Oh, I'm fairly certain you looked scorchingly sexy dishing out some whoop-ass on those jokers."

"When did you become so bloodthirsty?" His eyes closed as she slid down his chest and planted kisses on his pecs.

"Mmm, just since you. I would have loved to see all these muscles," she tasted each one, "bunching and straining as you laid them out."

Her tongue drew a line down the center of his torso, and he groaned deep in his chest. "Abs flexing, arms bulging." She reached down and took him in her hand. "Speaking of bulging."

Anna wrapped her lips around him.

"Oh fuck," he breathed out as his back bowed and his hips lifted toward her.

"That's the plan."

He didn't let her play very long before he hauled her up and rolled her underneath him. She knew anger was still riding him, and he needed a place to burn some of it off. He wasn't gentle with her, but gentle wasn't what she wanted. They'd both had an emotionally-charged day and, for now, they needed to take solace in each other.

His face was buried in her neck when he thrust into her in one swift and sudden move. She bit down on the top of his shoulder to stop the scream of pleasure that threatened to echo through the house.

He grunted and picked up speed. Over and over he drove into her.

Knowing what he needed, what she now craved, she whispered into his ear. "Harder."

His rough hands slid down her body to take hold of her cheeks, and he tilted her pelvis up to receive him deeper. The sounds of his thrusts were loud in the room as flesh slapped against flesh at a frenzied pace. He took her so completely, so fully, that Anna was lost in sensation. She felt her orgasm gathering, tightening every muscle in her body until she thought she'd splinter into a million pieces.

When it finally broke over her, she bit down hard on her lip as her nails dug into his back.

He didn't give her time to recover from the first when he was forcing her up again. Her head was spinning and she couldn't catch her breath. The heat their bodies were generating threatened to burn her up from the inside out. On and on it went until, when she peaked again, he was right there with her.

Afterward, he lay heavy on her for several minutes before shifting his weight to the side and standing up. Throwing on some pajamas, his eyes raked over her as she did the same.

When they crawled back into bed, he nuzzled the back of her neck and pulled her close.

"You bit me," Joe accused in a sleepy voice.

She snuggled into him. "I did."

"I liked it," he growled in her ear.

"Pervert."

She was still smiling when they slipped into sleep.

# 22

A few hours later, Joe and Anna were awoken by Jacob's screams. They tore from their bed and raced across the hall to find him thrashing and fighting in his sleep.

He cried out over and over. "No! Stop! No!"

Joe reached him first. He sat on the side of the bed and pulled him up and into his arms. Anna joined him and brushed her hand over Jacob's head.

"Shh, it's okay. You're safe, Jacob. I'm here. Anna's here." Joe repeated the soothing words countless times, hoping Jacob would hear it. "We've got you."

Jacob slowly settled, but tears still leaked from the corners of his closed eyes.

"We're right here, love," Anna assured him. "It's okay."

Big brown eyes fluttered opened and looked up at them.

She gave him a minute to realize where he was. "That was a pretty bad dream, huh?" Anna caressed his face, wiping away his tears.

Jacob nodded.

"Can you talk about it?" she coaxed. "If we get it out into the light, it can't hurt you anymore."

It's no wonder he'd had a nightmare, Joe thought. What he'd been through would take a toll on anyone. Joe was surprised he hadn't had more, since he'd seen his mother murdered and he'd been left for dead.

Anna soothed him now with her loving, calm nature. She was such an amazement to Joe, as was the boy in his arms.

Anna tried again. "Can you tell me what your dream was about?"

Jacob took a hitching breath. "The men were there. They were trying to take me again. Ethan was there, but he couldn't help me. I thought he was dead."

*Couldn't, or wouldn't?* Joe wondered. That uncertainty ate at him. Had Ethan had anything to do with Jacob's attempted abduction? He still wasn't sure.

"Ethan's okay, sweetie," Anna reminded Jacob. "He has lots of bruises, but he'll be okay."

Anna helped him through the trauma of his nightmare enough that Jacob fell back asleep in Joe's arms. Not wanting to leave him alone, he stood and carried Jacob into their bedroom. Joe positioned him between them, and even after Anna had dozed back off, Joe lay in the dark, wide awake.

~~~

Three days passed, and Joe still hadn't gotten a chance to confront Ethan. He'd been sequestered away at Mary and Paul's house since he'd been released from the hospital. They'd insisted on taking their son home with them to oversee his recovery.

Remembering how he'd looked, Joe figured it would still be a few more days before Ethan could open his eyes fully or even breathe without pain. Let alone talk and explain what the fuck he'd been thinking.

Forced to sit back and wait, Joe had tried to keep his days busy. Between running his business, training his clients, and pounding the heavy bags every chance he got, Joe had gotten through.

Mostly.
~~~

The nights were a different matter though. Thankfully, Jacob hadn't had any nightmares since that first night. Anna had taken him to see Ethan a few times and that had gone a long way in reassuring him that Ethan was okay and healing.

Joe on the other hand had yet to rest easy. He'd lain awake each night, listening for any sound coming from his son's room, ready to go to him at the first sign of trouble. The hours in the dark gave the questions swirling around in his head more opportunity to torment him.

Anna told him that Ethan had sworn to her that he hadn't had anything to do with Jacob's botched kidnapping. But Joe wasn't taking his word for it. He wanted Ethan to look him in the eye and swear it to him.

But when that would happen, Joe didn't know.

He pushed the frustration away and did the job in front of him. Today, that was putting the equipment away and then getting ready for his next client. When he walked out of the supply closet, Joe saw Ethan slowly crossing the floor towards him.

Surprise hit him first as he took in the improvement in Ethan's condition. All of the swelling from his time with Noor was gone, and the bruising was down to a mottled mixture of yellows and greens now. He still walked with a slight limp in his step, and his arm rested protectively around his middle, but overall he'd recovered quickly.

Joe added healing to this family's loaded bag of tricks and briefly wished he'd known them when he'd been in the ring.

He motioned Jay over. "Troy is due in any minute. Get him started with warm-ups. I'll be back shortly."

Jay nodded and took over pulling the pads he'd need.

"My office." Joe motioned to Ethan before turning and walking away.

Joe didn't look back. When he got to his office, he went directly to his desk but didn't sit. When he turned, Ethan was there, closing the door behind him.

"Where are Anna and Jacob?"

Joe cocked an eyebrow at his question. "Upstairs. Do you want me to call her down?"

"No. I wanted to talk to you alone." He paused. "How, uh, how is he? How's Jacob?"

Neither had yet to sit down. Joe stood behind his desk with his arms crossed over his chest. "He seems fine now. And he's here. He's not hurt. I guess I have you to thank. For that, at least."

Ethan took a cautious breath. "I'll be making the rounds to apologize and explain, but I thought I owed it to you to start here, with you. I want to make sure you know I would never have let Noor take Jacob." Ethan slid his hands into the front pockets of his jeans.

"Why should I believe you?" Joe held a hard line. He knew his face was set in a cold, deadly mask, because that's exactly how he felt. He'd been told by several people that he was one scary son of a bitch when he got like this.

He didn't care. He wanted assurances from this man that his son would be safe with him. If he couldn't make that happen satisfactorily, there would be nine kinds of hell to pay.

"No matter how much I wanted...*needed* to believe I had Honor back, I never would have sacrificed that little boy. I love him. He's become as much a part of this family as any of us. I may have taken stupid chances with myself and with my siblings, but I wouldn't *ever* put Jacob in danger."

Joe didn't say anything. He just watched Anna's brother, trying to gauge the truth of his words. He wished he had a little of Anna's empathy to find out for sure. But he didn't. All he had were his instincts. They usually led him pretty straight about people, and right now they were telling him this man was being completely honest.

He may have let a madman dick around in his head, but

he hadn't stepped over the line and endangered a six-year-old child for his own benefit.

The fear and anger Joe had carried since that night slipped away. The release caused him to drop into his desk chair. He motioned for Ethan to sit.

"I'm so glad to know I don't have to kick your ass," Joe told him, only half-joking. "You've just healed, and then your sister would have probably kicked *my* ass."

"I'm glad too." Ethan attempted a small grin and then sobered. "I've broken everyone's trust in me—I know that. I let Noor in. Welcomed him even, if it meant he'd give me more time with her." He dropped his gaze to his hands. "I knew it wasn't real, but I didn't care. She was there. I had her back. In my dreams, I could feel her, taste her, hold her."

He pushed up out of the chair, and Joe tracked his path as he stalked around his office.

"God, I was finally getting over her," Ethan confided. "After three hellish years, I was starting to feel alive again. I could laugh and be happy and not feel like I was betraying her. I was beginning to think about the future. I still mourned the loss of her, but I was beginning to learn how to live without her."

Ethan ran his hands back through his shaggy black hair. "Then the morning of our twenty-fourth birthdays came, and I dreamed of her. But it wasn't like any other dream I'd ever had. It wasn't a memory of someplace we'd been or something we'd done together. It was like our lives had simply continued on—picked up where we'd left off. We were living in this little apartment on the beach. We were happy. We had a fucking *dog*." He laughed humorlessly.

"Every time I'd close my eyes, it progressed." Ethan swung back around to face Joe. "I was finally living the life I should have had with her, and I couldn't make myself give that up."

Hearing Ethan talk about losing his love and finding her again had Joe thinking back to the question Anna had posed that day. She'd asked them to think about what *they* would do if they ever lost someone who was their whole heart.

Joe hoped that he would go on, but he just didn't know. Having Anna or Jacob dangled in front of him every time he slept had him doubting he'd do anything differently than Ethan.

"I'm sorry about Honor. Anna told me what happened. That had to be excruciating for you. And I'm sorry Noor used that love against you." Joe waited a beat. "But you have to know holding onto her like that wasn't healthy. She's gone. She's not coming back."

Ethan sat again. "I do know that. And that's the problem. I just miss her so damned much." His voice dropped to a pained whisper. "I'm afraid I'll let him back in."

His candor startled Joe. Maybe Noor had been right in a sense. "He called you an addict. That night we found you."

Ethan blew out a breath. "I guess I am. I think about her every minute of every day. What if I can't get over her again?"

"Like any addict, you take it one day at a time. If you can't do that, you get through one minute, and then you work on the next, and the next, and the next."

Joe thought about how he'd worked through some of his own troubles. "I might be able to help you with that."

"How?" Joe saw desperation in Ethan's coal-black eyes.

"Your brother and Seth are already working out here. Why don't you start coming in too? I can set you up with a rigorous training routine. It'll kick your ass and keep your mind and body so busy, you won't have so much idle time to dwell on her."

"That sounds like a good idea, actually." A real smile lit Ethan's face for the first time. "We'll set it up." Ethan stood. "I'd better get going. Dad had Mom tied up with a project so I could sneak out and get back before she noticed. She's keeping a pretty tight leash on me right now."

He offered his hand for Joe to shake. Joe accepted.

When Joe left his office a few minutes later, his mood was a lot better. He took over with Troy and enjoyed the workout and sparring.

Anna and Jacob found him at the end of the day in his office. He was chipping away at some of the never-ending paperwork that littered his desk.

He looked up at his amazing family and grinned. "Ready to head home?"

"Mom texted me. She called a family meeting for tonight."

Joe nodded and shortly after they were headed to the Burke home base. When they walked in, most of the crew were there already. Mary, Paul, and Aria were sitting in the living room, chatting.

Seth sat with Aria, but he wasn't talking. Periodically he would send glances towards the back yard, and Joe wondered what he was waiting for.

He found out a moment later when raised voices could be heard coming from that direction.

"What's going on?" Joe asked. "Is that Evan and Ethan out there?"

"They're hashing a few things out." Mary looked completely unconcerned.

Anna looked towards the kitchen like she could see them. "Oh boy," she muttered and went to join her sister on the couch.

"Do you know what you could have cost us?" Joe heard Evan's question loud and clear. Hell, the whole neighborhood had probably heard it.

"Yes, I fucking know!" Ethan shouted back. "Do you think I *wanted* all this shit to happen?"

"How the hell should I know? It's not like you clued any of us in on what you were going through!"

Paul rose from his seat. "Hey, Jacob. How about I let you beat me at that maze game you like so much?"

After a moment's hesitation, Jacob nodded and took Paul's

hand. They walked out of the room, headed to the opposite end of the house.

Joe appreciated Paul's efforts to separate Jacob from the argument that everyone could hear. The sound of the game should drown out the voices and distract Jacob from the tension.

Once they were out of earshot, Joe turned to the others in the room. "Should someone go out there?" He didn't want to be the one, but this sounded like it was going badly.

"Oh no," Anna warned with a grimace. "We learned a long time ago to just stay out of their way. This is how they settle things between themselves."

Joe looked at Seth who just shrugged. Joe shook his head and sat down. He tried to follow the conversation going on around him, but all of his attention was on the two men outside. The argument went on for a good ten minutes before it got quiet. Too quiet.

"Did they drown each other in the ocean?" Joe asked.

Mary laughed lightly and shook her head. "No. But they've come to some kind of agreement. They should be in shortly." She rose from her seat. "I'll go check on dinner. It's got about another hour. That should give the rest of us time to sort this out."

When she returned a few minutes later, Evan and Ethan were behind her. Joe noticed that where Evan's face was full of temper and color, Ethan's was ashen and pale.

He wasn't completely recovered from the massive beating he'd taken.

Once everyone was seated, Ethan began. "First, I want to tell everyone I'm sorry. I took a stupid risk and I have no excuse."

"You should have told us." Hurt was evident in Aria's voice. "We could have helped you."

"I didn't want anyone's help. I had what I wanted."

"But you didn't," Anna countered. "It was all a lie. One meant to pull you in and make you dependent on him until you'd do whatever he asked of you."

"I know," Ethan admitted. "I took what he offered and ignored the fact that it wouldn't be free. I knew he'd demand payment at some point."

"Were you supposed to stand back and let them take Jacob that night?" Anna's voice trembled at the thought.

Ethan drew in a deep breath and let it out. "I honestly don't know. If he was testing me, I failed."

"And you were punished," Mary concluded.

"If he thinks that's going to change my mind about helping him, he can think again. Noor can beat me to a bloody pulp three times a day, and I'll still protect that little boy with everything I have."

Ethan turned to Anna. "If it will ease your mind, read me. I swear to you—I would lay down my life for Jacob."

Anna's blue eyes shimmered with overwhelming emotion. She smiled at her brother. "I don't need to."

The topic of Jacob's safety was put to rest, but Joe was sure that Ethan's mental state would worry the family for quite some time. The loss of Honor all those years ago had traumatized him deeply and now, thanks to Noor, he would have to suffer through losing her all over again.

# 23

After that, life was quiet, and they enjoyed the downtime to rebuild broken bonds and grow new ones altogether. Noor was out of the picture after his fight with her and Aria, and Hagen was still MIA. Everyone kept a close eye out for him, but as yet there'd been no sign.

Ethan had taken Joe up on his offer and had started coming into the gym for daily workouts. He and Joe were over at the heavy bags, and Joe was showing her brother a few combinations to practice.

Anna had plans with Aria later to do some shopping for Jacob. School would be starting again before she knew it, and he needed new clothes and supplies. Plus, she needed a distraction to keep her mind off the fact that he would be transferring into a regular classroom this year.

She knew the teacher he'd have and loved her, but Anna was still nervous about him being away from her. He'd made so much progress since that first meeting a few months ago, and she was so very proud of him.

Anna was using the time until Aria got there to work with Jacob one-on-one. They sat together on the landing at the top of the stairs. Their legs dangled over the side as they rested their arms on the middle safety rail.

This vantage point let them see the entire gym beneath them, as well as everyone in it.

"How are you doing with your shields? Have you been able to build them up enough so you don't see someone's inner self?"

"Mostly," he told her. "Sometimes I forget and it slips."

"That's really good though. You're doing a great job," she praised. "Now, I want you to try something else for me. This will take some effort and lots of practice."

"That's always what Nana Mary says too." He didn't look too thrilled by the idea.

"I know. Where do you think I picked it up from?" She laughed a little. "Okay. Make your walls really solid. Block it all out. Can you do that?"

He nodded and looked out on fifteen or so people below. Rapt concentration overtook his face.

"You got it?"

"Yeah, it's only them."

"Now, pick one person."

His eyes scanned the room. "Okay."

"I want you to open up just enough to see only *his* inner self."

Brown eyes snapped to hers. "How do I do that?"

"That's up to you. Depending on what you made your walls out of, you could open a door or a window, or maybe just make a small hole."

"It's a castle," he offered, "with thick stone walls."

She should have guessed that. "All right, let's see..." She gave it some thought. "What if you make one of those thin slot windows that they use to shoot arrows through? That would give you a pretty narrow focus. You could look at one person through that and still block out everyone else."

His head tilted as he thought about it, and then he turned back to the men working out below them. Anna watched as he struggled to fine-tune his abilities. It wouldn't be an easy process, but in the long run, it would allow him to live a happier life.

"Ugh." His whole body slouched. "I can't do it. The whole

wall goes away."

Anna wrapped her arm around his shoulders. "Hey, don't get discouraged. It took me a long, *long* time before I could raise and lower my shields the way I wanted."

She pointed to Joe. "Joe's pretty good at what he does, right?"

"Yeah."

"Do you think he just stepped into the ring one day and started knocking people out?"

He thought about that. "No. He practiced. He still practices, even though he doesn't do that anymore."

"That's right." She was pleased he saw where she was going. "Well, your mind is just like any muscle. The more you use it, the stronger it gets."

Anna tapped on the side of his head. "You'll get there. You just have to keep practicing." She wrapped her arm around him and pulled him in close. "But always remember, I'm proud of you, no matter what."

She kissed the top of his head. "I'll make you a deal...try one more time, and then you can go down and help Joe until Aria gets here."

Jacob loved to help out, so Anna knew that would give him incentive to try again. He took a deep breath and set about training his mind to open and close at will.

He didn't have any better luck this time, but she knew he'd get it. It was enough right now that he could block out what he didn't want to see. Anna released him and he ran down the steps and straight over to Joe and Ethan.

When Aria walked in a few minutes later, Anna called to Jacob.

"Can't I stay with Joe?" There was the slightest whine in his voice. She loved it.

"Not this time," she told him. "I need you with me so you can try on your clothes and shoes. I don't know what size to get you."

Aria stepped up next to her as Jacob literally stomped his foot on the mat.

"Honeymoon over?" she teased.

"He *is* getting a little testier," Anna smiled. "He's acting more like a six-year-old little boy."

"That just means he's comfortable with you."

"I know. It's still cute right now, but I know it'll get on my nerves soon enough." Anna laughed as Jacob grudgingly walked over to where they were waiting for him.

"What do you say I make it worth your while?" Anna tempted him. "How about when we're done shopping, we go have lunch?" He didn't have to know that had already been the plan.

Anna grinned as his mood brightened, and he agreed with no further argument.

They ended up having a fun day of shopping. Anna picked out some jeans and shirts, socks and underwear. She let him choose his own tennis shoes, and he decided on bright red ones with a comic book character on them. By the time they stopped to eat, her car was loaded with everything Jacob would need to start school.

Full to their gills with burgers and fries, they talked and laughed on the trip back to the gym.

Until the world suddenly exploded into a waking nightmare of screeching tires, breaking glass, and tearing metal.

Anna hadn't seen the other vehicle coming at them until it was too late. Before she could fully comprehend what was happening, it was plowing into them. It hit dead center on the passenger side of her car, crumpling the door in on Aria.

The impact sent them careening off the side of the road and over a rocky embankment. The car landed with a jarring thud on the sandy beach below. Ears ringing and brain fuzzy, Anna looked around. It took her a moment to remember how they'd gotten there.

Then it came back in full, blaring detail. Oh God.

Jacob. Aria.

Anna turned towards her sister. Her upper body was sprawled across the center console between them. She wasn't moving.

She reached out with a shaking hand and checked Aria for a pulse. Anna exhaled in relief when she found it beating strong and true.

Anna twisted around and searched the back seat for Jacob. He was still securely locked in his booster seat. The preventative measures she'd taken to keep him protected had done their job and held him safe, but he was slumped over, and that scared her.

"Jacob? Can you hear me? Wake up, sweetie."

A faint cry came from behind her.

"Oh, thank God." Anna fought her seat belt to no avail; she was trapped. It tore her heart out that she wasn't able to go to him. "I'm right here, baby. Don't be scared. We're going to be okay."

He didn't answer.

Out of sheer desperation she reached out to him with her power, but the throbbing in her head made it nearly impossible to concentrate. She forced her mind to stay on task. Hopefully, he was aware enough that she could see something.

Anna inhaled and exhaled deeply, centering herself, and then bore down on her magic.

At first there was nothing, but then she began to sense his fear and confusion. Pushing further and into the realm of her new power, she got an image of his head. It must be hurting him. That would make sense after what they'd just gone through. She concentrated more and also got a glimpse of his shoulder.

Considering how her own felt where the belt had dug in, he had to be suffering the same.

The head injury would worry her until he was checked out,

but the rest seemed minor. He'd obviously been shaken up, but she was sure he would be okay.

With her worry about her family lessened, Anna's own injuries became suddenly more apparent. Pain bloomed over the left half of her body where it had slammed into the door and window beside her. Her head pounded and nausea rolled in her belly, warning her of a possible concussion.

Anna laid her head back on the headrest to catch her breath and try to form a plan. But then the edges of her vision started to blur, and she could feel herself being pulled into the black of unconsciousness. She fought it off with everything she had, trying to shake herself back to lucidity. She needed to stay alert and protect Jacob.

Because Kurt had done this.

In the split second when the vehicles had collided, she'd seen him. Hands on the wheel and an evil smile on his lips as he'd plowed purposefully into them. And in that moment, Anna had known this was the vision Aria had warned her about all those months ago.

Aria had seen Anna lying broken and bleeding after a horrific car crash. They'd never been sure how the accident would happen or if anyone else had been with her. But here, now, Anna could fit the rest of the pieces together.

The vision had shown the aftermath of Kurt coming for Jacob.

Cold, steely resolve settled over her. She'd die before she'd let him take her child. She had to do whatever she could to change the outcome of that premonition. Since she'd been out cold when Aria had seen her, she knew her first goal had be staying awake and aware. So with the desperation of a mother protecting her child, Anna battled back the waves of dizziness.

She would not lose Jacob. That monster would not take him from her.

Anna's trembling hand felt for the seat belt. She needed to

get free of it before Kurt came. She had to be ready. Fighting back the distortion that threatened to take her under, she tugged at the belt with her left hand while the fingers of her right frantically jabbed at the release button.

She was still wrestling with it when the door behind her suddenly jerked open. Anna's gaze wheeled around to glare at Jacob's father.

"Leave him alone!" she screamed. "Get away from him!" Pain burst through her head but she ignored it.

"He's mine, bitch. And there's nothing you can do about it." Kurt hauled Jacob's limp body up by his arm. When the seatbelt caught him, Kurt swore and produced a knife to slice through the strap across Jacob's chest. Once that was dealt with, Kurt yanked until the lower belt fell away and Jacob slid free.

With a sneer and laugh, Kurt was gone and so was her son. Anna screamed again, hysterically jerking and tugging at the restraint holding her captive.

She had to get a hold of herself or she'd be no good to any of them. She took a breath and finally used her brain to think through the problem. Anna gave herself some slack on the lap portion and was able to maneuver her small frame out from under the belt.

Once free, she grabbed the handle and shoved the door open. As soon as she had enough room, she launched herself out. She stumbled to her feet and ran for a retreating Kurt Hagen.

"Stop!" she yelled.

He ignored her as he easily maneuvered the ragged rocks with a limp Jacob hanging upside down over his shoulder. She glanced past him to the truck he'd used to ram into them. It was a big, heavy-duty pickup. The force of the collision had only slightly damaged it. Nothing that would slow his getaway.

As she ran to catch him, her head throbbed to every beat of her pulse. As her heart rate accelerated, so did the pain until it nearly blinded her. But she had no choice; she had to fight or risk losing Jacob forever.

He'd chosen his ambush site well. Along this stretch of road, there wasn't much in the way of help. Except her dear and trusted friend, she remembered. She had an ocean full of water at her call.

Anna stopped so suddenly she teetered before catching her balance. Taking a calming breath, she pulled hard on her magic and brought a spout of water up and out of the depths. It extended out over white sand and rugged land. With thoughts of Jacob's welfare uppermost in her mind, Anna split the wave.

With one tendril, she slammed it into Kurt, sending him sprawling. With the other, Anna gently caught Jacob and cradled him as tenderly as her own arms would.

As the water retreated from Kurt, it deposited Jacob on the sand a little way behind her. Well out of Kurt's reach should he try for him again.

Hagen regained his footing and spun around. He stalked back to the beach where Anna stood between him and what he thought of as his possession.

"You think being a witch makes any difference? I'll kill you *and* still take my son."

"If you think you can, then bring it." Anna readied herself. She was resigned to the fact that only one of them was coming out of this.

Kurt smiled and slowly advanced on her. She knew her small stature gave him a false sense of security. He was used to intimidating women and using his size and strength to overpower them. She'd use that to her advantage just as Joe had taught her.

Her mind wanted to think about the man she loved and the possibility that she'd never see him again. But she locked it all away. She needed every whit of strength and determination she possessed to deal with the threat in front of her.

Anna held her ground as he strode right up to her. She shifted her weight for whatever he threw at her and then watched and waited. She kept her focus loose, looking for any sign that he was about to strike.

When his right shoulder dropped just a fraction, she was ready. The fist that came after was easy enough to dodge. And she had the pleasure of seeing the shock on his face when her right hook connected with his ribs.

Kurt took a step back and rubbed his side. She saw murder in his grey eyes.

"What's the matter?" Adrenaline was pumping through her veins, sweeping away all the pain from the accident. She knew it would return with a vengeance later, but right now she didn't care. "Not as much fun when we fight back, is it?"

His hands dropped to his sides where they clenched and unclenched over and over as his temper boiled.

Kurt swung out again but he expected her evasion. When she dipped low, his hand snaked out and grabbed a fistful of her hair. Anna gritted her teeth against the tearing pain and stepped in close to him. The move not only released some of the pressure on her scalp, but it also put her within striking distance.

Anna reached down and grabbed hard at his crotch. She squeezed and twisted until she could almost feel them crunch inside her fist.

Kurt sucked in a tortured breath. When he brought one hand up to dislodge the grip she had on him, the one holding her hair loosened. As she pulled free, she used his bent position in her favor. Anna wrapped both hands around the back of his head and pulled it down at the same time she brought her knee up.

At the last second, Kurt shifted and her blow skidded across his cheek. Off balance now, the advantage was his as he roared like a bull and lunged forward, bowling her over and taking her down.

They landed on the sand hard enough to drive the air from

her lungs. She was still trying to draw oxygen in when his fist came down and into the side of her face. Knocked senseless for a moment, Anna was too late to deflect when his hands went to her throat. Her vision began to dim as he squeezed and repeated over and over, "You're dead."

Anna knew she didn't have much longer before her strength ran out, so she gathered what she had left and pushed her hands up through his arms. Entwining her fingers at the back of his neck, she quickly pulled his face into her chest.

With his arms now bent, the leverage he'd had for the stranglehold was gone. Life-giving oxygen rushed back into her starved lungs. She wanted to lie there and just gasp, but she knew she didn't have time for that. Her life still hung in the balance.

Muscle memory had her hips shifting underneath her until she could initiate a move she'd practiced countless times. A quick flip and suddenly she was straddling him. Without hesitation, she slammed her fists into his face until she couldn't feel her hands anymore. Kurt's eyes rolled back and his body went slack.

Anna hefted herself off of him and stood with her numbed hands braced on her knees. She dragged huge draughts of air in and out past her abused throat. Glancing over to where she'd left Jacob, she saw him sitting up, watching her.

Mustering her energy, she straightened her battered body to go to him.

She'd taken several steps in his direction when she jumped at the sound of two gunshots ringing out almost simultaneously.

# 24

Anna spun around to see Kurt crumpling to the ground. He'd gotten up to come for her again but her back had been turned.

Movement on the street above drew her attention to where Joe, Ethan, Seth, and Evan were standing. Seth and her brother both had their guns in their hands.

Joe broke ranks and ran to her. She saw a multitude of emotions racing across his face as he drew near. Anger gave way to relief when he saw she was alive and safe. Sorrow was next as he took in what Hagen had done to her. And then finally there was love. A love that overwhelmed her with its intensity.

When he reached her, he folded her gently into his arms.

They held each other for a few moments before Joe drew his head back enough to see her face. "Haven't I always told you never to turn your back on your opponent unless you know for sure he's down and not getting up?" His deep voice was raw, his amber eyes searching.

Tremors were wracking his body as he held her. Or maybe that was hers; she wasn't sure. What she did know was that they needed each other in this moment, so she sank into him and drew on his strength.

"Lesson learned." Anna smiled and then remembered, trying to push out of Joe's arms. "Jacob!"

"Evan has him. He'll be okay for a minute; let me look at you."

His eyes roved over her entire body and, apparently satisfied that her injuries weren't serious, his attention landed on her throat. His fingers caressed over what were surely bruises, the marks from Kurt's hands darkening and spreading the longer time went on.

In an attempt to divert Joe's attention, she asked him a question. "Not that I'm not grateful, but how are you here?"

"Aria called out." Joe finally pulled his gaze away from her neck. "Evan heard her, but got scared shitless when he tried to respond and couldn't reach either one of you. He called and said you were in trouble and to come quickly. They used the GPS on your phones to find you."

"I thought she'd been knocked out when Kurt rammed us." The sounds of the accident echoed in her mind as she replayed the moment of impact. "She must have been able to send the alert just before she lost consciousness."

"Were you knocked out too?" Joe's golden eyes turned hard at the thought.

"I don't think so." Anna tried to think back. "If I was, it was only for a second."

"Why didn't you answer your brother?"

"I honestly didn't hear him calling to me," Anna said truthfully. "I was so focused on keeping Kurt away from Jacob, I must have blocked everything else out."

"Tell me what happened."

Anna recounted the events up to the time the others had found them.

Joe brushed her hair away from her face to inspect where Kurt had punched her. He rubbed his fingers gently over the sore spot.

"If he weren't already dead, I'd kill him myself." Joe's face was hard as stone and his voice just as cold.

Before Anna could say anything else, Aria joined them, assisted by Seth and Ethan. Evan was right behind them holding Jacob in his arms.

"Are you guys okay?" Anna asked her sister and Jacob.

"Woozy, but all right, I think." Aria moved gingerly.

When Jacob only nodded, Anna was afraid he'd taken a huge step back. That the trauma of what had happened here was too much for him to handle on top of everything else he had gone through.

But she should have had more faith in her amazing little boy. "I'm okay."

Anna smiled at Jacob and then turned her gaze back to Seth. She wanted to make sure Aria didn't brush off what had happened to her. Without asking permission, Anna lowered her barriers and searched Aria's mind to see how badly she was hurt.

She saw a flash of Ari's ribs on her right side. And of course the head wound. Though she'd taken the brunt of the hit, Anna was relieved to discover that her sister wasn't hurt worse than she was.

"She'll need to go to the hospital," Anna told Seth. "She's thinking about her ribs, and I'm pretty sure she has a serious concussion."

Seth nodded tightly.

"You and Jacob won't be too far behind her," Joe stated flatly. She humored him and didn't argue, because she knew he was only worried about them, and she wanted a doctor to look Jacob over too.

"We have to call this in," Evan spoke into the silence. "It was a righteous shoot, but they'll still have to investigate. Plus, the authorities will want to know that Kurt Hagen is no longer a threat."

Evan passed Jacob to Joe and stepped away to make the call. Anna wrapped her arms tightly around her boys and saw that Aria had also burrowed closer into Seth. They all took comfort in the fact that other than a few injuries, they'd made it through another battle.

<center>~~~</center>

A few hours later, after Anna, Aria, and Jacob had been checked over and released from the hospital, they all gathered at the family home.

Anna and Aria sat with their guys on the couch, sipping their mother's heal-anything tea from their cups, while Jacob, tucked up against Anna's side, drank from his own small mug. When Anna noticed his weight had become heavier on her, she looked down, surprised to see that he'd fallen asleep. She took the tea from his limp fingers before it could spill.

Her dad rose from his chair and picked Jacob up. Anna watched as her son was carried off to be laid down. She glanced at her mom and saw that her gaze too was following their exit. She caught a glint of something in her eyes.

Raising an eyebrow with an amused grin, Anna pinned her with a look. "Did you spike his tea?"

"Maybe just a few extra herbs," Mary said nonchalantly. "The excitement of the day would have worn him out eventually. I just gave him a little nudge. Since he doesn't have a concussion, sleep will do him good. And it'll give us a chance to talk about what happened."

Anna nodded, seeing the truth in her words.

"It was Aria's vision." She started with that, leading up to the actual crash. "I knew if I let myself go under, Jacob would be gone."

"And in doing so, you were able to alter what I saw." Aria stirred next to her. "Instead of Jacob being taken, Kurt was taken down. Permanently."

Anna nodded. "I still can't believe he's finally out of Jacob's life for good."

Joe turned to Evan. "Were there any problems with the

reports you filed?"

Evan shook his head. "Everyone involved is satisfied with the way things turned out. Kurt was already wanted for the murder of his wife; they knew he was dangerous. When he attacked the girls and Jacob, Seth and I were well within our rights to act as we did."

"Noor lost another soldier," Paul warned. "One with a blood tie. He's bound to retaliate."

"Hopefully not any time soon," Anna said. "Ari and I did a lot of damage the night he took Ethan. It'll take him a while to come back from that."

"But when he does, he'll be that much stronger," Mary reminded them.

Anna looked at each of her siblings. "Yeah, but so will we. We're not cowering and hiding from that bastard. We live and we go on, and we throw it all in his face. We show him that we're not afraid of him. We've beaten him back every time he's come at us, and we'll continue to do that until the final battle arrives and we send him to hell for good."

"Ditto, sis." Evan sent her a huge grin.

"Me too," Ethan nodded.

Aria grinned. "Oh yeah."

~~~

Anna and Joe were enjoying a quiet Sunday at home. They snuggled on the couch watching TV while Jacob lay on the floor, drawing in the art book Aria had given him. He loved it, and it was never too far from his hands.

Joe nodded to Jacob. "What do you think he's working on down there?"

"I don't know." Anna observed him for a couple of minutes. "Whatever it is, it's important to him."

Joe's cell phone rang on the side table. Reaching over, he
~~~

picked it up and accepted the call.

"Hello?...That's good news...No, I don't think that's the best thing right now. Can someone arrange to put it all in storage? Just send me the bill...Yeah, okay. I'll tell her. Thanks. Talk to you later."

"Who was that?" Anna asked.

"Evan. He wanted to tell us that the police in Georgia closed the case." Joe kept his voice low. "He also asked if we thought Jacob would want his and his mother's things from the house. I thought it might be too soon for that, so I asked if it could all be stored until he's ready."

Anna nodded. "Good thinking. It will all have to be sorted through at some point, but I think it can wait for a little while. He has that picture of his mom Evan had them email, and we can get it framed to put on his nightstand. We'll hold off on the rest for now—let him put a little more distance between himself and what happened there."

Joe kissed her hair.

Anna hugged him closer. Their little family was safe and secure.

They turned their attention back to the television until Jacob, finished with his drawing, stood and brought it to her.

She smiled when she saw it and looked up to see Joe grinning too.

Jacob had given Anna's angel shiny metal armor.

"Well," Anna felt a surge of pride wash over her, "it looks like you're not the only knight around here anymore."

# EPILOGUE

Evan hung up his phone and leaned back in his chair. He wasn't scheduled to be at the station today, but he'd come in because these three open murders were pissing him off. They had no leads and no suspects. All they did have was a cause of death.

In all three cases, these seemingly non-related men had had their throats cut with a thin, sharp blade. They didn't have a definite ID on the weapon because the killer had always taken it with him.

So, Evan was spending his day off reading through the reports and statements yet again. Frustrated that nothing new had jumped out at him, he set them aside and looked over the crime scene photos, hoping he'd catch something he'd missed the first half-dozen times he'd studied them.

A phone call from Georgia, and a subsequent one to Joe, pulled his mind out of the endless loop of questions it had been swimming in for the last few hours. He took in the mess of paper on his desk and knew he couldn't just sit here and stare at it anymore. Doing it this way wasn't getting him anywhere.

Evan rolled all the facts around in his head, trying to stack them up in different ways as he reached out for his old PD mug. A quick shot of caffeine would kick his brain back in gear so he could figure this out.

Finding his cup empty, he swore and pushed away from his desk. He wove his way through the other desks in the bullpen to the coffee pot that sat on a long table against the wall. Taking the carafe from the hot plate, he poured another cup of the overcooked, strong-as-diesel-fuel brew.

Evan took a drink as he turned and walked back to his desk. He grimaced. "This tastes like ass."

He sighed and thought about making a fresh pot. But now that the craving had been triggered, he wanted a decent cup. Setting the mug down on his desk, he picked up his phone and slid it into his pocket. There was a little café a few blocks over on Main Street that had really good coffee.

And getting out and taking a walk might be just what he needed.

Stepping into the late summer heat from the air-conditioned coolness of the precinct was a shock to the system. It pressed on Evan like a weight and had his white cotton dress shirt sticking to his body. The slight breeze drifting in off the water was enough to tousle his black hair, but it did nothing to cool the air.

Resigned to the temperature, Evan took his sunglasses from his breast pocket and slipped them over his midnight-dark eyes. Behind the mirrored lenses, he took in his city as he walked.

Another sunny weekend was coming to an end. He couldn't believe it was August already. That left him and his siblings only six months to figure out how to combine their four elements. His sisters had been successful in merging theirs, but he and Ethan had yet to try it.

Evan and his twin weren't on the best of terms as of late. Ethan had pulled some pretty stupid shit, and Evan still wasn't sure how he was going to get past it. They were twins for fuck's sake; they were supposed to be able to tell each other anything. But Ethan had hidden so much. The worst of which was that he'd let Noor dick around inside his head and manipulate him.

The secret to becoming one as the prophecy demanded had a lot to do with trust—being able to completely give yourself over to the joining. If you held anything back, the merge wouldn't work.

Evan was afraid that he and his brother wouldn't be able

to reach that level of faith in each other again. If that were the case, they were screwed. Because they all needed to work together as one to finally defeat Noor.

Lost in thought, Evan was just crossing in front of an alley when someone came barreling out and plowed right into him. He vaguely heard something clatter to the ground but dismissed it as his mind continued to process the collision.

"Whoa." His hands automatically came up to grip the arms of the stranger to steady them, at the same time their palms landed flat on his chest and clutched reflexively at the material.

Evan looked down into the most stunningly beautiful face he'd ever seen. Her wide, black-lined doe-eyes were the same color as old Kentucky bourbon. As they stared up at him, the rest of her registered on his senses.

Her hair was short and choppy, like she'd hacked at it herself. It couldn't be described as merely brown, because it actually carried every color of the spectrum. Though a deep, rich mahogany was at the base, it also shone with blondes and reds and even some darker hues. Her features were sharp and angular, and he got the impression it wasn't for vanity's sake. She seemed to be thin to the point of gaunt. Like she'd missed too many meals.

She was tall, probably around five nine or ten. Where his hands gripped her upper arms, she felt slender but toned, telling him the weight loss may have been recent.

Under his fingers, the leather of her brown jacket still held the warmth of the sun. She wore a plain white tee beneath that hugged her body. And what a body it was. Her breasts weren't overly large, but they also weren't too small. To his muddled mind, they were perfect. *She* was perfect.

Evan was finally able to stop the speeding and out of control train his thoughts were on. This woman was a complete stranger; he didn't need to be ogling her and wondering what she wore under that cotton top. Gathering his manners again, he put his gentleman hat on.

"I'm sorry. Are you..."

The sound of his voice must have shocked her out of whatever daze she'd been in, because the rest of his question was lost as she tore free from his grasp and ran off down the street. Her booted feet slapped the ground as her long, denim-clad legs quickly put distance between them.

"Well, that was odd." Evan muttered as he automatically straightened his shirt and made sure it was still tucked in. When he glanced down, he saw the red stains that her small hands had left behind.

"Son of a bitch." Evan's brows came together and his gaze snapped up to where he'd last seen her. Had someone attacked her? Was she hurt? He hadn't seen any obvious injuries, but then again, his mind hadn't been on assessing her medical needs.

He made a half-turn, contemplating going after her, but his shoe connected with something lying on the ground.

Evan looked down and saw a blood-slicked knife. "What the hell?" He ripped his glasses off, and black eyes rose to scan the shadowed alleyway.

About midway down, he saw a body sprawled out on the ground. He took off running, and a moment later was standing over the downed man. Careful not to disturb the scene or contaminate the evidence, Evan crouched and got a good look. What he saw stopped his heart and ripped a curse from his lips.

"Fuck!"

Evan pulled out his phone to make the call back to the station to report the crime. At the same time, he reached out and carefully checked for a pulse.

"Yeah, this is Detective Burke. I've got a dead body." He relayed his location. "Male. Caucasian. Mid- to late-twenties. COD is pretty apparent. His throat's been cut."

He also gave them a description of the woman, leaving out his personal observations, and told them where he'd last seen her heading.

Rising to his feet again, Evan walked back out to the mouth of the ally. He squatted down and studied the murder weapon with a practiced eye. Overall length looked to be around seven inches. The blade itself was three-and-a-half to four inches and maybe two inches wide.

It was currently covered in what he assumed to be the victim's blood, and Evan could just make out good, usable prints in the blood on the wooden handle as the sun glinted off of it. With any luck they'd be in the system, and then they'd have her.

Evan lifted his gaze and stared off in the direction his suspect had gone and cursed for letting her slip through his fingers.

Misha McKenzie has been an avid reader since learning how at four years old. Countless books later, she still loves to immerse herself into the lives of the people within those pages. After graduating high school, she went on to earn a degree in Business Administration, married her high school sweetheart, and had two beautiful boys. At thirty years old, while working as an office manager for a construction company, a family of witches began to brew, and The Magic of the Heart Series was born.